Here You Come Again

Tracie Momie

ISBN:978-0-692-05004-0
Copyright ©2018 TRACIE MOMIE
Original Front Cover illustration by Gorbash Varvara via Shutterstock
with vector edits by Tracie Momie.
I Wonder song lyrics by Tracie Momie ©2017

I Wonder

I see her every night in my dreams
I wonder if she ever even thinks of me?
She's a girl that I used to know
I carry her picture everywhere I go
My heart will always belong to her
I doubt that she knows this, but I wonder
I see her every night in my dreams
I wonder if she ever even thinks of me?
There is no woman that could take her place
Whenever I close my eyes- I see her face
My heart will always belong to her
I doubt that she knows this, but I wonder
If I could go back in time
I'd find a way to make her mine
We'd be together and she would see
No one would ever love her like me
I just want one chance to see what could have been
So much time has passed since I've seen my friend
My heart will always belong to her
I doubt that she knows this, but I wonder

August

2013

Sometimes the smallest things can have the biggest impact on your life. Sometimes innocent comments open wounds you thought had healed long ago.   And sometimes the most random numbers appear and your past suddenly collides with your future.

Fifteen.

I glanced at the clock on my computer– it was fifteen minutes past five on the fifteenth day of August and at that exact moment my assistant, Christina walked in holding an envelope.

"Guess what I have!" she said in a sing-song voice. She smiled brightly and waved the generic packet in the air. "It was just delivered!"

"A winning lotto ticket?" I teased.

She rolled her eyes. "No, you have to play to win and I wouldn't waste my money on lotto tickets. Besides this is bigger, *better* than that!"

"Really? Okay, I'm intrigued." I leaned back in my chair and gave her my full attention.

She walked closer to my desk and placed the envelope in front of me but before I picked it up, she squealed.

"It's an invitation to your fifteen-year high school reunion!" she announced excitedly. "Open it! I can't believe my favorite group is performing at your class reunion!"

High school reunion? My heart fluttered as I pulled a cream-colored card from the envelope, which she'd already opened. I immediately recognized the Charles Drew High School mascot and colors emblazoned on the front. The reunion was in one month, on September 15th in my hometown of Buffalo.

"Did you know Xavier Ross?" Christina asked.

I glanced up at her and took note of the awestruck expression on her face.

"What? How do you know Xavier Ross?" I asked confused.

"Turn it over, Soul Skylight- he's the lead singer. Please, tell me you've heard of Soul Skylight?"

I tuned Christina out and stared down at the invitation. My hands shook as I turned it over. There was a photo of a group of guys and sitting on a stool in the center, clutching a guitar, was Xavier Ross.

My breath caught in my throat and I found it difficult to breathe. I looked at Christina as I gasped for air.

"Oh my god, Angela!" She came behind the desk and patted me forcefully on the back.

I gulped and forced air down my windpipe. "I'm okay! I couldn't breathe, I'm not choking!" I exclaimed as I moved away from her heavy hand against my back.

"You scared me! Do you have asthma or something?" she asked concerned.

"Um, no- I just- I-," I stammered as my eyes darted back to the invitation.

Christina's eyes followed mine and her mouth fell open. "You and Xavier Ross?" she whispered. "No way!"

I didn't know whether to be embarrassed or insulted by her reaction.

"It was just a silly high school thing," I said dismissively.

"Oh really?" She smirked. And I knew she wasn't convinced.

Christina had worked for me for almost three years. She'd started as an intern during her last year of college and after graduation, she received an offer for a permanent position. Our work relationship was solid but we'd also established a close personal bond, I considered her a good friend.

"Seriously, it was nothing. We went to high school together, dated briefly, went to prom and he took me home early. I haven't seen him since." I quickly recapped my relationship with Xavier and slid the card back in the envelope.

"Why do I get the feeling there's much more to that story?" she folded her arms across her chest and tilted her head.

"Christina please, I can't do this with you right now. I've got to go, I'm meeting someone for an early dinner," I reached forward to turn off my computer and she picked up the invitation.

"Do you want me to RSVP for you?" she asked hopefully.

"I don't really have a reason to attend my high school reunion, it's my past." I declared. But there was a small part of me that wanted to see Xavier in person one more time.

"But what about the performance? Maybe we could go just to see the band play,"

"*We?*" I looked at her and raised an eyebrow.

"I tried twice last year to get tickets to see them. They did a show at the Apollo and a pop-up performance in Jersey but both shows sold out! This might be my only chance to ever see them perform live." she pouted.

"Fine, you can use the invitation. Take Greg and have a great time," I stood and grabbed my jacket from the back of my chair as she moved around to the front of the desk.

She sighed. "Angela, I can't take Greg. I have to go with an alumnus. And besides, Greg and I are taking a break," she said quietly.

"What?" I asked surprised. I thought she and Greg would be engaged before year-end, they'd been dating since college. I could tell by her tone that the "break" wasn't her idea.

I walked over and placed a hand on her shoulder. "You okay?" I asked.

"Not really, but I know what would make me feel better." She sighed dramatically.

"What's that?"

"Seeing Soul Skylight live," she smiled.

"Wow, I fell right into that one," I laughed and shook my head.

"Okay, we'll go! But right after the performance, we're leaving."

"Yay!" she exclaimed with the excitement of a little kid.

The thought of seeing Xavier Ross again made me feel like a kid as well. A kid afraid on her first day at a new school, afraid of being judged by the entire student body but she ends up forming an unlikely friendship with the most sought-after boy in school and eventually falls in love with him, only to have him break her heart.

Oh wait, that actually happened.

I had been content not knowing the whereabouts of Xavier Ross for the past fifteen years; I'd buried him in the memories of my past life. And now he had been resurrected. I couldn't believe he'd become a famous singer. Soul Skylight, huh? I was definitely Googling that when I got home.

"I'll see you tomorrow, Christina," I announced as I left my office and headed toward the elevators.

After exiting the building, I hailed a cab and had the driver take me to The Modern, a restaurant located inside the Museum of Modern Art. I stood out front of the building, smoothed down the sides of my blunt cut bob and took a shaky breath before I entered.

I approached the hostess stand but as I looked around the restaurant, the person I was meeting waved from a table near the bar.

"Hi, I'm meeting someone for dinner and I think I see him," I pointed towards the bar. The hostess looked over her shoulder and saw Rodney smiling widely at us. She smiled and led me over to his table. He automatically stood and pulled out my chair.

"Angela! Hey, it's good to see you, you look great," he smiled.

Rodney Anderson was my ex. *Fiancé.* He was tall, lean and boyishly handsome. His mocha skin was smooth and free from any facial hair, providing the perfect view of the dimple in his left cheek, which made him appear younger than his thirty-seven years. He was currently living in Houston working as a vice president for Ernst & Young.

I was initially attracted to Rodney because of his outgoing personality but he was also intelligent, kind, and ambitious. During our time together, we'd traveled and had some amazing experiences. It was also with Rodney that I'd felt comfortable enough to become more adventurous in the bedroom. I'd had some terrible sexual encounters in the past that left me jaded but Rodney was a generous and patient lover.

He was a good partner most of the time but Rodney could be stubborn and he drove me crazy wanting to plan every second of our lives. It was his inflexibility, lack of patience and decision to accept a job sixteen hundred miles away that ultimately brought our three and half year relationship to an end. But that was *my* side of the story, Rodney probably blamed me and my faults just as much. Although he was the one who had made the first move (literally) by accepting the job in Houston without talking to me about it.

When I told him I wasn't going to quit my job in New York to follow him to Houston, he was so angry that he'd left town without even saying goodbye. We'd lost contact for a little while but he called me a few weeks ago and apologized. He wanted us to try and be friends.

I didn't exactly understand the point of people being friends with exes. But that was before I had an ex. I really liked Rodney. We were friends before we started a romantic relationship, so I accepted his apology and decided there was no need to burn that bridge. Rodney had been good to me and I didn't have any animosity towards him. I was glad that we'd dodged a bullet by not getting married, it probably wouldn't have lasted a year.

I believed in the sanctity of marriage but I couldn't be a traditional wife, relying solely on my husband to take care of me. The thought of depending on anyone that much terrified me. I'd seen first-hand how women in those types of marriages usually got the short end of the stick.

Rodney called me two days ago and told me he would be in New York for a business meeting and suggested we meet for dinner. We used to love going out to experience the culinary delights of New York's restaurant scene. I'd missed that while he was gone.

"You look good Rodney. Houston seems to agree with you," I returned his compliment after I sat down and placed my bag on the empty chair next to me.

"It's nice. Really humid," he laughed.

We stared at each other for a few seconds before lapsing into an awkward silence. I didn't want to talk about the breakup and he most likely didn't either, but it was hard to pretend everything was normal.

He cleared his throat. "So, how have you been?"

"Great, just finished a big campaign, so I've got some downtime for a couple of weeks," I smiled.

"Lucky you, we're already ramping up for year-end." He groaned.

"The life of a numbers man," I teased.

"Yeah, but hopefully things won't be that way for long," he remarked cryptically.

I was about to ask what he meant by his remark when a waiter appeared to take our drink orders. We ordered a bottle of Cabernet to share. There were a few times when the conversation seemed forced but after our second glass of wine, we were laughing and talking like old friends.

"Do you remember that trip we took to Martha's Vineyard, and that guy we met-," he started.

Of course, I remembered. The guy resembled Morgan Freeman but had long gray locs and a Jamaican accent. He talked to us for almost two hours entertaining us with amazing stories about all the places he'd traveled in his life.

"Yes! I loved him, he was so full of wisdom and all those incredible stories of the places and things he'd seen," I gushed.

Rodney laughed. "You know that was a bunch of bullshit, right?"

"What are you talking about?" I asked confused.

"I think he was just making that stuff up," he sipped his wine.

My eyes widened. "No, why would he? I refuse to believe it!" I shook my head. The guy had seemed sincere.

"Because he had the attention of a beautiful woman who was hanging on his every word," Rodney chuckled.

"But he obviously made an impression on you too since you still remember him." I pointed out.

"That's only because I remember how you looked that night sitting in front of that fire pit. Your skin was glowing and you were smiling at him, showing all your teeth," He grinned. "And your eyes were sparkling. . .you looked so carefree and happy," he said with a hint of melancholy.

And I knew I was blushing.

"Shut up," I giggled. I also remembered that night we'd gone back to our room and had the best sex we'd ever had during our relationship.

And the way Rodney was staring at me across the table, with a mixture of desire and wonder, it was obvious he remembered that part too, which explains why instead of going our separate ways after dinner, we ended up at my apartment. One thing led to another and soon we were kissing and groping each other on my couch. I hadn't been with anybody since we broke up and being in Rodney's arms felt good and familiar but I knew it was wrong. Just as our kissing escalated and he pawed at my breasts, I snapped out of my lust induced haze.

"Stop!" I yelled.

He jumped liked he'd been burned by fire and stared at me wide-eyed from the other end of the couch.

"What are we doing? We can't do this," I straightened my blouse and hung my head.

He exhaled harshly. "I know, I guess we both got caught up in the moment. I'm sorry. I didn't mean to take advantage," his voice was barely above a whisper.

"Oh no, God no– Rodney we're both slightly intoxicated right now and if anything is at fault it's the alcohol and our hormones but you absolutely did not take advantage of me or the situation. We just– we can't,"

Having sex with Rodney would have significant meaning to him–

he would take it as a sign that I wanted us to get back together or start a long-distance relationship. And I didn't want either of those things, we had too many unresolved issues to just pick up where we left off.

He smiled faintly and raised his head to look at me. "I know it's too little, too late but I wanted to say again that I'm sorry about how things ended between us. I should have never left the way I did. I guess a part of me thought it could be a fresh start. I never considered your career, it was selfish of me. You were important to me and I'm really proud of your accomplishments, Angela. And I sincerely wish the best for you and that no matter what you find happiness."

Tears clouded my vision and spilled over on to my cheeks. I moved closer to him and wrapped my arms around his waist and hugged him.

"Thank you, Rodney I want that for you too. I don't know, I don't think you and I are- we're just not-," I started at a loss for words.

"We're not destined?" he questioned.

I nodded my head. "Yeah, I don't think we're destined," I said sadly.

He stared at me quizzically before he stood abruptly and put on his jacket. "Well, I should get going," he announced.

It was pretty late, so I walked him to the door and he kissed my forehead before saying goodbye.

I closed the door and leaned my back against it. *Destiny.* Did I even believe in destiny? It sounded like something out of a Disney fairytale. I turned off the lamp in the living room and walked down the hall to my bedroom letting Rodney's words sink in.

After I removed my makeup, I wrapped a silk scarf around my hair and changed into my pajamas. I arranged the pillows on my bed before getting comfortable with my MacBook on my lap. Once I signed in to my email, I laughed out loud at the ridiculous number of messages from Christina. Most of the subject lines were "High school reunion", "Soul Skylight" or "Cute outfits" about ten in all. I didn't need to Google Soul Skylight because Christina had sent me several links and photo attachments.

I opened one of the "Soul Skylight" e-mails and clicked on the first attachment. The computer buffered for a few seconds before a huge image of Xavier Ross appeared and filled my entire screen. He had an intense expression on his face. I shifted my body from left to right and his eyes followed me! Or it could've been me moving the computer on my lap. I laughed and a snort escaped.

I covered my mouth and stared at the screen horrified that he'd heard me. I cleared my throat and took a deep breath. "It's just a picture," I muttered. I closed out that picture and moved on to the next one.

My hand instinctively reached out to trace the features on the screen. Time had been more than kind to him; he had aged well. His green eyes were bright and shining, his hair– that I remembered being so soft, curly and thick– had grown out and he had a full beard, which made him look older, more mature and *sexier*.

My fingertip moved away from his face and down the opening in the denim vest he wore without a shirt. He had always been lean with some muscle definition whenever we were teenagers but now he was toned and muscular. His abs were tight and his chest well-defined; it was obvious that he worked out to get in that kind of shape.

I felt myself getting excited about the idea of what he looked like without any clothes and decided I'd had enough eye candy. I opened one of the links to the band's website.

I'd apparently been living under a rock. Soul Skylight had been around for about five years and had won two Grammy's. They'd also sold millions of albums worldwide. I wasn't a big fan of current music; when I listened to the radio it was usually an oldies station that played '80s Pop or '90s R&B. But after I clicked the site playlist, I was surprised that I'd actually heard a few of their songs.

I was mesmerized by Xavier's voice– it was remarkable. He was able to pull off softer R&B ballads just as well as party anthems. As I read the accompanying lyrics, I was shocked to learn he'd also written the majority of the songs in their discography. I removed my phone from the docking station and downloaded several of the songs from iTunes.

I wasn't aware how long I'd been online until my eyes began to drift shut. I yawned and noticed the time was 1:15 am. *Shit!* I had an early morning meeting. I reluctantly powered down my computer and placed it on my nightstand before rearranging the pillows again. I pulled the chenille blanket up over my shoulders, closed my eyes and began to dream of another place and time.

****

I vividly remembered the first day I'd arrived at Charles Drew High School. I had transferred there after my mom moved us to a two-bedroom apartment when she and my dad divorced. I was so mad at her! But not mad enough to stay with my dad, who I'd blamed for the divorce in the first place. It just sucked to transfer in the middle of the second semester of my junior year.

On my first day at Drew, there was a pep rally in the gymnasium. I'd sat at the bottom of the bleachers close to the exit, so I that could be the first person out of the gym when it was over.

"Hey, new girl, you need to find somewhere else to sit!" I heard someone say. I looked up and saw a skinny girl in a cheer uniform frowning at me. She was short, with dark brown skin and her big brown eyes were outlined in bright blue eyeliner. And her hair was in a long, braided ponytail.

She put her hands on her bony hips. "Are you deaf? *Move!* This is where the players sit."

That explained why no one had sat next to me. I stood and fought the urge to punch her in her rude ass mouth. I looked around and a few people stared at us like they expected a fight.

"Dang Rashida, cut the girl some slack," came a voice behind her.

Rashida smiled brightly before she even turned around. When she did turn around, I caught a partial glimpse of a boy's face.

"What you talking about Xavier? I was being nice," she giggled.

"Oh- okay," he replied like he knew she was full of shit.

"You too pretty to be so mean," he said as he walked past her and pulled her ponytail. When he came into view he was smiling and my mouth fell open.

The first thing I noticed about him was his eyes, they were a light piercing green, the same color as a freshly sliced kiwi. And his skin reminded me of melted caramel and looked just as smooth. But it was his smile that made me practically turn into a puddle on the gym floor.

"Hey, I'm Xavier. We can go sit up there," he pointed to the top of the bleachers as he walked towards me. "Since this is reserved for the basketball boys," he remarked in a teasing tone as he looked over his shoulder at Rashida. She smiled at him but as soon as he turned away, she frowned at me.

I followed him to the top of the bleachers as more cheerleaders piled on to the floor. "Who the hell is that with Xavier?" one of them asked. But I didn't catch the reply if there was one, I was too busy trying not to fall. The last thing I needed was to embarrass myself in front of the cutest boy I'd ever seen and give the cheer squad something to laugh at.

When we finally made it to the top, Xavier sat down and patted the spot next to him.

"Thanks," I mumbled.

"So, what's your name?" he asked.

"Huh- oh, I'm Angela but everybody calls me Angie,"

"Okay, Angie. Is today your first day at Drew?" he asked.

"Yeah," I replied.

"You know that's what this pep rally is for, right? To welcome all the new students. When they call your name, you have to go down and say a few words,"

My eyes widened as I turned to look at him. There was no way in hell I was doing that!

He laughed loudly and few people looked in our direction.

"You're too easy. And too serious." He leaned back against the wall and stared at me.

"Ha ha," I said and smiled despite myself. I hoped I didn't start blushing; it was a horrible and uncontrollable trait. When I was embarrassed or happy my face betrayed me even when I tried to act unfazed.

"Why did you come to a new school in the middle of the last semester?" he asked.

Before I could answer his question, the band started playing and everybody stood up and cheered. After the school song, introduction of the cheerleaders and basketball players, the principal took to the floor and offered some encouraging words to the basketball team since they were headed to the state championship.

"You gone leave me hanging?" Xavier scooted closer to me.

"Huh?" I asked confused.

"Why did you come to Drew? Did you get kicked out of your other school?" he smirked. He'd still been waiting for an answer to his question.

"Um, no. Me and my mama moved and it was out of the district from my other high school, so here I am," I sighed. He was cute but very nosy.

"And you hate it." He stated.

"First day. Don't know enough about the school to hate it yet."

"*Yet*. You're funny," he chuckled. I diverted my gaze back to the gym floor.

"Did you leave your boyfriend at your old school?" he asked. I looked at him and focused on the intricate design cut into the side of his tapered hair. It was a zigzag line that ended in a swirl near his ear.

"You ask too many questions," I snapped.

"Sorry," he held his hands up and moved away. "You just look like you could use a friend,"

I rolled my eyes. Boys like him didn't want to be friends with girls. I may have been a virgin but I wasn't stupid.

"Friends? *Really?*" I smirked at him.

"Oh, what you think I'm trying to push up on you?" he laughed. And I was instantly offended. Maybe he didn't think I was pretty enough for him.

"Whatever," I muttered.

"Nah- that ain't a diss or nothing, I have a girlfriend," he announced and for some reason it made me a little sad even though I'd only known him for all of thirty minutes.

"Well, where is she?" I questioned.

He smiled. "She's absent today but I'll be sure to introduce you.

Peace," he stood as the pep rally ended and bounded down the steps ahead of the hundreds of students merging from the bleachers.

And that was the first time I met Xavier Ross.

The next time I saw him was in Biology class two days later. He walked in with his arm around a girl who looked more like a swimsuit model than a high school junior. He kissed her and they broke apart to take their seats. She sat in the front of the class and he sat in the back. When he passed by my desk he tapped it with his pencil. I looked up at him and he winked before he continued to the back of the class.

I wouldn't have another conversation with Xavier Ross until the first day of our senior year.

"Hey, I was hoping you'd be coming back this year," he sat next to me at lunch and I glared up at him.

"What? Oh, hey." My frown was replaced by a small smile.

"What's up? How was your summer?" he asked grinning at me.

"It was good. Fine." I shrugged. I wondered why he was going out of his way to talk to me. Maybe he felt sorry for me because I eating lunch alone. I was about to tell him I didn't need his pity when he spoke,

"I thought about you over the summer. A lot." He said suddenly.

And I laughed. "Yeah, right,"

"I'm serious," he said convincingly.

"Do you even remember my name?" I challenged.

He rolled his eyes. "Angela Barnes. You transferred from Grant in March. We had Biology together. You used to take bus 710 home or sometimes your moms, I guess it was your mom, would pick you up in that blue Honda,"

My eyes widened in surprise. "You're a stalker." I couldn't

believe he knew that much about me. Or that he'd been thinking about me. I'd actually thought about him a couple of times too.

"Nah- I ain't like that," he laughed. "You're just not easily forgotten,"

"Where's your girlfriend?" I asked.

"She moved to Georgia and we broke up," he said quietly. "Is it okay to be your friend now?" he asked.

I thought about it for a legitimate ten seconds before I smiled and rolled my eyes. I doubted that he only wanted to be friends but I was more than okay with that too. I was probably the only high school senior, in the city of Buffalo, that was still a virgin.

"I suppose we could be friends," I smirked.

"Good. I don't really have any friends," he said and there was a hint of sadness in his voice.

"Boy, are you serious?" I laughed loudly drawing stares from the other tables. "You're the most popular boy at this school. Half the girls in this cafeteria are mean mugging me right now because you're sitting with me,"

"They're fake and shallow. Trust me, if I was dark skinned and didn't have green eyes none of them would have shit to say to me," he said bitterly.

His reply had shocked me. I hadn't expected him to be so self-aware but I also knew that he used his pretty boy looks to his advantage. Yet, he didn't seem like the same boy who had tried to charm me on the bleachers last year. He had hardened a little.

"Sorry. I didn't mean to get all deep on you," he grinned.

"Well, I guess since we're friends now, you can tell me what's on your mind," I smiled at him.

"And what about you? Are you gonna tell me what's on your

mind? Like why you always so mad?"

"I'm not always mad," I said defensively. He'd had some nerve trying to psychoanalyze me. He hadn't even seen me since May. It was September.

"My bad, just sometimes," he teased.

I sighed and decided to throw him a bone since he'd been so honest with me. "I guess I'm like you, I can't stand the fakeness. I'm not trying to kiss any of these girl's asses to be friends with them and I don't need to be in a clique. We'll be graduating soon and if I'm lucky, I won't have to see any of them ever again." And I'd meant every word of it because most of the girls at Drew were mean and catty. The only female I trusted was my Mama.

Xavier and I talked until the bell rang and then he walked me to my next class. We didn't have any classes together our senior year but we did eat lunch together every day and pretty soon we became inseparable. At the end of the school year, we went to prom and I was prepared to give him a piece of me that no one else had ever possessed but instead the night came to a sudden end and he became a stranger to me once again.

****

I woke up the next morning with a headache undoubtedly from the three glasses of wine I'd drank at dinner with Rodney. I swallowed two Advil to ease the dull pain but was still moving slower than usual because I couldn't get Xavier off my mind. I'd caught myself daydreaming about him over coffee, in the shower and while putting on my makeup.

I glanced down at my watch and remembered my meeting would be starting in twenty minutes. It would take me almost thirty minutes to get to work! I placed my mug in the sink and called Christina on my way out the door to push the meeting back fifteen minutes.

Once I arrived to work, I put my purse and laptop in my office before heading to the conference room. I was still five minutes late even with the new start time. As I listened to a presentation about the upcoming holiday campaigns my thoughts drifted back to Xavier. I couldn't believe he'd become a famous singer. Back when we were in high school, I remembered him playing the guitar but he'd never said anything about wanting to pursue music.

"What are your thoughts, Angela?" Moses, the project manager for the campaign had interrupted my musings. He looked at me expectantly.

I cleared my throat, placed a finger to my chin and pretended to be contemplating his question.

"I tell you what– let me think about it. Send me an email recapping everything and we'll reconvene. I apologize but something has come up, so I need to end the meeting early," I looked down at my phone and hoped my stall tactic didn't come back to bite me in the ass later.

"Is everything okay?" Christina asked after I returned to my office. "I thought the meeting was for two hours?"

"We finished early." I lied.

"Were you able to-,"

"Excuse me, Angela I have some invoices I need you to sign,"

One of the accounting managers appeared at my door and cut Christina's comment short. I was grateful for the interruption.

"I need to take care of this, we'll talk later." I said to Christina.

I definitely wasn't going to tell Christina that I had been distracted in the meeting because I was thinking about my high school boyfriend, who I hadn't seen in over fifteen years. Although it was technically her fault. If she hadn't mentioned Xavier, I would have never taken a second look at that reunion invitation or even considered going. But I had looked and listened and downloaded and now I was on Xavier overload.

After signing the invoices and checking my email, Christina told me I had a call waiting.

"Angela Barnes," I said picking up the receiver.

"Hello, Angela," It was Rodney.

"Hey, Rodney,"

"Hi, sorry to call you at work. I just wanted to make sure you were okay after last night, I um- things were a bit fuzzy and-,"

"Rodney, we're good," I assured him. I felt bad because I actually hadn't thought about Rodney or our almost hook up since he'd left my apartment.

He sighed deeply. "Okay, good. So, how are you? How is your day so far?"

I shook my head and closed my eyes. I definitely didn't have time or interest in small talk.

"My day is going well but I'm extremely busy, so I actually need to go but thanks for calling and checking on me," I said with a hint of impatience.

"Okay, well it was really good to see you and I'll be sure to keep in touch." He said and his tone sounded hopeful that I actually wanted to keep in touch. Although Rodney had said he understood that we weren't destined, he still probably thought there was a chance for us to get back together. He wasn't easily persuaded.

"Sounds good. Take care, Rodney." I hung up the phone before he could say another word. I hadn't meant to be rude but after last night I felt I'd gotten some closure.

Christina had read my mood and sensed that I wasn't up for chatting, so she stayed out of my way until after lunch.

"Hey, you got a minute?" she stood in the doorway of my office after I returned from eating at the deli downstairs. I knew I couldn't avoid her forever especially since I had agreed to take her as my date to the reunion.

"Sure, come on in."

"Did you get my emails?" she smiled. She sat down in the chair across from my desk without an invitation.

"All twenty-five of them." I teased.

"Sorry, I think I got a little carried away." She laughed.

"Just a little." I smiled. "No, it's okay. I downloaded a few of their songs." I said nonchalantly. I actually ended up downloading two of Soul Skylight's entire albums.

"And?" she asked curiously.

"They're really good," I said still holding back.

"Yes! The band is good but Xavier's voice is what makes them great! He's just so amazing! He can hit falsetto's like Maxwell but he also has timbre like old school Jeffrey Osborne and he exudes sexuality like Prince." She smiled dreamily.

"Wow," I said surprised and a little jealous of her assessment.

"I told you I was a fan," she said slightly embarrassed.

"I see," I laughed. "I actually agree with you."

We chatted a little more about Soul Skylight before ending the conversation with what outfits might be appropriate for a high school reunion that was taking place in the auditorium of the newly rebuilt school.

We managed to get through the rest of the day and the next couple of weeks with only minimal conversations about Xavier and the band. I'd also added an extra mile to my treadmill workout each day to minimize the jiggle. Not because I was trying to impress Xavier Ross, I was doing that for the mean cheerleaders who I hoped had gained three hundred pounds each.

September

Soon the week of the reunion arrived and for as much as Christina talked about going to see Soul Skylight, it just wasn't meant to be. The Monday before the reunion she started coughing, by Wednesday she was sniffling, and Thursday night she had a one hundred three-degree fever.

"Oh my god Christina, you should go to the emergency room! I'm on my way over there," I exclaimed.

"No- no, you don't have to come," She croaked out.

"You need someone to look after you." I insisted.

"Greg is here. He's going to take me to urgent care."

Greg? The boyfriend who wanted to take a break? Maybe he wasn't a total asshole after all.

"Are you okay with that?" I asked.

She chuckled and then started to cough. "More than okay."

"Good, well make sure they give you some prescriptions for the good stuff and I'll stop by and check on you tomorrow."

"No, you can't check on me," She coughed. "You'll be at your reunion."

"Um, no I won't. The only reason I was going was so that you could cross off seeing Soul Skylight from your bucket list. There is no reason for me to go now."

"Seriously? Angela, you have to go."

I heard Greg in the background telling her they should leave.

"Greg is right, you need to go." I cosigned.

"And so do you! Promise me you'll still go. I want to live vicariously through you! Please!" She begged. Then she started to cough again. "I'm not leaving until you promise."

Greg threatened to throw her over his shoulder.

"Why is this so important to you?" I questioned.

"I worry about you. You work too much. Go, please?"

I sighed. "Okay, fine. But be prepared for a boring report on Monday morning."

"Can't wait. Have fun!"

"Feel better."

After I ended the call with Christina, I held the phone close to my chest. The thought of going to the reunion without her made me nervous. I'd wanted her there for support. What if Xavier had totally forgotten about me? I laughed out loud. I was being absurd, he would be there to perform and I probably wouldn't even get to see him. It's not like we were still friends or had kept in touch over the years but I'd always wondered why things ended the way they did.

I took a calming breath and placed the phone on the couch next to me. I would go and take a few pictures and videos for Christina. I'd be in and out before anyone even knew I was there.

The next morning my flight from LaGuardia was delayed two hours. It was pretty ridiculous considering the flight itself would only take a little over an hour. Once we finally boarded, I got settled in my seat and decided to work on a few emails to pass the time on the short flight but before I could get my laptop from my bag someone sat next to me.

"Angela Barnes?" A woman gasped.

I turned my head and tried not to appear annoyed. I wasn't much of an airplane conversationalist. A heavy-set woman with long curly hair, which I suspected was a weave, stared at me with a big smile. She obviously knew me from somewhere but I couldn't place her.

"Hi....," I said drawing out the syllable.

She laughed. "You have no idea who I am, do you?"

I winced. "Sorry."

"Dana Simmons. Well, it used to be Simmons, it's Robinson now. I married Danté Robinson, he was our quarterback. I had a conference in New York and decided to fly from here. He's going to meet me in Buffalo. We live in Florida now. He got drafted by the Dolphins after college. . .,"

She rambled on and on telling me things I didn't give a shit about and it wasn't until her long-winded introduction was almost over that I realized who she was– Dana Simmons, captain of the varsity cheer squad at my former high school and leader of the original mean girls.

I couldn't believe she was being so chatty since she barely talked to me in high school except to criticize my clothes or ask me what kind of spell I'd put on Xavier.

"Yeah, Dana I remember you." I smiled. I was positively giddy that her perfect cheerleader body no longer existed. I pulled my laptop from my bag and hoped she'd take a hint and cut the conversation short.

"I was captain of the varsity cheerleaders. We won state twice." She said proudly. She was too much of a cliché for me to handle.

"I think I remember that too," I said not even pretending to be interested.

"What have you been up to? You haven't changed much." She tried and failed miserably to be inconspicuous as she looked me over.

"Thanks," I said even though she probably hadn't meant it as a compliment.

"You must not have any kids? Since I had the twins it's been hard for me to lose this weight. It came right off after my first two but it's been a struggle with the last two. Not to mention I'm really busy, I'm a Brand Ambassador for Amway. We had a business retreat in New York for three days, which is why I was here. It worked out perfectly." She said finally taking a breath.

"Sounds like it." I pushed my bag under the seat and slid my laptop in the seatback pocket after the flight attendant announced we'd been cleared for take-off.

"Do you have any kids?" she inquired pulling the seatbelt across her ample chest.

"Oh no, not yet." Not sure why I added, 'not yet.' It's not like I had any real desire to have kids but I didn't want to add to Dana's already smug attitude.

"Girl, I don't blame you. Take your time but don't take too long because it's harder to get pregnant the closer you get to forty. I would've waited but Danté was such a caveman, he wanted me pregnant right away." She laughed.

"Well, since I'm only *thirty-four* I think I still have a few good years left." I turned away from her and looked out the window.

"You live in Manhattan?" she pried some more.

"Yep." I answered without making eye contact.

"I should have known you'd be coming to the reunion." She laughed lightly.

I turned toward her again. "Why is that?" I asked, this time not even masking my annoyance.

She rolled her eyes and smiled. "Xavier Ross."

"Ha!" I tried to sound indifferent but my voice betrayed me and came out high pitched and weird sounding. I cleared my throat, "Girl, that was a long time ago. I haven't seen or talked to Xavier since we graduated."

"I bet you hate you lost touch. I mean he was fine back then but now– ooh wee! *And* he can sing and he's famous. You know Danté was actually cut from the Dolphins after a year; he had issues with his hamstrings. He ended up coaching at Miami Senior High." She whispered. "But you and Xavier- everybody was shocked that the two of you were even a couple and then you broke up with him." She shook her head in disapproval.

I broke up with him. Is that what he told everybody? I took a deep breath and decided not to get into the details of my past or present life with Dana.

"Yeah, like I said– it was a long time ago."

I took a nap once the plane took off and woke up as we were landing. Dana told me goodbye and said she'd look for me at the reunion. I was going to make sure she didn't find me.

After deplaning with my carry-on bag, I headed to the car rental lot at the end of the airport. Once I got settled, I entered the address of the hotel where I was staying into the GPS. My parents had divorced when I was in high school and they'd both moved from Buffalo a few years ago. Since I didn't have family in the area I had no choice but to get a hotel room for my one night stay.

Once I'd checked in, I stared around the small, drab hotel room and wondered what I was doing in Buffalo. After Christina was unable to make it, I should have canceled. I had no genuine interest in seeing anyone I went to high school with and I didn't have that many fond memories. I had skipped the ten-year reunion altogether and should have skipped the fifteen as well.

It was almost four o'clock– the networking reception started at six and the performance would begin at eight. My plan was to get to the auditorium just in time for the performance, that way I could avoid any awkward run-ins with former classmates.

I started watching a *House Hunters* marathon on HGTV and before I knew it, it was 6:30. I jumped from the bed, unzipped my travel bag and decided to take a quick shower.

An hour later, I stood in front of the floor length mirror and studied my appearance. I smiled as I looked at myself from all angles in the navy blue, off the shoulder, fitted jumpsuit. Not bad. Not bad at all.

I had pulled my hair into a bun and touched up my makeup before grabbing my clutch from the bed and heading out the door.

When I arrived to my former alma mater, I was impressed by the new school and state of the art auditorium. The lights were low and the emcee, one of our former guidance counselors, was about to introduce the band.

The auditorium was packed and I wished I'd gotten there earlier to get a better seat. Most of the people had probably come for the free show to see a Grammy-winning band and not to actually reconnect with high school friends. I made my way up the stairs to the top seats closer to the stage. There were a lot of people standing in front of the stage, mostly women. No doubt trying to get Xavier's attention; some things never changed.

"Soul Skylight is a Grammy award-winning, internationally renowned band and we are so honored to have them here at the fifteen-year reunion for the class of 1998. We want to give a special thanks to one of Drew High's own, Panther alumni- Xavier Ross," The women in front of the stage started screaming like thirteen-year-olds at their first concert.

It was really juvenile but I wasn't in a position to judge since I was sitting on the edge of my seat vibrating with equal excitement.

"Please put your hands together and give a big Drew High

welcome to Soul Skylight!"

The crowd went crazy! Even the guys were barking and pumping their fists in the air.

When the curtains opened, soft lights illuminated the stage and a lone figure approached the microphone. The keyboard player started the opening chords of a familiar song and then a spotlight brought Xavier into view.

Cue more screaming.

"Hello Drew Class of 1998!" he yelled. "I know you know this song." He smiled widely and my heart fluttered.

The keyboardist started playing again and I recognized it as our school song. Xavier laughed before he started to sing and encouraged the crowd to sing along with him. He signaled the keyboardist to stop playing as the auditorium erupted into the chorus of the Panther fight song. I found myself unable to resist joining in as I sang loudly and off key.

"That was good! Give yourselves a big round of applause!" Xavier clapped after the song ended. "We are so happy to be here tonight and hope you enjoy yourselves as we take a trip down memory lane."

He walked over to the edge of the stage, picked up a guitar and joined the band as they played a medley of songs that were popular when we graduated before giving the people what they really came for– Soul Skylight. They performed a few of their most popular songs and people sang and danced in the aisles. I sat mesmerized by this boy, now a man, that I used to know so many years ago. The way he led the band, commanded the crowd and performed so effortlessly gave me goosebumps. He was magnetic. I took my phone from my purse and snapped a few pictures and sent a video to Christina. I traced the image on my screen and wished I could have seen him face to face one more time.

After the last song, I walked down to the auditorium floor where several people had gathered and were discussing the show and reminiscing about the past. A couple of classmates spotted me and I was pulled into the conversation. We all took turns reporting our whereabouts and achievements over the last fifteen years. I was shocked that the majority of the group still lived in Buffalo.

I looked back at the stage and hoped to get another glimpse of Xavier but he was probably already on his way to another city. I desperately needed to get some fresh air, so I excused myself from the group and headed towards the side exit.

Outside I leaned against a brick column and stared at the night sky surprised so many stars were visible. A slight breeze ghosted through the air and I rubbed my arms briskly to generate some heat. I'd left my wrap in the rental car.

I turned around and decided to go back inside, and less than five feet away from me stood Xavier Ross. My mouth fell open and my heart began to beat erratically.

"Hey Angie," he said and a lazy smile graced his face. The husky tone of his voice combined with the slight Brooklyn accent, which had faded some over time, sent a chill down my spine.

The Internet images did not do him justice. Up close and personal he was so much better looking. He no longer had a beard, so I was able to see more of his flawless skin and sexy jawline.

My inner sixteen-year-old started squealing when he used my nickname from so many years ago. No one really called me Angie anymore except my family. I took a deep breath and remembered I was no longer a child, I was a thirty-four-year-old professional woman.

I cleared my throat and raised my head a little higher.

"Hello." I smiled back at him.

We stared at each other for a few minutes before either of us spoke again. I was still trying to reconcile the boy I once knew with the man that stood before me and I'm sure he was doing the same.

"How have you been? It's been so long since– wow, you look amazing," he said softly. He thought I looked *amazing*? That one word tumbling from his lips caused a warm sensation in the pit of my stomach or it may have been lower, it was hard to tell.

"Great, I've been great. Yeah, it's been a long time, a really long time. How have you been?" I shifted nervously under his gaze. His eyes were still hypnotic and his penetrating glare caused me to feel short of breath.

"I've been good. Just playing in this little band," he grinned.

"Oh yeah, the band! You guys are good, really good! Great performance!" I clasped my hands together to avoid breaking out in spontaneous applause.

He lowered his head and appeared to be embarrassed. "Thanks," he muttered. Then he suddenly raised his head and narrowed his eyes at me. "You had no idea who we were, did you?"

Busted.

"What? Yeah, sure I did," I lied.

He laughed. "You're still an awful liar,"

"Okay, okay. So, I'm a little out of the loop. But in my defense, I've been busy climbing the career ladder." I smiled.

"You know what they say about all work and no play," he winked.

It was an innocent comment and I knew there was no malice behind his words but it reminded me of the time I'd felt the sting of his rejection.

I swallowed my smile and took a deep breath.

"You know, I was actually just leaving," I said strongly as I gripped my clutch under my arm. My voice reflected the bitterness I felt.

His eyes widened. "Oh shit, I'm sorry did I say something wrong?" he asked. The look of confusion and distress on his face burned a hole right through the protective armor I wore around my heart.

I closed my eyes and sighed. "No. . . it's just getting late." I said dejectedly.

"Oh, yeah– is your *fiancé* here?" he asked and his tone seemed to harden.

"My fiancé?" I asked confused. How had he known I was engaged? Was he stalking me? More importantly, why was I happy about the idea of him stalking me?

"Sharon mentioned you'd gotten engaged." He had apparently read my thoughts. He turned away from me and stared up at the sky.

Sharon Perry had been one of my only other friends (besides Xavier) in high school. She was currently living overseas with her husband and three children. I only knew this because of Facebook. And she probably only knew about Rodney because I'd posted a picture of the ring after we got engaged. We hadn't exactly kept in touch after we graduated.

"When did you talk to Sharon?" I asked.

"She lives in Abu Dhabi, right? We did a private show in the Emirates not too long ago." He said as if that explained everything. I didn't need to know the rest of the story, the fact that he had asked about me was enough.

"Actually, I *was* engaged but not anymore. We broke up." I admitted.

"Sorry to hear that," he looked at me and smiled broadly.

My mouth fell open and I narrowed my eyes at him this time. "I don't think people usually smile quite so big when someone mentions a failed engagement."

"You're right, that wasn't cool. It was rude of me, I'm sorry." he said and appeared to be sincere.

I resumed my spot against the brick column. "Yes, it was rude," I said lightly. I didn't why he seemed to be happy that I was no longer engaged. I allowed my mind to run wild with scenarios about rekindling our teen romance.

"Did you love him?" he asked out of the blue.

The no-nonsense side of me knew I should have told him it was none of his business and walked away. But I was feeling quite nonsensical at the moment. Strange how he still managed to make me feel that way after all the time and distance that had been placed between us.

"Yes, I did. But at some point, things started to fall apart and neither of us tried hard enough to stop it. Then he ended up taking a job in another city and left without me." I said sadly as I thought about Rodney.

"Hmm," he said thoughtfully. "Sometimes I think things fall apart because we try so hard to please other people and we lose ourselves in the process."

When did Captain Clueless become so profound?

"Yeah well, the story of my life, I suppose." I ran my hands up and down my arms again.

"Are you cold?" he asked and before I could answer he had removed his leather jacket.

"I'm okay, but I should probably go, I mean I think the party is pretty much over anyway." I looked up at the windows around the top of the building and saw the lights on in the auditorium. I could also hear people in the parking lot on the other side of the building.

"Yeah," he said.

"You know I just realized something– how did you manage to make it out here without causing a riot?" I asked confused.

"I have my ways." He smiled.

"I bet you do." I shook my head and sighed. "I'm sure you probably have to go too, right? Where are your bandmates? Do you have another gig tonight?" I tried to sound cool and knew I'd failed when he laughed at me.

"No. No more *gigs* tonight. Actually, they already left. I wanted to see you before– hey, there's a coffee shop around the corner, come have a cup of coffee with me?" he asked hopefully.

"Really? Don't you think it will be full of people?"

"Nah, there's actually a party at some club that everyone is headed to." He announced.

Nobody had mentioned anything about a party to me. I was glad because I wouldn't have gone but I was also offended. Apparently not much had changed since high school, I still wasn't part of the popular crowd.

"I don't know-," I hesitated.

"Please?" He asked and there was a hint of desperation in his voice.

I stared at him and wondered why he was so anxious to talk to me. He'd never made an effort to reach out to me in fifteen years.

"Sorry, I know you don't owe me anything. It's just, we leave on tour in a week and I was hoping to talk to you some more. I've thought about you a lot over the years," he confessed and then hung his head as if he wished he could swallow the words back down.

"Sure, coffee sounds great," I replied. I was shocked that he'd thought about me over the years. Maybe he'd explain why over coffee.

He draped his jacket over my shoulders and I was immediately engulfed in his scent. It was something sexy and masculine combined with the smell of expensive leather.

"Should we drive? I have a car." I offered as we walked towards the parking lot.

"No, it's just one block up and over. Unless you want to drive," he shrugged. He took a baseball cap from his back pocket and pulled it down almost covering his eyes, no doubt trying to create some anonymity.

Once we made it to the coffee shop, we ordered and took a seat at a table in the back. It was a cute little shop with eclectic farmhouse décor. I sipped on my latte while he emptied an artificial sweetener into his plain black coffee.

"Do you still live in town?" he asked.

I chuckled. I'd outgrown Buffalo a long time ago. "No, I live in Manhattan."

He took a tentative sip of his coffee before asking, "So, what corporate ladder have you been climbing? What do you do?"

"I'm the Associate Director of Marketing Media Strategy for Clinique," I said proudly. I felt it was quite an accomplishment for someone my age.

He smirked at me. "Can you break that down for me in English?" he teased.

"Oh yeah, well my department makes sure our product line is advertised in magazines and media outlets. Wherever it makes sense for our end users to see our products, our team makes sure it happens."

He nodded. "Cool. I think I may have used some of your product before."

"I don't think so, I'm in the cosmetics division." I chuckled.

"I went through an eyeliner phase– huge Prince fan." he said and gave an exaggerated sigh before he continued, "Didn't help me play as good as him though."

I laughed loudly and as he joined me I wondered when he'd learned to be so self-deprecating. The past fifteen years had obviously matured him in more ways than one.

"But I bet it made your eyes look even more fabulous," I instinctively placed my hand against his cheek. His eyes widened and he swallowed hard. I felt a tingling sensation in my fingertips before I quickly dropped my hand.

"Sorry," I mumbled as I took a sip of my latte.

"Don't be," he smiled.

"So-,"

"How-,"

We both tried to conceal the uneasiness of the moment.

"Go ahead, what were you about to say?" he grinned.

"I downloaded some of your music. You have a great voice. I remember you played guitar in high school but I didn't know you could sing or were even that serious about music."

He smiled shyly. "I wasn't that serious about it. It's one of those things that just kind of happened. I won an open mic night at a club after performing on a dare. There was an agent in the audience that night and things moved pretty fast from there and the next thing you know we were in a studio recording a demo and signing a two-album record deal."

"Wow! Why didn't you go the solo route? Don't you sing the

majority of the songs?" I asked. It seemed it would be a lot more lucrative to be a solo act.

"Most of them but Johnny sings on some tracks plus he's my writing partner. Those are my boys, I don't know that I could do this without them. It's been an amazing, wild ride."

I tried to keep my expression blank but I was sure a 'wild ride' meant a groupie in every city.

"You mentioned a tour? Where are you going?"

"Our new album is called 20/20 you know like perfect vision— clarity, seeing things clearly. That's also the name of the tour. We're doing 20 U.S. cities and 20 cities internationally."

"That sounds exhausting. How long will you be gone?" I frowned.

He smiled faintly. "Six or seven months. We've only toured once before and it was just a few dates. Our fans have been begging for this for two years, so we decided this album would be a perfect time."

For some reason, my heart sank. It wasn't that I expected him to keep in touch with me but being on tour was definitely going to make it impossible.

"That's. . .whew," I said at a loss for words. "I bet that's hard on your girlfriend." Talk about a pathetic attempt at being nosy.

He sipped his coffee and chuckled after he swallowed. "Are you being inquisitive?" he asked.

I raised an eyebrow. "That's an awfully big word," I said and immediately covered my mouth. "I'm sorry- that was- I don't know where that came from."

"No apologies necessary. You haven't seen me since high school and I didn't have the biggest vocabulary back then," he admitted.

"So, I guess I am being inquisitive." I shrugged.

"There is no girlfriend. It makes it easier to leave."

"Sounds kind of lonely."

"Only when I come off stage," he remarked sadly.

We settled into an easy conversation reminiscing about the good times we shared in high school all the while carefully avoiding anything about the last night we saw each other.

"Sorry, but we're closing now." A young barista announced from the counter.

I looked around the coffee shop and was surprised when I realized we were the only customers. Xavier looked at his watch and his eyes widened.

"Man, we've been here for a while, it's a little past midnight."

"Are you serious? We're so sorry." I apologized and we hurried out into the frigid night air. The temperature had dropped at least ten degrees.

"Guess we really did have a lot to catch up on," I smiled as we walked back to the school.

"Yeah." He stuffed his hands into his pants pockets and hunched his shoulders like he was freezing.

"Oh my god, here take your jacket!" I offered.

"No. I'm fine, really."

I smirked at him and locked my arm with his. "Such a gentleman," I snuggled closer to him under the pretense of trying to share body heat.

"Yeah, right," he muttered.

"What is that supposed to mean?" I laughed. Had he read my mind?

"Nothing," he sighed.

"So, can I give you a ride back to your hotel or something?"

He shrugged. "Sure, I guess, I mean if that's okay. Otherwise, I can call our driver to come and get me."

"You have a driver?" I teased.

He scratched the back of his neck and appeared embarrassed.

"I'm just teasing! Come on, get in," I opened the driver door and disengaged the locks.

He got in and told me the name of his hotel, it wasn't too far from where I was staying; much nicer than my hotel but still close. Both hotels were only about twenty minutes from the school.

He seemed really uneasy once we got on the highway and shifted uncomfortably in his seat for most of the ride. I tried to ignore it but once his hotel came in to view, I finally said something. I didn't want the night to end with the weird vibe that had settled over us.

"Okay was it me this time, what did I say? Seems like the mood changed drastically." I gripped the steering wheel as I pulled into the valet area of his hotel.

"Come upstairs with me?" he asked quietly. He said it so softly that I almost didn't hear him.

An invitation to his hotel room could only mean one thing.

"Look, it was good seeing you but I'm not some groupie who's trying to get laid," I was mildly offended that he thought he could treat me like a dumb fangirl who would do whatever he wanted. Only *mildly* offended. Another part of me was extremely flattered. But I had to maintain some dignity, right?

"No, nothing like that!" he protested. "I just– I'm not ready for you to leave yet. I go on tour soon and I probably won't see you again for another fifteen years or ever again. I guess I want to keep talking to you- keep you here until-," he rambled.

I stared blankly out the front window as the valet appeared at my door. I gripped the steering wheel tightly and contemplated my next move, and what it would mean.

"Okay," I agreed. Because he was right, I'd probably never see him again after tonight not to mention, I'd hoped to finally get some answers about what had bought our relationship to an end fifteen years ago.

After we entered his hotel room, Xavier offered me a bottle of water and I took a seat on the plush couch in the living area of the suite.

"I meant what I said, I didn't invite you up here expecting anything would happen," he reiterated.

I removed my shoes and sat with my bare feet curled under me on the couch while he reclined in the chair across from me. For a moment, it felt as if no time had passed between us at all. But a great deal of time had passed and I was still hung up on what could have been.

I took a deep breath and cleared my throat as I tried to find my voice.

"What happened the night of prom? Did I do something wrong? Or did you just change your mind?" I asked and hated that my voice trembled and made me sound like a pitiful woman who never got over that one moment in her past because that's exactly who I was.

"What?" he asked obviously shocked by my line of questioning.

"The night of prom, we had it all planned out and then nothing. You took me home and acted like you couldn't stand the sight of me." I said angrily.

He moved and sat next to me on the couch.

"Are you serious?" he frowned.

"Xavier, you dropped me off, and left without even a kiss goodbye and then you were pretty much a ghost at school that last week."

He sighed harshly. "I don't remember all of that but I did want to be with you. That night– I wanted to be your first," he said. "But I overheard what you said to Sharon and I couldn't go through with it."

"What are you talking about?" I asked. I didn't even remember a conversation with Sharon that night.

He stared at me and his expression suddenly changed. "You told her you couldn't wait to get it over with, that you were probably the only virgin in the whole school and you should have just done it a long time ago with your ex-boyfriend. You said that's why he broke up with you."

"So?" I shrugged.

"So? I was under the impression it meant something to you, that you wanted it to be *me* because of how you felt about me not because I had a willing dick." he frowned. "I thought you were like all those other girls, just pretending they liked me, so they could say they had been with Xavier Ross." He shook his head obviously recalling a specific incident.

I winced. "First of all, I don't remember saying that to Sharon. And second, after everything we'd shared is that what you really thought? That I was just using you to scratch an itch?" I scoffed.

"I didn't know what to think-,"

"And you didn't bother asking me." I exhaled harshly.

He sighed. "I know, I'm sorry. It was a long time ago and we were so young. Plus, you were leaving to go to college in Michigan and I didn't know what I wanted to do. It just seemed like it was the right thing to do since we'd more than likely break up anyway." He reasoned.

He was probably right but I had been distraught by the way he just stopped talking to me. "I know it was a long time ago and we were young but I loved you, Xavier. You were one of my best friends. It was hard after my parents divorced and I ended up at Drew but you always made me feel like I belonged." I smiled. "And I really wanted you to be my first, I always regretted that you weren't. I thought you rejected me because there was something wrong with me, and it definitely affected most of my early sexual experiences." I confessed and instantly wished I could take it back.

His eyes widened.

"And on that note, I'm going to leave now." I felt mortified for admitting that to him.

I stood and my foot felt like a million pins were pricking it all at once. "Shit, my foot fell asleep," I hopped around on one foot and tried to make it over to my shoes.

He realized I was going to pick up my shoes and beat me to them. He gathered them by the heels and moved around to the other side of the coffee table.

"No, don't go. Please, not like this." He begged.

"Xavier, give me my shoes. This was a mistake I shouldn't have come up here and unleashed all this stuff about the past. It's been over fifteen years, we've both moved on." I said.

"What if I haven't moved on?" he asked.

"Yeah, right. You're Xavier Ross, an international star. You can have any woman you want."

"I want you. Can I have you?" he asked staring at me.

I diverted my eyes away from his gaze. I wasn't going to get caught by those laser beams.

"You said that's not why you asked me up here." I threw his words back at him.

He walked towards me and I backed away.

"You have haunted my dreams for the past fifteen years," he said softly as he took another step towards me. "Every love song I've written, there is a lyric that says how I felt about you."

I looked at him with a gaping mouth and he continued to advance towards me but I was frozen in place. He extended the shoes towards me.

"Thank you for having coffee with me and for coming up to talk. I know its fifteen years too late but I really am sorry. I never meant to hurt you and for the record, I loved you too." He said and I felt all my resolve disappear.

I took the shoes and threw them aside as I fisted his shirt and brought my face to his, he was stunned for a minute but then he grabbed me around my waist and I kissed him.

His full lips were firm against mine but the skin was smooth and soft. When he opened his mouth, I decided to let my intentions be known and sucked on his tongue.

He groaned before he pulled away panting hard and staring at me wild-eyed. "I swear I didn't ask you up here for this-," he started and I thought he had second thoughts but instead he said, "But I do want you, I've always wanted you."

A trail of shed clothing followed behind us as we made our way to the king-sized bed in the second room of the suite. I closed my eyes and smiled as I reveled in the sensation of floating, I had to be dreaming there was no other way to explain what was happening. Because I did not do things like this, although I knew him this was technically a one-night stand. And the way. . . . .

"Hey, where are you?" he kissed my nose and interrupted my thoughts.

I opened my eyes to find his hooded eyes staring back at me. His irises had turned a dark green.

"I'm dreaming, right?" I smiled.

He smiled back at me. "Nah, you're not nearly this beautiful in my dreams and you're not as soft as you feel now," he ran nose along my neck before inhaling deeply.

"And I don't remember you smelling this good. So, this must be real."

"Hmm," I hummed and closed my eyes again. My entire body buzzed with anticipation but I was also extremely nervous.

Xavier's finger trailed up my inner thigh before moving to the apex of my thighs. I gasped and kissed him again. When he pulled away, I gently ran my finger over the tattoo on his forearm, an ornate design of a guitar.

"I used to love kissing you," he breathed against my lips as he continued to stare into my eyes.

His finger slid under my lace panties and stroked me lightly. The sensation made me whimper and I wrapped my arms around his neck.

"Wait a minute," he sighed as he gently pried me away. I watched as he left the bed and headed for his discarded pants. He dug around in the pockets until he found his wallet. Once he opened he it, he smiled and returned to me. I stared at the large bulge in his underwear and bit down on my bottom lip to suppress the moan that was threatening to erupt.

"I only have one so we better make this count," he said as he tossed a condom on the bedside table.

"Do you want to turn off the lights?" I was suddenly a little self-conscious. I thought my body looked pretty good but my breasts were small and my stomach wasn't completely flat no matter how many ab extenders I did at the gym. He'd probably been with women with perfect bodies.

"No, leave them on. You're beautiful and I want to see all of you." He declared and the throbbing between my legs intensified.

Xavier placed a knee on the mattress and reached behind me to unhook my bra, then he pulled me onto his lap. I straddled him as he kissed and caressed me; I was so worked up that I found myself grinding over him before grabbing his wrist and placing his hand on my waist.

"What?" he breathed and gave me a teasing smile before pulling away. "Tell me. What do you want?"

I wasn't used to this. The talking and direction. I found it slightly annoying but I was also very aroused.

"Take them off," I sucked in a deep breath and he smirked.

He fisted the waistband of my underwear and I was about to lift up, so that he could pull them down but instead he gathered the material tightly and ripped it away from me.

"Ah!" I hissed as the fabric scraped my skin making it feel like it had been ignited. I looked at him and he had a wicked grin on his face. For a second, his grip on me loosened as he reached over and grabbed the condom. After wriggling out of his briefs and fully sheathing himself, he kissed my neck. I could feel him stiff and ready beneath me but he didn't make a move to do anything.

"Xavier," I whispered his name as I inched even closer to him.

"Take what you need," he rasped in my ear and I lost all restraint. I sank down on him and he gripped my hips as our bodies moved together in sync. After only a few minutes, I could feel a familiar pressure building and suddenly I was flat on my back against the mattress. Xavier had flipped me over and changed our positions.

"You feel so good," he grunted and thrust at the same time. I arched like a cat and met each thrust until my body start to tremble.

"Stay with me a little longer," he begged.

I tried to force away the feeling of wanting to explode and allowed myself to be consumed as I clung to him.

Xavier was a confident and skilled lover and I wondered how different things would have been if we'd had sex fifteen years ago. He probably wouldn't have known how to hit my body at the perfect angles the way he was doing. And he definitely wouldn't have had me shouting the choruses of "oh shit's" and "fuck yeah's" that had involuntarily come out when his hand moved between us and his fingers stroked me while he moved deeper inside me.

I felt the sensation of falling and just when I thought I was about to hit the ground, I started falling again. It was mind-blowing. About twenty minutes later we were both sweating and convulsing as we reached a simultaneous climax.

Afterwards, I lay in his arms and stared up at the ceiling. We were both silent except for the sounds of our harsh breathing. His fingertips gently brushed against my shoulder.

"Be right back," he got up from the bed and headed to the bathroom. A few seconds later I heard the toilet flush.

When he came back he lay down next to me and put an arm around my waist.

"I'm so glad that we reconnected but damn I hate the timing. Tomorrow I fly back to L.A. We've got rehearsals for a week before we head out on the 20th," he said softly.

I swallowed back my emotions and smiled. "I know it sucks. But I'll never forget this night. *Ever*." I said sincerely. We had come full circle and I could finally close that chapter in my life.

He propped himself up on his elbow and looked down at my face. "So, wait- was this just a one-time thing?" he questioned.

I sat up a little higher and looked at him. "I mean what were you thinking?" I asked confused.

"I don't know that we'd see each other again- that we could try to see where this could go?"

I laughed lightly. "Xavier, you're going on tour. *For six months.* How are we supposed to see each other again?"

"Phone calls, texts, Skype or Facetime- I can send you tickets and you can come to some of the weekend shows." he offered.

"Oh wow, you're serious," I said in disbelief.

"Yeah- unless- shit. This isn't something you want." He fell back on the bed obviously disappointed.

This time I propped myself on my elbow and stared down into his face. He wouldn't make eye contact with me. I gently grabbed his chin and turned his face towards mine.

"I don't know. I don't want to get my hopes up. You'll be on the road, I know there are a lot of women, plus the distance and fifteen years is just a long time. . .we've both changed so much," I rattled on.

Seeing Xavier was one thing but starting a relationship with him, I didn't know if I was ready for that especially a long-distance relationship. That was one of the reasons I had ended my relationship with Rodney.

"I don't want anybody else but you. I know we can make this work, I lost you once, I don't want to lose you again." He grabbed my hand. "Do you think you could at least be open to trying? Getting to know each other again?"

I couldn't believe what I was hearing. The rational side of my brain knew a relationship with Xavier would never work but I was tired of always being so rational. I thought about it for a few seconds. Did I want to be in a relationship with Xavier Ross? Hell yes!

I smiled and nodded slowly. He smiled and grabbed my face and kissed me firmly on my lips.

Before I left his hotel, we exchanged phone numbers and email addresses. I couldn't wait to get home and tell Christina all about my trip.

****

When I returned to the office Monday morning following the reunion, Christina gave me exactly five minutes to get settled before she appeared at my door with coffee and a big grin on her face.

"I looked at your calendar and you don't have any meetings until ten, so is this a good time to talk?" she placed my coffee mug on my desk and had already sat down across from me.

After thinking about it, I'd decided not to tell Christina that I'd indulged in groupie-like behavior and had sex with Xavier. I also didn't want her to know that I had agreed to try a long-distance relationship with him. She respected me and considered me a mentor. I didn't want to ruin that image.

However, I couldn't control the big smile that appeared on my face. Christina jumped up from her chair and rushed over to close my office door before returning to her seat. She placed her elbows on the edge of the desk and leaned forward.

"So how are you feeling? You look and sound much better." I commented.

"I'm good. I slept most of the weekend."

"Did you get my video?" I asked.

"Yes! Oh my God! They sound even better in person." She gushed. "Did you see him? Did you talk to Xavier?"

I smiled showing all of my teeth as I nodded.

She smiled widely and squealed. "Did he remember you? What did he say?"

"Oh yeah, he remembered me. We actually went out for a cup of coffee after the reunion was over." I said taking a sip from my mug. "You know just catching up and stuff," I remarked vaguely.

"Are you serious? I would've died!" Her eyes were wide.

"I tell you what– time has been more than kind to him!" I fanned myself with my hand.

"Really? I didn't think the man could get any finer," she snickered. "I can't believe you had coffee with Xavier Ross!" Christina gushed.

Coffee wasn't the only thing I'd had.

"You should have taken a picture with him! Did he say anything about keeping in touch? Maybe you can get tickets when they come to town!"

"Yeah, he kind of mentioned that." I shifted in my seat. "I'll have to make sure we get you a ticket to see the band the next time they're here. I feel really bad that you missed out." I said sincerely.

"That would be so awesome!" she exclaimed.

While she was momentarily dazed I was able to quickly change the subject.

"So, was Greg your knight in shining armor?" I asked referring to her ex-boyfriend taking care of her while she was sick.

She smiled and leaned back in the chair.

"Yeah, he called me and when he heard my voice, he asked if I was sick. I told him I wasn't feeling well and twenty minutes later, he was at my door."

"Are you guys back together?" I asked carefully.

She shrugged. "We're moving slow. I don't want him to think

he's doing me a favor by being with me. I mean I appreciate him taking care of me this past weekend and I know he still loves me but he can't just decide to push me aside when he gets bored. It's all or nothing, you know."

I smiled. "Good for you. You deserve someone whose love is consistent. I'm glad you're standing up for yourself. Excuse me for saying this but Greg is an idiot if he doesn't see what he has in you-you're beautiful, smart, funny and you have the biggest heart of anyone I know."

She smiled. "Thank you for saying that Angela."

"I mean it! Now we should probably get some work done today." I laughed. "I sent you some information to add to the Macy's package. We need to make sure that gets out today."

"No problem. I'm so glad you went to your reunion." She smiled walking over to the door.

When she opened it, one of the other office assistants stood in the doorway holding a vase with a beautiful assortment of daisies and roses.

"I was just about to knock. These were delivered a few minutes ago." She smiled.

"Thanks, Sherry," Christina said looking at me.

I tried to suppress my smile, they were probably from Xavier.

Christina looked at the card and laughed nervously.

"They're for me." She said softly. She read the card silently and closed her eyes. "Greg," she said as her voice cracked.

I smiled at her. I was happy that Greg had made such a considerate gesture but I'd be lying if I said I wasn't disappointed. Xavier sent me a text when he boarded his flight yesterday and another one after the flight landed in L.A. but I hadn't heard from him since.

Christina cleared her throat. "I better put these down. I'll update the package and send it out this afternoon." She said hurrying from my office.

The day moved by at a snail's pace and after two back-to-back meetings, I grabbed a sandwich from downstairs and ate lunch at my desk.

"Angela, you've got a call on line one. Should I tell him you're at lunch." Christina's voice came over the intercom.

Him? Was it Xavier?

"No, I'll take it."

I cleared my throat before picking up the line.

"Angela Barnes."

"Hey, did I catch you at a bad time?"

It was Rodney. For a second I had an irrational feeling of guilt about my weekend with Xavier. But then I remembered Rodney and I were no longer together, which is why I couldn't understand why he was calling me so much.

"No- not really. I was just about to eat lunch at my desk." I sighed and unwrapped the wax paper from the deli.

"Okay, I won't hold you, I just had a quick question: Did you ever find that painting you were looking for?" he sounded like he was whispering.

"Calm Sea?" I asked absently. I opened the sandwich to make sure there was no mayonnaise.

"Is that the one with the woman at the park?"

"She's at the beach. But no, I never found it."

I first saw the reproduction print when Rodney and I had gone to an art festival in Dumbo, Brooklyn. We walked around for a while and when I'd gone back to get it, it had been sold. I'd immediately fallen in love with it because of the vibrant colors and the carefree feel of the piece. I'd spent the next few months looking for another copy but had eventually given up.

"I'm at an estate sale and I think I may be able to get the original for you if you're still interested."

"What? Are you serious? Yes, I'm definitely interested! Thanks, Rodney!" I said excitedly.

"No problem,"

"Do I even want to know why you're at an estate sale in the middle of the day, it's noon there, right?" I looked at my watch before taking a bite of the turkey sandwich.

"Believe it or not, this is actually work." He sighed.

I swallowed. "I didn't think you ever got to leave your desk," I said only half joking.

"Extremely rare occasions. Although I would prefer to be at my desk right now," he said and this time he was definitely whispering.

He told me that he was doing some personal appraisal and tax eligibility assessments for one of the partners going through an ugly divorce. I talked to Rodney for about ten minutes before he said he had to go.

I was reviewing a contract when my phone beeped thirty minutes later indicating I had a text. I picked it up and was a little deflated when I saw it was from Rodney. I was about to ignore his text but there was an attachment, I opened it and it was a picture of the Romare Bearden painting. I smiled and replied: **Thank you, thank you, thank you!** And I added a heart emoji. After I sent it, I regretted it. I didn't want him to think it meant anything. I had to keep reminding myself that we were no longer a couple and I'd made a promise to Xavier.

He texted back: **You're welcome. I'll have to figure out how I can get it shipped to you or I can bring it in person in a few weeks, if u can wait?**

AB: Shipping will be fine. You don't have to come to NYC just to drop off the painting.

RA: I've got a meeting there in three weeks. So, it's no problem.

AB: Okay whatever is easier. Thank you for thinking of me!

A few minutes passed before he responded, **I'm always thinking of you.**

My eyes widened and I turned off my phone.

****

Later that evening after I'd made it home from work, I sat on my couch watching TV and drinking wine– actually I was drinking wine and the TV just happened to be on. It was a distraction to keep me from looking at my phone and growing more and more disappointed that I hadn't heard from Xavier all day.

One of the main reasons I never wanted to be in a long-distance relationship was the lack of availability and accessibility. I didn't want to become an anxious, needy woman waiting for a phone call from a man. Or wondering when I'd see him again.

Xavier had probably just said he wanted to keep seeing me because he didn't want to hurt my feelings or make me think he'd used me. I was more than fine with having just one night with him, no expectations. But now, like a fool, I'd gone and gotten my hopes up.

I knew Xavier was busy preparing for a tour but I had hoped to hear from him before he left. I picked up my phone and decided I would send him a "good luck on tour" text just to see if he responded.

We also had a three-hour time zone difference between us that would make it hard to connect, and it was getting close to my bedtime. It was almost ten o'clock in New York but only a little to seven in L.A.

Right after I unlocked my screen, my phone rang. It was Xavier. I took several deep breaths and tried not to seem too eager.

"Hello," I said casually. I stood up from the couch and knocked over the bottle of Chardonnay sitting on the floor. "Damn it," I hissed.

"Hello? Angie?" his voice came on the other end. Whenever he called me by my old nickname, it gave me butterflies.

"Hey, it's me, sorry about that,"

"Did I catch you at a bad time?" he asked.

"Um, no- no. Now is good. Hey, what's up?" I asked. I felt like I was back in high school talking to him on the phone for the first time. I walked to the kitchen to get a towel.

"I am so sorry for just now calling you. I know you probably think I'm full of shit but yesterday after I called you, a car service picked me up from the airport and I left my phone in the car. I hadn't memorized your phone number yet so I couldn't call. I went to rehearsals and spent most of the day trying to get my phone back. A courier delivered it about an hour ago and it was dead, so once I charged it, I was able to call." He said out of breath.

I smiled. He hadn't forgotten about me.

"No problem. I know you're getting ready to go on tour, so I understand you're busy." I said as I bent down and blotted the wine from the rug.

"Yeah, but I don't want you to think I'm too busy for you. I mean that's the only way this is going to work, if we are able to communicate with each other, right? Or have you changed your mind?" he asked quietly.

This was my chance to tell him I didn't want the stress of wondering if and when he was going to call or when I'd see him again. But when it came to Xavier Ross my head rarely got a say in how things went down.

"Of course, I haven't changed my mind," I said quickly. A little too quickly. I wondered if he had changed his mind. "Have you?"

"No, definitely not. I was so unfocused today not being able to talk to you. I can't wait to see you again." I could tell by the sound of his voice that he was smiling. My smile widened.

"I can't wait to see you either. You mentioned your first stop on the tour was there in L.A.? Where are you off to after that?"

"Hold on- let me- I'm going to put you on speaker while I email you the tour dates. We're going to be performing at Radio City Music Hall on New Year's Eve and we have a few days off, so I thought maybe we could make plans then?"

New Year's Eve? It was September. I would have to wait almost four months to see him? I wasn't prepared for that and he must have picked up on my silence because he started speaking quickly.

"We're also going to be in Denver in a few weeks and Chicago in late October if you wanted to fly out to that show. I mean you're welcome to come to whatever show you want or all of them," he laughed. "I don't want to take your schedule for granted. I know you have a life, so just let me know what you want to do once you get the email and I'll have someone arrange travel and tickets for you,"

"Okay, that sounds like a plan. I'll take a look and let you know." I said. "So how did rehearsal go?" I asked changing the subject.

We talked on the phone for about forty-five minutes before the time difference got the best of me and I reluctantly had to say good night.

"I promise I'll do better about calling and being mindful of the time difference." He said. "I really do want this to work."

"Me too," I yawned and he laughed. "I am so sorry," I said embarrassed.

"Good night beautiful. Sweet dreams," he breathed into the phone.

"Good night Xavier.

October

*I*t had been almost three weeks since I'd seen Xavier at our fifteen-year reunion but he called me three to four times per week always being mindful of the time difference. He'd made plans to fly me out to Denver for the show on the eighth, which was in four days, so I worked from home a few evenings to make sure I was caught up on everything before the long weekend.

I was in the middle of reviewing an ad contract when my phone rang, I reached over and pressed the accept button realizing too late that it was Rodney.

"Hello," his voice came across the line.

"Hey, Rodney,"

"Hey Angela, how are you?"

I cleared my throat. "Good. I'm just trying to catch up on some work. I was in back to back meetings most of the day,"

"Will you be in the office tomorrow?" he asked.

"Yeah, what's going on?" I tried not to sound aggravated by his question.

"I'm flying to New York tomorrow and I'll have an hour after my meeting before I need to be back at the airport, so I can bring that painting to you." He suggested.

"Oh yeah, I almost forgot about that- um, what time?" My mood instantly brightened.

"Around one-thirty,"

I clicked on my calendar and looked at my schedule. I was

actually free after one o'clock. "That should work, do you want me to meet you somewhere?"

"No, I can stop by your building since I'll be in midtown," he yawned. "Excuse me, I guess it's past my bedtime."

I looked at my watch. It was nine o'clock Eastern time, which meant it was only eight o'clock in Houston.

"Your bedtime? You sound like an old man," I laughed. When Rodney and I lived together he'd been a night owl.

He laughed as well. "I know. My hours have been crazy. I've been up since five this morning and my flight tomorrow leaves at six,"

"Oh wow, well I'll let you go. Call me when you're on your way tomorrow and I can meet you in the lobby,"

"Sounds good. Good night Angela."

I hung up the phone and looked around my home office for a place to hang the painting. Although Rodney had started calling me a little too frequently, I was excited about the painting and that he'd even remembered I wanted it after all the time that had passed. He was sweet and thoughtful but after I got the painting I would tell him I was seeing someone. I didn't want there to be any misunderstandings.

The next day was a day from hell! I'd spent most of the morning putting out fires due to a marketing error and to top it off one of our largest publication partners wanted to reschedule our meeting for Friday. I was supposed to be leaving for Denver on Friday morning.

"I'm sure your family will understand if you take a later flight Friday or earlier flight on Saturday. I can double check the flights and make the arrangements," Christina had offered. I'd told her I was going to Philadelphia to see my family. I still hadn't told her about Xavier. It's not that I was trying to hide our relationship but I didn't want it to become a source of gossip.

"No, don't worry about it, I'll figure out something. Just make sure we call Sephora to pull those flyers effectively immediately,"

I talked to the ad project manager at Glamour and was able to reschedule our meeting for next week but instead of getting the back cover, our ad moved inside to an anchor page. It wasn't what I wanted but I'd made the compromise so that I wouldn't have to move my flight.

I couldn't wait to see Xavier. I smiled and thought about all the naughty things I hoped we'd get to do when my phone vibrated indicating I had a text:

My car is pulling up to your building.

It was Rodney. It was so strange how he would call or text me whenever I was thinking about Xavier.

I grabbed my phone and wallet before I told Christina I was going downstairs.

When I saw Rodney, I was a little shocked by his appearance. Three weeks ago, he looked like he had gained a little weight but it filled him out nicely. However, today it looked like the weight had been transformed into muscle mass. It looked good on him. Really good.

I chuckled. "Look at you- have you been lifting weights?"

"Girl, stop playing," he blushed as he flexed his right arm and I laughed.

"I recently got into cross fit." He admitted.

I raised an eyebrow, Rodney had jogged every now and then when he lived in New York but he never spent any time in a gym working out.

"Don't ask," he sighed. "Here's the painting, sorry I couldn't get the frame for it too," He handed me a packing tube.

"No, this is more than enough. Thank you again. So how much do I owe you?" I opened my wallet and hoped I had enough cash, I had stopped by the ATM that morning.

He titled his head and smirked. "Really? You don't owe me anything. I didn't have to pay for it and even if I had you know I wouldn't take money from you."

I shrugged. "I had to try," I actually wanted to pay for the painting, so that I didn't feel like I owed him anything.

"Anyway, the driver is waiting. I better go. I don't want to miss my flight. Maybe next time I'm in town, I'll have more time and we can grab lunch or something," he shrugged.

"Sounds good. Just give me a heads up, so that I can make sure I'm in town," That would be my way of paying him back and I would also tell him about Xavier. I wanted him to know I'd moved on.

"They have you traveling now?" he asked.

"No, it's not a permanent thing but you know sometimes client site visits," I said quickly. I actually didn't have to travel for my job anymore, I suppose my mind was on my upcoming trip to Denver.

"Oh okay, well I'll let you know when I'm back out this way. Take care," he leaned in and gave me a one arm hug.

I hugged him and could feel the additional muscle around his solid midsection.

"Ouch, I think you broke one of my fingers with those abs," I joked.

He laughed and then a serious look crossed his face. "Sorry, that's been happening all day,"

I laughed so loud my voice echoed in the vestibule. He grinned at me and shook his head. Rodney and I had always shared a silly sense of humor.

"I've got to run. I'll see you next time," he waved before disappearing through the revolving door.

When I went back upstairs, I removed the painting from the tube to look at it.

"Is that the Glamour mock up?" Christina asked entering my office.

"No, it's a painting Rodney got for me," I gently unrolled it and spread it across my desk.

"Rodney- Rodney Anderson? Your ex? Are you two back together?" she asked.

"No, we are not. Just friends"

"I thought you said exes couldn't be friends," she smiled.

"I'm not having this conversation right now. Oh my God! This is huge, I need to get it framed. I wish I could hang it this weekend," I smiled running my fingers over the texture of the painting.

"You want me to take it in? There's a shop near my apartment."

"I actually have a frame already picked out. I'll take care of it when I get back." I was mesmerized by the woman in the painting, something about her was so relaxed and confident. Calm Sea was the perfect name because that's exactly how it made me feel– awash with calmness and peace.

"It's really pretty, that was so thoughtful of Rodney," she said and when I looked at her she was batting her eyelashes at me.

"Was there something else you wanted?" I asked. I'd made the mistake of crying, literally, on Christina's shoulder after my break up with Rodney. I cherished my relationship with Christina but we couldn't get too relaxed and jeopardize our work relationship. There were only three black people in the cosmetics division, we needed to remain professional especially at work.

Christina gave me a strange look before shaking her head. "You okay?" she asked.

I sighed. "It's just been a crazy day with all that's going on, I really need this long the weekend."

The day finally came to an end and sixteen hours later I arrived at the Denver International airport. Xavier had me booked on a first-class flight and when I made it through baggage claim there was a driver holding a sign with my name. He was an older black man with a graying beard. He reminded me of my father.

"Hi, I'm Angela Barnes," I smiled.

"Hello Miss Barnes," he smiled. "I'm Sam. Let me take your bag," He took my rolling suitcase and led me outside to a Lincoln Town Car. After opening my door, he put the suitcase in the trunk.

I'd only been to Denver one other time and it was a night; I was excited to see the mountain views in the daylight. It was always so surreal to travel to places with actual landscapes that didn't include a skyscraper. Whenever I left Manhattan it was like being on another planet.

When we arrived downtown and Sam pulled the car into the valet area of the Ritz Carlton.

"We're here," he announced as he exited the car and walked around to open my door. He then went to the trunk and removed my suitcase. When I got out of the car, a bellhop had taken the suitcase and pulled it to the front door.

"Thank you, Sam," I smiled and extended a twenty-dollar tip towards him.

"You're welcome, and Mr. Ross has taken care of everything," he refused the tip and walked back to the driver side of the car.

"Welcome to the Ritz Carlton, Miss Barnes," the bellhop greeted me as he pulled my luggage inside the lobby. He led me to the reception desk. "Elissa will complete your check in," he smiled.

"Thank you," I was used to VIP treatment with a couple of the business trips I'd taken before, but this was on another level.

"Hello Miss Barnes, welcome to the Ritz Carlton Denver. How was your flight from New York?"

"It was great," I smiled offering her my ID. She took a cursory glance and smiled before typing information into her computer. "We have you staying two nights in our luxury suite."

She placed a card key on the counter. "Raymond will show you to your room," she smiled at a young man who approached the counter.

"Hello Miss Barnes, allow me," he said taking my suitcase.

The room was beautiful and entirely too large for one person. It was twice the size of my apartment. There was an incredible mountain view from the living area and a fresh rose arrangement on the large table in the dining room next to a platter of fresh fruit and cheeses. The bedroom had a king size four poster bed and another fresh rose arrangement was on the bedside table with a bottle of champagne. The bathroom included a huge soaking tub and a separate shower with multiple shower heads. And in addition to the regular bathroom there was also a powder room!

"Does the suite meet your satisfaction?" Raymond smiled as he took in my awed expression.

"It's incredible!" I replied.

"Excellent. Please do not hesitate to let us know if there is anything we can do to make your stay more enjoyable. Here is your room key. You will need to use this after midnight to access the elevator to your floor." He said giving me the key card. "If there is nothing else, I will let you get settled." He headed towards the door.

"Wait– here," I tried to give him the same twenty-dollar bill Sam had refused.

"That won't be necessary," he smiled kindly. "Enjoy your stay,"

After roaming through the suite, eating a handful of grapes and smelling roses, I sent Xavier a text.

I'm here! In Denver.

He called me a few minutes later.

"Hey, so you made it? Are you at the hotel?"

"Yes! And this room was totally unnecessary," I laughed.

"Only the best for you. I can't believe we're in the same city!" he said excitedly.

"Me either. So where are you right now? Are you staying at the Ritz?" I removed my boots and tights before sitting down on the couch. I flexed my bare feet on the rug and smiled down at the bright red polish on my toes.

"I'm at rehearsal for the show tonight. The band is staying at another hotel but I'll be at the Ritz with you. We're almost done and I'll be there as soon as we finish up. The venue is only about ten minutes from the hotel."

Soul Skylight was performing Friday and Saturday at the Bellco Theater. Tickets to both shows had sold out.

Less than an hour later Xavier knocked on the door of the hotel suite. Coming face to face with Xavier after a few weeks of nothing but phone calls and texts, I didn't realize how much I'd missed him. He smiled broadly when I opened the door. He grabbed me around the waist and walked me back inside the room. I wrapped my arms around his neck as he closed the door and we both laughed. His eyes seemed brighter, he had a fresh haircut and was cleanly shaven. And his scent was intoxicating. He smelled of citrus, sandalwood and something else that was manly and sexy!

"I missed you," he whispered against my mouth before kissing me deeply.

"I missed you too," I sighed as we broke apart.

"Have you eaten? Are you hungry?" he asked still holding me close.

The only thing I hungered for was him. "Maybe we can order room service afterward," I said kissing his neck.

"After what?" he asked hoarsely.

I kissed him again and then nipped at his chin.

"After I show you how much I missed you," I grabbed the hem of his t-shirt and moved it up exposing his abs. I was prepared to make my intentions known after our last encounter where he wanted me to take the lead but this time was different. Very different.

He removed his t-shirt, kissed me and then turned me so that my face was against the wall and my back was to him. His hands splayed across the sides of my thighs before roughly hiking up the sweater dress I'd worn. I shrieked when I felt his warm breath followed by his tongue on my left ass cheek. I looked over my shoulder and watched as he removed my thong with his teeth. I sucked in a sharp breath when he looked up at me and smiled around the fabric.

He stood and unbuckled his pants before taking a condom from his wallet. Pressing his body against mine, he spread my legs apart with his foot while ripping open the condom. I placed my hands against the wall as he gripped my hips and slammed into me.

I whimpered and felt my entire body go limp from the sensation.

"You okay," he asked as he panted against my neck.

"Yeah, yeah, don't stop!" I pleaded. I should have felt ashamed for begging him to continue pounding me into the wall but I found immense pleasure in surrendering to my base instincts.

Xavier obliged and gave me more and more until I was shaking and stuttering his name. I collapsed against the wall and he gathered me up into his arms and took me to the bedroom where he peeled the sweaty dress away from my body.

"Here," he gave me a bottle of water and I took a long swallow before handing the bottle back to him. He drank what was left over.

"That was- wow," I looked at him smiled.

He scratched his head. "Sorry, I didn't mean to-,"

I laughed and shook my head. "You definitely don't have to apologize for that," I assured him.

"I just missed you so much," he hugged me tightly and pulled me down next to him on the bed.

"The show starts at seven," he looked at his watch. "But I have to be there at six. We can order something to eat and then we need to shower and get ready to leave. You can hang out in my dressing room until the show starts.

"Are you wearing the same thing you had on?" I asked. "Where are your clothes?"

"I have some stuff at the venue but there is a bag in the closet," he leaned over and picked up the menu from the bedside table. "What are you in the mood for?"

"It's kind of early– maybe just a salad or something. What about you? Are you hungry?"

"I don't usually eat anything too heavy before I perform. I'm already nervous and I'd hate to throw up on the people in the front row," he grinned.

"Ew, that's gross!" I covered my face and closed my eyes to get rid of the image of Xavier vomiting.

"You asked," he chuckled.

"No, I didn't." I frowned and dropped my hands from my face. "You still get nervous after all this time?"

He sighed. "Yeah. Crazy, huh? I don't know- my biggest fear is that I'll go out there and forget the words to a song or how to play my guitar," he stated quietly.

"You seem like such a natural, so comfortable," I ran my finger over the sharp contour of his jawline. He grabbed my hand and kissed my fingertips.

"I am, once I get going…then I'm fearless. It's such an incredible high to be up there in front of all those people and they are singing the words to a song you wrote," he smiled widely.

"Has fame been everything you thought it would be? I can't imagine what it must be like to be recognized and mobbed every time you go outside,"

He looked at me and laughed. "It's not quite *that* bad. But yeah, there are times when you're minding your own business, just out buying underwear or something else insignificant and you see a camera flash and there's a paparazzi snapping a picture. I'm like, damn bruh, I'm just buying a pair of drawers. Nothing newsworthy,"

I laughed. "But I guess the money makes up for a little loss of privacy," I figured Xavier was pretty well off financially since he told me about a house that he'd recently purchased in Malibu.

"Nah- not really. The money is great to have, *really* great but there are still some downsides. The worst thing about fame is not knowing who you can really trust, you know? Are they around because they care about you or is it the money or attention or whatever else might benefit them. Plus, it took me a while to get a team in place that I can truly rely on to handle the business side of things. When we first started, we all had the same manager and even though a bunch of groups before us should have been cautionary tales, we still got screwed over with the money, taxes, and contracts. After our first contract ended we all got separate managers,"

"Seems like that would be too many people involved,"

I was glad Xavier was sharing this part of his life with me. Most of our phone conversations were the mundane, 'how was your day' or conversations about things from high school. I hoped I didn't sound like a reporter with all the questions I was asking. I was only trying to get a feel for what life was like for him.

"Actually, having more people involved is much better because it's harder to try and cheat the system when you got four other managers trying to make sure their client's money isn't messed up."

"How do you and the rest of the band get along, *really*? Do they mind that you get so much attention as the lead singer?"

"We have a good relationship. More like family- brothers- and you know brothers fight and argue. But they each know what they bring to the table, so they aren't really bothered by any extra attention I might get. Because at the end of the day it gives the band publicity. And I think they prefer being low key, so they don't get recognized as often or called out in interviews,"

We talked a little more about his experiences as a famous musician before taking a shower and getting ready to leave.

"Damn, look at you! Now I'm going to be distracted knowing you're a few feet away wearing this," Xavier groaned when I walked into the living area of the suite.

I smiled, pleased to know my outfit had an effect on him. "I'm glad you like it,"

By most standards it was pretty modest– dark denim skinny jeans and a black, sleeveless jersey tee but the entire back of the tee had been cut out and replaced with thin, gold chains leaving most of my back exposed. It may have also appeared that I was braless, but I was wearing a backless, push up. I completed the look with my burgundy, knee-high suede Yves Saint Laurent boots. I'd also brought my cashmere Burberry coat because it was cold in Denver.

We took the service elevator downstairs and Sam, the same older gentleman that had picked me up from the airport, was waiting for us at the back entrance of the hotel. Xavier mentioned that he preferred hiring older drivers in the different cities he traveled to because he trusted them more than the younger guys. A couple of years ago, he had gotten robbed by a driver who took him to a bad part of town after a show.

Once we arrived at the venue we went inside and were escorted to a hallway of private rooms.

"Do you always get your own dressing room?" I asked staring around the space.

"It just depends. . . I requested a separate space this time because you were coming and trust me you don't want to hang out with the fellas," he laughed. He took my coat when we entered the room and hung it on a hook in the corner.

I was surprised by the plainness of the space. The walls were white and two beige oversized chairs, and a cream-colored couch sat in the middle of the room. There was also a counter along the back wall with a mirror and vanity lights above it. The mirror ran the entire length of the counter with two bar stools flanking it and some random items on top including incense, which was burning in a jar in the corner.

On the opposite end of the counter was a framed photograph. I walked over and picked it up. I was shocked to see an autographed photo of Prince. It looked like it had been taken during the *Purple*

Rain era, he had on a white ruffled shirt and his head was thrown back as he played the guitar.

"He doesn't sign autographs but he signed this one for me. He's one of my idols. I bring this on tour for good luck," he smiled.

"That is really cool!" I exclaimed. I would faint if I ever met Prince in person.

"There is a mini fridge with fruit, water, beer and I think a bottle of Rosé, that's your favorite, right?" he asked.

I placed the picture back on the counter and nodded. Cabernet was actually my favorite, but Rosé would do.

"We'll go out and grab something to eat with the guys after the show." He announced. We had never got around to ordering room service at the hotel.

"With the guys?" I asked nervously.

I hadn't met the guys from the band yet but Xavier had told me all about them. However, the thought of actually meeting them terrified me. Two months ago, I had no idea who they were and now I was dating their lead singer.

"Yeah, don't worry, they're cool. Before I forget, there is also a restroom behind that sliding door," he pointed to the corner of the room. "I need to go out and do one final sound check. I'll make sure someone comes back to show you where you can sit and watch the show,"

Xavier kissed my lips and left me alone. I paced the room while nursing a bottle of water and thought about texting Christina to tell her I was in Xavier's dressing room. She would probably have a heart attack.

I felt bad that I still hadn't told her about me and Xavier. I was just enjoying keeping a piece of him to myself. I decided I would ask him for extra tickets to the New Year's Eve show at Radio City and maybe she and Greg would get a chance to meet him.

Less than twenty minutes passed before someone came and led me to the side of the stage where two empty stools were waiting. I had a perfect view of the audience; the theater was packed. I sat down just as the lights dimmed and an announcer introduced the band. This was one of the first concerts I'd ever been to that didn't have an opening act. But by the sounds of the ear-splitting screams from the crowd, it was obvious they only cared about Soul Skylight. All five of the guys came out together and I didn't think it would be possible for the crowd to get louder but they did. The band fanned out across the stage and waved at the crowd before taking their places with their instruments. Xavier picked up his guitar and pulled the strap over his head allowing the guitar to rest against his chest.

Although I was less than fifteen feet away from Xavier I was disappointed that I wasn't in the audience watching him perform. All I could see was his side profile. However, I could see the faces of the women in the front row. Most of them scantily dressed and screaming Xavier's name probably hoping he'd look in their direction or pull them on stage. Or maybe even bring them backstage.

I thought about how many times that exact scenario had probably played out and how many groupies Xavier had taken back to his hotel room. I closed my eyes and shook my head to get rid of those thoughts, the last thing I wanted to imagine was Xavier with another woman. I took a deep breath and tried to focus my attention back to the stage.

"Is Denver, Colorado in the building?" Xavier yelled and the audience yelled back in response. "We want to thank you for coming out to see us tonight and we hope you enjoy the show. Johnny are you ready?" Xavier asked and turned to the man on his left.

Johnny was Xavier's writing partner and best friend. He also played the guitar and sang co-lead. Xavier had known Johnny since they were kids. Johnny was a few years older than him and had been like a brother and sometimes father figure. Johnny was tall, lean and his head was shaved bald but he had a full beard. The black hair from his beard almost blended into his dark chocolate skin.

"I'm ready! What about you, Eric?" Johnny looked over his right shoulder.

"I was born ready!" Eric assured Johnny.

Eric was the backup bass and saxophone player. Xavier mentioned that Eric had had a drug problem but he'd been clean and sober for over a year. Eric was Johnny's first cousin. He was taller than Johnny and although he was younger, he looked much older. His long locs were almost to his waist and tattoos were visible from the sleeveless t-shirt he wore. They completely covered both his arms.

"But we need to make sure the Maestro is ready!" Eric laughed.

Maestro was the band's nickname for Michael. Michael was a classically trained pianist, who had been a child prodigy. He was the band's keyboard/piano player. He was biracial and the only member of the band with a college degree. Xavier had met him at a music store right before they officially started the band and decided he would be a perfect fit since they were still looking for a keyboardist. Michael looked like he belonged in a rock band from the eighties with his big curly hair, and eyebrow and lower lip piercings.

"The Maestro is ready if the drummer is ready," he replied.

The drummer, Chris did some theatrics on the drums driving the audience into a frenzy.

Chris was the baby of the group, five years younger than the rest of the guys. He had grown up with a father who was in the military, so he'd lived all over the world. Chris was slightly overweight, he also had a beard and wore safety goggles on stage. Xavier said he had poked himself pretty hard in the eye during a show and had worn goggles ever since. Chris had the distinction of being the only member who had auditioned for his spot.

"Well, I guess the drummer is ready. Soul Skylight, let's do this!" Xavier said and the band launched into their latest song.

Soul Skylight was a really tight band. They sounded even better live than on their recordings, which was almost never the case with most artists. I bobbed my head as they played some of their new up-tempo songs and a medley of old songs. Every now and then a roaming spotlight would hit the stage and blind me for a few seconds. I blinked to adjust my eyes as Chris finished up an incredible drum solo and the crowd started applauding.

Xavier walked towards the side of the stage where I was sitting and my heart pounded in my chest. I hoped he wasn't about to bring me on stage. He picked up a towel on the way, smiled directly at me and winked. Then a guy stepped in front of me and handed him a stool.

Xavier took the stool and turned back to the center of the stage and the ladies screamed. He placed the stool in front of the microphone stand and adjusted the mic before wiping his face with the towel and sitting down.

"Denver, are you guys still with us?" he asked. And the crowd answered with shrieks and shouts. I couldn't understand how these people found the energy to keep screaming the way they did.

"Do you mind if we slow it down a minute? I want to sing one of our first songs, a ballad that I wrote about a girl who I never quite got over," he continued and again turned in my direction and smiled.

The tinkling of piano keys cut through the crowd's cheers and then Xavier grabbed the microphone with both hands.

"*I see her every night in my dreams, I wonder if she ever even thinks of me?*" he sang and the rest of the band joined Michael on their instruments. I'd heard that song on the radio when it came out a few years ago, I couldn't believe he'd written it about me.

My breath caught in my throat and tears filled my eyes.

"*She's a girl that I used to know, I carry her picture everywhere I go,*" Xavier belted out the song and I felt it in my soul.

"Can I get some help?" Xavier asked.

And the audience was more than happy to oblige. The entire auditorium started singing the next verse: "*My heart will always belong to her. I doubt that she knows this. . . but I wonder.*"

Tears spilled over on to my cheeks and I couldn't stop the goofiest grin from spreading across my face. A couple of the stage hands glared at me but I didn't care.

Once the concert came to an end I was ushered back to Xavier's dressing room. I took a quick glance in the mirror and reapplied my lipstick. As I was putting the tube back in my purse, I heard loud voices in the hallway and then the door opened. It was Xavier.

"Shut up!" he laughed.

"Hey, Angie!" An obvious male voice said in a high-pitched tone followed by other men's laughter.

"Quit being stupid! No, stop!" Xavier tried to close the door before it was pushed open and he stumbled back into the room.

Chris leaned against it to keep it open. "See, this thickness comes in handy sometimes," he said to Xavier before waving at me.

The rest of the guys crowded the doorway and Xavier hung his head in his hands before looking over at me. "Sorry," he shrugged.

"Hi Angie, we just wanted to stop in and officially say hello before we go to dinner. I'm Johnny," Johnny said.

"Hi," I smiled and tried not to sound as nervous as I was at the moment.

Eric made his way inside and Xavier tensed. "She is way too fine for you," he smiled appreciatively at me. "I'm Eric," he extended a hand.

Xavier walked over and pushed Eric's hand away. "Watch it E. She doesn't want to shake your sweaty hand, you need to go get cleaned up so we can leave!" Xavier said.

I reached my hand out despite Xavier's protest. "Hi Eric," I said and he shook my hand but lingered too long before Xavier pushed him towards the door.

"I'm Chris by the way and this is Michael!" Chris yelled before being forced out by Xavier.

"I am so sorry about that," he leaned against the door once they left.

"It's fine," I laughed.

"So, how'd you like the show?" he walked over and stood in front of me. He was so close that our toes touched. "I want to kiss you but I'm sweaty. I need to take a quick shower and-,"

I cut him off by throwing my arms around his neck and kissing him.

"I loved the show. My favorite part was the song about this woman you never quite got over," I smiled and tiptoed to press my forehead against his.

"Oh, you liked that, huh?" he asked kissing me again.

"Yes, it was beautiful. But, also a little creepy," I said pulling away from him.

"Creepy?" he asked in an offended tone.

"Do you really carry my picture everywhere you go?" I asked recalling the lyrics.

He tapped the side of his head. "Photographic memory."

I looked into his eyes which had changed colors again. Now they were the color of emeralds. "You're not easily forgotten," He smiled at me and I felt a tingling sensation start at the tip of my toes then it traveled up to my thighs and lingered between my legs before it made its way to my chest and settled on my heart.

I cleared my throat, dropped my hands to my sides and stepped away from him. "You should probably go change or shower or whatever you need to do. Because if you don't, I'm probably going to straddle you on that couch and we won't be making it to dinner."

He let out a ragged breath. "We're not staying long," he picked up his bag and hurried into the bathroom.

We were meeting the guys at Panzano, an Italian restaurant only a few minutes from the theater. Xavier told me the restaurant usually stayed open until eleven, but the owner was staying open late for the band. It was 11:15. Although he was well aware that the restaurant was waiting for us, it didn't keep him from pinning me to the couch in his dressing room and kissing me senseless for almost ten minutes.

When we arrived to the restaurant there were a dozen or so people hanging around outside.

"Shit," he muttered. "Go ahead inside and I'll take a few pictures and sign a couple of autographs. Just wait for me at the hostess stand,"

Our driver, Sam, opened the car door and I stepped out followed by Xavier. As soon as they spotted him, the people assembled started calling Xavier's name and snapping pictures. I hurried inside the door where the owner was waiting. I wondered how those people even knew Xavier would even be there.

"I don't know how he stands all that attention," The owner remarked shaking his head.

"Neither do I," I replied softly as I watched Xavier smiling and talking to his fans. I would never want to live my life in such a fishbowl. Xavier signed a few autographs and took pictures before he headed inside. We followed the owner through the restaurant to a private room and there was a lot of laughter on the other side of the door, but once the door opened the laughter immediately stopped.

"There they are, I was about to send the police to look for the two of you!" Johnny said loudly from the far end of the table.

I was so embarrassed that we were the last to arrive. All of the guys were there and seated with women who reminded me of the scantily dressed women from the front row of the concert.

"Sorry we're late," I said.

"No worries, X is always late," Eric said meaningfully while the woman with him looked me over from head to toe.

Xavier scowled at Eric before he turned his attention to me. I took off my coat and folded it over the back of the chair.

"Everybody this is Angie, Angie this is everybody," Xavier grinned. "But I guess you knuckleheads already met her earlier," He pulled out my chair before sitting next to me.

"Since when you pull out chairs for people," The woman with Eric cackled. She wore a low-cut, purple dress that barely contained her large breasts and her arms were covered in a mish mash of tattoos.

"Brenda, chill," Eric smirked.

Johnny cleared his throat to cut through some of the tension. "This is Mimi," he placed an arm around the woman next to him. Her face remained blank but she gave me a small wave. She had long platinum blonde hair but she looked to be Puerto Rican or of Hispanic descent.

"Hey Angie, remember me- Chris? This is my fiancée,

HERE YOU COME AGAIN

Diamond," Chris smiled as he motioned to the woman sitting beside him. She had a curly, red afro and wore a bright pink tank and big hoop earrings.

"Nice to meet you," I smiled. She smiled in return.

"I'm Michael, this is Tay Tay," Michael grinned and motioned to his date.

"Taylor," she rolled her eyes at him before smiling at me. "Pleased to meet you." She appeared to be the only normal woman in the room excluding me. Her mahogany skin was accentuated with a small amount of make-up and her hair was up in a flawless bun. And she wore a black turtleneck dress with shoulder cutouts.

"Okay, now that we all know each other, can we order? I'm starving!" Eric exclaimed.

We ordered dinner and a few bottles of wine and talked about the show while we waited for the food. I'd made small talk with Taylor after the entrees arrived and learned that she was building her online brand and hoped to become a social media coach for entrepreneurs. I had no idea what that meant but I smiled and nodded my head anyway.

I felt awkward and out of place. It seemed I was the only woman, who had an actual job. Taylor mentioned that Diamond made earrings and I got the feeling Brenda and Mimi didn't work either but it was none of my business, so I didn't ask. I was willing to bet they relied on their men to take care of them financially.

There was a lull in the conversation around the room, so Mimi used that as an opportunity to put Xavier and me on the spot:

"So, where'd you and Xavier meet?" she asked in a confused tone.

Xavier put an arm around me. "We were high school sweethearts," he smiled wide and I couldn't help but blush.

"I know you haven't been together since high school," Brenda laughed like there was some inside joke.

"No, we um, we actually recently reconnected at our high school reunion," I smiled at him and he kissed my lips.

"Aw, y'all are too cute," Chris teased and everybody in the room laughed except Brenda.

Fortunately, Taylor asked Chris and Diamond about their upcoming wedding and the focus was off me and Xavier but I saw Brenda scowling at me from the corner of my eye. After we finished dinner I was thankful we all went our separate ways.

"What was the deal with Brenda?" I'd asked Xavier once we were settled back in the car.

He rolled his eyes. "She was one of the first Soul Skylight groupies. She tried to get with me and when I turned her down she sank her claws in Eric."

"Get with you? You mean have sex?" I asked.

He smiled. "First time I met her she had somehow convinced the hotel manager that she was my girlfriend. I came to my room and found her naked in my bed. I called hotel security and had her removed. I think she's probably bitter. And definitely jealous of you,"

"She doesn't even know me. Does Eric know she was naked in your room?"

"Eric isn't as discriminating or judgmental as most people. And she's jealous because I've never introduced them to anyone or even brought anyone around. I'm always alone, keeping to myself. Just writing and coming up with new music. She knows if I'm bringing you around, it's serious."

"Does she think she still has a chance with you?" I didn't want any drama but I would definitely let Brenda know he was off limits the next time I saw her. Just because I was an educated professional didn't mean I was to be played with, I was a hardcore New Yorker through and through. And I'd hate for Brenda to find that out the hard way.

"I sure as hell hope not. I don't want to talk about crazy Brenda. I want to show you something," He told the driver to take us to a place called Lookout Mountain.

"I thought we were going to finish what you started earlier, I don't really want to go out anywhere," I complained. I was done sharing him for the night.

"You started that but I will definitely finish it," he promised. "Lookout Mountain is a scenic thing. I've always wanted to see it at night,"

Once we made it to the top of a long winding highway, there was a spectacular view of the city below. It was lit up like Christmas. Sam parked the car and Xavier opened the sunroof. He pulled a thick, cotton blanket from a bag in the backseat and helped me stand so that we could stick our heads through the sunroof. It was freezing.

He quickly wrapped me in his arms after draping the blanket over us.

"Look up," he whispered in my ear.

The sky over lookout mountain was magical and the stars looked like a million twinkling, Swarovski crystals. And there were so many shooting stars I couldn't keep count.

"This is incredible," I whispered in awe.

"I don't usually get a chance to see the cities that we travel to because most of the time I'm in my hotel room. Man, I'm so happy that you're here and I got to share this with you." He smiled and kissed my cheek. We stared up at the sky and at the scenery below until my teeth started chattering and Xavier pulled me back into the warmth of the car.

On the way back to the hotel, Xavier fell asleep. I figured he was probably exhausted. I woke him when we got back to the hotel and was prepared to let him get some rest once we made it to the room but he'd made good on his promise and finished what was started in his dressing room.

The sex was slow and he was very methodical, paying attention to every inch of my body. I was so tired afterward that *I* fell into a deep sleep.

I spent the next afternoon at the hotel spa getting a massage while Xavier headed to a band meeting and another sound check. We met for a light lunch and cocktails around three o'clock at Peaks Lounge, which had some amazing views of the city. And a few hours later, it was time to head to the theater for the show.

Michael's girlfriend, Taylor joined me on the side of the stage for the second show. She pointed to the audience and sure enough, the other ladies were front and center including Brenda who kept her eyes trained on Xavier during the entire performance.

After the concert was over Xavier and I went back to the hotel, watched TV and ordered room service before taking a long, hot bubble bath together. I had an early flight, so we just cuddled and fell asleep in each other's arms.

The next morning while gathering my things, I noticed how quiet Xavier had been.

"This weekend was amazing! My only complaint is that it was over too soon," I pouted.

"I can't wait for this tour to be over," he walked up behind me and hugged me tightly.

"It kind of just got started," I remarked.

"I know. I've just been feeling really disconnected from the experience but I feel like these past two shows have been our best because I was so happy knowing I'd be coming off stage to you,"

"Aw, that's sweet but we'll see each other soon. The time will pass by quickly," I said and willed myself to believe it. We most likely wouldn't see each other again until the end of December. Things were about to get incredibly busy for me at work with the upcoming holidays, so I wasn't going to be able to make it to another show until he came to New York.

"You sure you can't come to Chicago in two weeks?" he asked.

"I'll have suppliers in town through Friday of that week and we have dinner planned Friday evening,"

"You could fly up Saturday morning, it's only an hour and a half and then go back Sunday evening,"

"I wish I could, I really do but-," he cut me off with a kiss.

"Please, just think about it," he breathed against my mouth.

"Okay," I relented. "I'll think about it."

November

*T*he weeks following my trip to Denver were really busy at work as we prepared for our holiday campaign and the release of three new products for Valentine's day. I didn't make it to Chicago, so I wouldn't get to see Xavier until he made it to New York next month. We were both disappointed but knew the time would fly by. Not to mention it was something about absence making the heart grow fonder. The more I missed him, the more I looked forward to seeing him again.

My feelings for Rodney were fading and I felt maybe Xavier and I could actually make a long-distance relationship work. I hadn't seen Rodney since he'd dropped off the painting last month but he continued to call, email or send texts at least once a week just 'checking in'. I foolishly thought they were harmless especially since we didn't live in the same state. Until one night Rodney called and dropped a bomb:

"Hey, I wanted you to be the first to know, I'm moving back to New York." He announced.

"Really, why?" I asked baffled.

"I've gotten a promotion that will bring me back home," he said excitedly.

"Rodney, you're from Sacramento," I reminded him.

"I know, but New York was home for over six years,"

"I don't know what to say- well, I guess congratulations first off. When do you start the new position?" I asked.

"Thanks, I start the week after Thanksgiving,"

"Oh," I said at a loss for words. I think the reason I had been able to get over Rodney, even before I started seeing Xavier, was because he lived in another state. I'd been able to move on because I didn't really have a choice. I had mixed feelings about him being back in the city.

"Angela, I know you and I are- things are over but I'd be lying if I said I didn't miss you and-,"

I couldn't let him finish.

"Rodney, I'm seeing someone," I said quietly. I hated to tell him over the phone but I needed to put an immediate end to any hope he had of us getting back together.

He was silent for a minute and I thought he'd hung up until he cleared his throat. "Oh. Okay. Wow, so who's the lucky guy? Or is that an inappropriate question to ask?"

"No, it's not a secret. We went to high school together and reconnected during our reunion a couple of months ago,"

"A couple of months? Sounds like it's getting serious,"

"A little, look I just wanted to be honest with you. I know we-,"

"You don't owe me any explanations. I um- I've got to go- the uh- the FedEx guy is pulling up and I have to sign for some stuff." The hurt in his voice was apparent and he'd probably made up an excuse to get off the phone but I didn't push.

"Okay, well I guess I'll talk to you later."

I hadn't meant to hurt him with my news, but I didn't want him to move back to New York to be with me because I felt that ship had sailed. I hoped his new position would keep him busy for a while and then maybe he'd find a woman who could be whatever he needed her to be.

It was a crazy coincidence that one week after Rodney told me about his promotion, I'd also gotten a promotion at work. I was promoted from Associate Director of Marketing Media Strategy to Director of Visual Merchandising. Before I accepted the new position, I made sure Christina was bumped from her administrative position to a Marketing Associate position. I wanted her to continue to advance through the company as more than an administrative assistant. I would definitely miss having her as my assistant and seeing her every day but she deserved the new role.

I told Xavier about my promotion and he said he was happy for me but he was also in the middle of boarding a plane, so he'd offered a distracted, 'congratulations' and got off the phone after about five minutes. They were doing a show in Atlanta and he would be spending Thanksgiving with Chris and his family. I didn't even get a chance to tell him what I would be doing. For a brief second, I considered calling Rodney and telling him my news. I knew he'd be excited for me and offer up the perfect words of encouragement for success in my new role but I decided against it. I didn't want to send him mixed signals.

This would be my first Thanksgiving without Rodney in three years. We used to visit my family for Thanksgiving and travel to California to see his mom for Christmas. Unfortunately, when a relationship ended those traditions that became a part of your life ended too.

I was willing to bet Rodney's mother was happy about the breakup. I got the feeling she didn't think I was good enough for 'Roddy'. He was an only child and when he was around his mom his spine conveniently disappeared. He said it was difficult for him to confront her when she did something wrong because she'd had a hard time raising him by herself after his dad died. He'd also admitted she could be overbearing, which is why he'd moved across the country. But his mother had survived by marrying a wealthy man ten years older than her.

Not that I had any room to criticize his family situation considering the dysfunction of my own family.

I'd taken the train to Pennsylvania on Wednesday before the holiday to spend the long Thanksgiving weekend with my mother. I was aware that my uncle, my brother and his kids would be coming to Thanksgiving dinner but I was shocked to find out my dad would be there as well, I was even more surprised when I found out that he had been spending nights with my mother.

"So, what's up with you and daddy?" I asked as I removed the macaroni from the oven and placed it on the counter.

"What you mean 'what's up' with us? Hand me that slotted spoon out the drawer."

"Are the two of you getting back together?" I asked. I opened the drawer and passed her the spoon.

"Girl, no. Your daddy works my damn nerves!" she frowned taking the spoon from me.

"Well, why is he spending the night over here?" I whispered. He was in the other room with my Uncle Larry, my mom's older brother, and his wife.

"You might need to get you some business," she laughed.

"I'm serious, Mama, I don't want to see you get hurt," She'd forgiven him for roaming around during their marriage but I'd never quite gotten over it.

"Ha! You think your daddy can hurt me? Child please, those feelings left a long time ago, if you must know we hook up every now and then but that's it,"

I glared at her. "Hook up?" Surely, I'd heard my fifty-eight-year-old mother wrong.

"Yeah, *sex*. I'm too old to be out here dating and dealing with all these crazy people. Plus, the sex with your daddy is ah-ma-zing," she giggled.

"Excuse me but I think I just threw up in my mouth a little. Have you ever heard of TMI?" I groaned.

"You asked!" she shrugged.

I just stared at her. My mom was a petite and curvy woman with skin the color of cinnamon. She'd cut off all her hair last year and was sporting a reddish blond teeny-weeny afro. Not only did she look stunning but she had a sassy attitude that stunned you as well.

I'd always felt my mother's main goal in life was to shock me and my brother. Her behavior had always been inappropriate. I think it was because my grandmother had raised her and her siblings in a nightclub that she co-owned with her third husband. They spent time around adults and in adult conversations from the time they started walking and talking, so she had no filter or reference for what was socially acceptable.

She and my dad had met in college but after my mom got pregnant with my brother she dropped out. I was born three years later and she'd never gone back to get her degree. I got the feeling it was something she'd always regretted.

My dad had gotten a master's degree in engineering and he provided well for our family and my mom had been a stay at home mom. My parents were never a lovey-dovey couple (at least in front of us) and my dad spent a lot of time working out of town. When he was home my mom waited on him hand and foot. She had totally sacrificed who she was as a person to be a wife and mom. It wasn't until she and my dad divorced that she actually seemed happy. She got a pharmacy tech certification and had worked for Rite Aid for the past fifteen years. But getting the certification was just something she'd done to give her a sense of self-worth because she didn't necessarily need the money. My father had sent her large sums of money every month and continued to do so long after they'd divorced.

Seeing how my parent's marriage dissolved hadn't necessarily jaded my view on marriage but I could never be the type of wife my mother had been. I could never cater to or become totally dependent on a man and lose myself in the process, which is why I worked so hard to make my own way.

"What about you? You getting any nookie since you and Rodney broke up?" my mother winked.

"Mama, stop." I rolled my eyes and took the cranberry sauce from the refrigerator.

"What? So, you're not seeing anyone?"

"Now, that's more of an appropriate question to ask. And actually, I have started seeing someone," I smiled.

"Really?" she sounded doubtful.

"Yes, really. He's a musician," I smiled as I thought about Xavier.

"Have I ever heard of him?" she asked.

"Maybe," I responded vaguely.

"Ooh, is it Drake?" she wondered.

I laughed. "What, how do you even-,"

I was interrupted by my brother as he came into the kitchen talking loudly on his phone.

"Paula, I'm not playing with you! I swear if you don't bring my kids to my mama's house right now, I'm taking your ass to court!" he yelled before disconnecting the call.

"Uh-oh, you okay AJ?" I asked.

He sighed harshly before kissing my mom on the cheek and then pulling me into a hug.

"I'm supposed to have the boys on Thanksgiving- actually I should've had them this entire week but Paula lied and said they had doctor appointments. I found out when I talked to Kyle and he asked me why they were going to their other grandma's house for Thanksgiving instead of Grandma Gloria's,"

My brother Allen Jr., had been legally separated from his wife Paula for almost a year. They had two handsome little boys, Kyle and Brandon. The reason they weren't divorced yet was because they were in business together and hadn't been able to come to an agreement on how to split the assets. They co-owned Swerve, a hair salon and barbershop that also offered unisex spa services.

"I hate how the two of you put the kids in the middle of all that mess," my mother said and the crease in my brother's forehead deepened.

"She's the one who's acting stupid! She's just mad because I'm not calling or begging her to let me come back home,"

That was news to me. I thought he left her.

"Wait, I thought you left her?" I asked.

"I did. And instead of regretting it, every day she makes me glad I did. I don't want to talk about Paula. What you need me to do?" he asked mama. The only reason Allen had volunteered to help was so that he wouldn't have to make small talk with my dad.

Although Allen had graduated high school and was in basic training for the Army when my parents divorced, he was still hurt by it and also blamed my dad.

Mama placed a hand on his cheek. "Why don't you take the turkey out to the table. Everything else is just about ready," she smiled.

Allen helped us bring the food to the table while my dad sat like a king on his throne and didn't lift a finger to do anything. My mom had refused help from my Uncle Larry's wife saying she was letting her take a much-needed break.

Uncle Larry and his wife of forty years, Loretta reminded me of how my parents used to be. Even after all this time, Aunt Loretta still catered to my uncle. It seemed like she was his employee instead of his wife. Yet another example of the kind of relationship I did not want to be in. I wanted to be an equal partner, not a servant.

Uncle Larry and Aunt Loretta had four sons and she had also catered to all four of them, which is why they were disappointing women in four different states around the country.

We sat down to eat and my dad immediately took the seat at the head of the table. I looked over at my mom but she was oblivious or at least pretending to be. My brother looked at me and rolled his eyes.

"AJ, you sure you don't want to wait for the boys?" I asked.

"My grandsons coming over?" My dad smiled. "What about Paula, where is my pretty daughter in law,"

"Al, you know they separated," my mom interjected.

"We can go ahead and eat. I don't know what time they'll be here," AJ responded.

After Uncle Larry blessed the food, daddy stood and carved the turkey.

"This is a good-looking bird, Glo," he complimented my mom and placed some of the meat on a platter.

We passed around the other serving dishes filled with food as he finished carving the turkey.

"Angela where is that handsome beau of yours, Roger? I think that's his name," Aunt Loretta asked.

"Rodney," I corrected. "Um- we're not together anymore," I said placing a big spoonful of my mama's dressing on my plate. I thought about Rodney and wondered where he was spending Thanksgiving. He loved my mama's cornbread dressing; her secret ingredient was caramelized bacon.

"Aw, I hate to hear that. First, AJ and his wife and now you and Roger. I guess you young folk don't have the staying power like us old school folks," she chuckled and I bit my tongue to keep from being disrespectful.

"You forget I'm old school and divorced," my mama said pointedly. She didn't have anything against Aunt Loretta but she didn't like anybody saying anything out of line to me and my brother. That was Mama's job.

"Gloria, you and Al might be divorced on paper but the love is still there," my uncle commented.

"She will always be my first and only love," Daddy said sweetly as he smiled at Mama.

"Gone on with all that nonsense," she rolled her eyes at him but she couldn't hide her blush. Yeah, I got it from my Mama.

My brother groaned audibly and I kicked him under the table.

Fortunately, the subject of love and relationships quickly changed when my dad pulled my brother into a conversation about football. My brother was a die-hard Philadelphia Eagles fan and couldn't resist talking about them even with my father.

Just as Aunt Loretta was about to serve some of her delicious sweet potato pie, Paula showed up with the boys. They immediately ran to my brother and the three of them embraced as if they hadn't seen each other in years.

"Daddy, daddy," they squealed and I got a little teary-eyed.

Allen was a great father and I was glad that he had given my parents something I probably never would– grandchildren.

Paula offered a quiet hello and refused my mother's offer to stay for dessert. She told Allen she'd call him tomorrow for arrangements to pick up the kids.

It was apparent that the boys also loved my parents. Especially my dad. They hugged and kissed him and my mom before giving me an obligatory hug after being urged by my mother. I felt bad that I was their only aunt (Paula had two brothers) and didn't see them that often.

Later that evening after Uncle Larry and Aunt Loretta left, Allen and I washed dishes while our parents played a board game with Kyle and Brandon.

"So, you and Rod called it quits for good?" he asked.

He and Rodney used to play poker together, which is how I'd met Rodney.

"Yeah, I guess we weren't a good fit, you know? And it's good we found out before we got married," I gently ran the scrubber over my mom's ceramic platter and sighed.

"I wish I would have found out Paula's ass was crazy before we got married," he said drying the last glass and putting it away.

Growing up, Allen and I were close because we were the only kids in the house but we were just siblings, not really friends. However, as adults, we'd forged a solid friendship.

"Actually, she was crazy when you married her, you were just too sprung to see it," I teased.

"Agh, I know, why didn't you tell me!" he pretended to choke me.

"Boy, stop! If you make me break mama's heirloom platter. . .," I warned as I tightened my grip on the platter.

He looked at me strangely. "Her what?" he asked.

"This platter is an heirloom, she got it from her grandmother," I said admiring the ornate floral design around the edge. It was still in pristine condition.

"Angie, Mama bought this from TJ Maxx last week!" he laughed loudly.

My mouth hung open. "Are you serious?" I asked.

"I swear! I was there with her. You know you can't believe half the stuff she says," he snickered.

"What is wrong with her?" I wondered aloud still being careful with the platter as I passed it to him to dry.

"You know how she is," he shook his head as he gingerly took it from me.

"Did you know daddy was spending nights here sometimes?" I whispered.

He sighed harshly. "Doesn't surprise me. I don't know what she's doing. He was missing in action for two months, said he was doing some contract work out of town and then he just showed up here one night while I was putting up a ceiling fan."

"She told me to mind my business and that it wasn't serious," I kept my voice low.

"That sounds like a good idea. The less I know the better." He sighed. "You ever think maybe we have issues with relationships because of them?" he asked seriously.

"Definitely," I chuckled.

"But what about you? Don't you want to settle down, get married and have kids?" he inquired.

"I don't know about marriage and kids but I am seeing someone," I smiled. Allen had graduated from the high school we'd attended before we moved, so he didn't know Xavier.

"Look at you blushing like your mama," he teased. "So, you kicked Rodney to the curb and found you a new man? That's harsh,"

My eyes widened. "It wasn't even like that! I've only been seeing him a couple of months,"

"I'm just kidding," he grinned. "Good for you. You deserve to be happy,"

"Thanks. And so do you. You don't think you and Paula will be able to work things out?" I asked carefully.

He shrugged. "I doubt it. I can't handle the drama. And I really hate that our business is tied up in all this mess." She had accused him of cheating, which was the catalyst for their separation. AJ had vehemently denied it. I believed him. Not just because he was my brother but because he was really one of the good guys. Not to mention, my mama believed him and neither of us had ever been able to lie to her.

"Have you guys considered counseling?"

"We went and she accused me of flirting with the counselor who was a woman, which is what *she* wanted." He said in a frustrated tone. Paula was definitely a piece of work.

"Well, the most important thing is that you're there for your sons. They adore you. You're a great father, AJ,"

"They're my world." He said as his voice cracked.

AJ and the boys stayed a little while longer but after Kyle fell asleep, he decided it was time for them to leave. I spent the night in the guest room at my mom's house and tried to ignore the fact that my mother and father were two doors down probably 'hooking up'. The next morning me and Mama went to a few stores for some Black Friday sales and that evening AJ and the boys dropped me off at the train station.

I always enjoyed spending time with my family but after being away for a few days, I started to get antsy. I missed the hustle and bustle of New York, the crowded streets, the bright lights of Times Square and the smell of pizza on every block. I smiled as I exited Penn Station and hailed a cab. I was home.

The Monday following Thanksgiving, I was surprised to get a call from Rodney. He had called to let me know he was officially back in New York and asked if it would be okay to call me from time to time. He said he didn't want to cause any problems between me and my new boyfriend. Rodney was a man of his word and if I would've told him to not call anymore, he wouldn't. But I valued him as a friend and I didn't want him to disappear from my life forever. So, I'd told him it was okay to stay in contact as long as he respected the fact that I was in a relationship and didn't cross any lines.

The conversation was a little uneasy after that, so to break the ice, I mentioned my promotion. As I'd predicted, Rodney knew just what to say and his excited reaction made me smile. I felt my confidence reinforced when he told me I'd worked hard and deserved it. He also asked if it would be okay to meet for lunch to celebrate. I was about to decline until he mentioned Carbone. I'd been trying to reservations at that restaurant for almost six months!

I was filled with anticipation when I met Rodney at the newest Italian Ristorante in Manhattan two days later. There had been a review in the Times raving about the food, location, and service. I was a true foodie and had tried the majority of restaurants in Manhattan. I was excited about adding Carbone to the list.

"I want to apologize again for falling off the radar for a few weeks, I was busy with the move and new position," Rodney said after we were seated.

"You don't owe me an explanation, Rodney," I repeated his words from our previous conversation.

"I know but honestly, I was caught off guard when you told me you'd started seeing someone. I guess that made it more *real* that things are over between us, if that makes sense. But if you're happy then I guess. . . ," he sighed and then forced a smile. "I'm happy for you,"

"Thank you, Rodney," I said and couldn't contain my smile as I thought about Xavier.

"Good, so what are you thinking about getting?" He looked away and turned his attention to the menu. I'd probably made him uncomfortable smiling about my new man but I wasn't going to downplay my relationship. However, I decided not to gloat too much, that would be cruel.

"I've heard they have the best lobster ravioli! I have been wanting to try this restaurant since they opened. How did you get reservations?" I gushed.

"Called in a favor." He smiled slyly.

"I bet," I laughed. It was no secret Rodney's connections ran deep. "So how is your new position? What are you doing exactly?"

"Great, it's busy but good. I'm the Global Vice Chair of the Tax Division. But we're here to celebrate *your* promotion. Congratulations again, how is it going?"

"It's crazy, but I thought I'd be busier since my team has expanded, yet I'm delegating just about everything."

"That's not a bad thing, is it?" he questioned.

I shrugged. "I guess not,"

The waiter interrupted us to bring our sparkling waters and bread. We still hadn't decided on our entrees.

"You know that's how it is– the further you go up the ladder, your actual assignments decrease but your responsibility increases.

I'll check in on you in a few months to see if you're still bored," he laughed.

"You're right it's just a change of pace. I guess I'm not used to having so much free time," I groaned.

He smiled faintly. "Well, while things are slow, you should use this time to make sure you know every single thing about the employees and positions that fall under your responsibility. Just in case there is ever an issue where someone drops the ball, and the executive team is looking at you for an explanation," he advised. "Now is the time to focus on crisis management before there is a crisis to manage."

I exhaled sharply. "I definitely don't want to be coasting along and then something pops up unexpectedly and I'm not prepared. There are already people waiting for me to fail because they think I'm not qualified. Thanks, that's great advice, Rodney." I said sincerely.

Rodney was hands down one of the smartest and most business savvy people I'd ever met. His professional advice was always on point.

He waved me off and smiled as he took a sip of water.

"No seriously, you're the only person I know, who actually understands what it's like to be a black person working at this level in a company where there are so few of us," I said.

He nodded in agreement. "Yes, I do. And don't you let those haters and naysayers get into your head. You are highly competent and more than qualified to take on that role," he said strongly.

He looked up at me and I smiled brightly. Rodney had always been extremely supportive of my career. He made me feel invincible with his advice and encouragement.

"Thank you," I said softly as I tried to swallow down the sudden lump in my throat. I didn't know why his comment had made me emotional.

"I mean it," he smiled warmly. "Hey, I wanted to run something by you- I've been waiting until I got to my current level to propose a mentoring program for other young black men who want to work their way up to senior management. They have absolutely no resources or people that look like them to share inside information about the company and how to rise in the ranks,"

"You'd be perfect at something like that!" I encouraged. At that same moment, I heard the tone I'd set up for Xavier's texts.

"I'm so sorry," I whispered as I removed my phone from my purse and looked at the screen. Xavier was letting me know he was in New Mexico and would call me later tonight. I quickly responded to let him know I'd gotten the message.

When I looked up, Rodney dropped his gaze back to the menu. I felt I owed him an explanation, so I didn't think to censor myself when I responded.

"Sorry, he was letting me know his plane landed. He travels a lot so we've been doing the long-distance thing." As soon as the words left my mouth, I regretted it.

His eyes widened in surprise.

"What? Are you serious?" he asked angrily. "So, let me get this straight, you're in a long-distance relationship? Something you said you didn't want?"

"I know how it must sound but he's a musician. He's not living in another city, he travels all around-," I tried to justify my decision even though it was none of his business.

"That makes it better?" he yelled and then lowered his voice. "And a musician, really Angela?" he said disapprovingly.

"I don't have to explain myself to you!" I said angrily.

"You know what, I'm suddenly not hungry," he placed the menu flat on the table and stood. He gave me a harsh glare and for the first time, I could see the pain in his eyes. He shook his head, turned and walked out of the restaurant.

The waiter came over with a puzzled expression. "I'm sorry, is everything okay?" he asked.

"Yeah, turns out I'll be having lunch alone today," I managed a smile. No way I was missing out on the chance to try the lobster ravioli.

For the rest of the week, I ran the gamut of feeling sorry for Rodney to being mad at him for storming out on our lunch. But I decided not to dwell on it. If things were reversed I probably would have done the same thing. Besides I'd gotten to try a new restaurant and the lobster ravioli was fantastic!

By the time Friday evening rolled around, I'd put the disastrous lunch with Rodney out of my mind. I soaked in a hot bubble bath before putting on my favorite pair of silk pajamas and waited for Xavier to call.

"Hello," I answered on the second ring.

"Hey you," he said sweetly. "What's up, did I catch you a good time?" he asked.

"Anytime is a good time if I get to talk to you," I assured him.

"It's so good to hear your voice," he sighed.

We hadn't seen each other since Denver but we Facetimed or talked on the phone every other night.

"I can't wait to see you," I said.

"Thirty days and counting," he responded and my heart fluttered at the idea that he was counting the days until he saw me again. "Hey, I meant to ask– our team made arrangements for me to stay at the Renaissance but I didn't know if you. . . did you want me to stay with you?" he asked.

I smiled brightly even though he couldn't see me. The thought of Xavier Ross in my apartment tangled up in my sheets gave me goosebumps.

"Sure, yes, that would be great! You can definitely stay with me," I tried to tone down my excitement. "I must warn you though, it's not as big as the Ritz,"

"Anywhere I'm with you is paradise," he replied.

I was really glad he couldn't see me because now I was smiling really big and goofy. Instead I said, "I feel the same,"

I asked him about the tour and he rattled on for a few minutes before I interrupted. "Hey, speaking of the tour, I promise I won't become a pest or ask for any more favors but I was wondering if you'd be able to get me tickets and a backstage pass for the Radio City show for a friend?"

It had been a while since Christina and I had seen each other and I wanted to do something really special for her. I still hadn't told her about me and Xavier but I'd rationalized it was because I didn't see her that often.

"She's a huge fan of the band and of you in particular, if I have to pay for it-,"

He laughed. "Seriously? You want to pay for a backstage pass? Okay, but I don't want money. I'll take my payment another way," he said suggestively.

"I'd be willing to make it worth your while," I whispered coyly.

"How many do you need? You can have two, ten- hell, one hundred!" he exclaimed.

I laughed. "I think one will be enough. Or maybe two, if she's bringing her boyfriend,"

"Consider it done, just send me a text or email the names and I'll make sure to have them sent with yours,"

"Don't you want to know who it is?" I asked.

"I trust you, so it's cool," he assured me.

"I know, but her name is Christina, we work together but we're also really good friends. She used to work for me before my recent promotion-," I paused realizing I had never told him about my new position. I had just mentioned it in passing. I waited for him to say something but when he didn't I decided to continue.

"Anyway, she was the one who convinced me to go to the reunion because I wasn't going to go at first,"

"Oh really? Well, I definitely want to meet the woman responsible for getting you back in my life,"

I was about to mention the promotion again but he spoke before I got the chance.

"Sorry, I have to cut our call short, I need to run. But listen make sure you send me those names and I'll try to call you tomorrow,"

"Okay,"

"Thirty days!" he reminded me.

"Thirty days," I echoed before the line disconnected.

I lay in bed thinking about my conversation with Xavier. It concerned me that he hadn't asked me about my job since that first night in the coffee shop after the reunion. I knew he was in the middle of a tour but it seemed only natural to express interest in your girlfriend's career.

I decided not to give it any more thought but would definitely bring it up on our next call, I didn't want this turning into a one-sided relationship where it was all about him. Just because he was a famous musician didn't mean my work or my life for that matter was unimportant.

December

The holiday shopping season had officially started on Black Friday but December was when the entire division went into overdrive. All departments in our division from sales to marketing were extremely busy. I was actually thankful my workload had picked up. I was also in a merry mood because I'd be seeing Xavier at the end of the month.

A few weeks before the concert, I met Christina for lunch at the Plaza Food Hall to tell her about the tickets.

"Ah! It's so good to see you!" I exclaimed hugging her tightly. "I love your hair."

She appeared more grown up, more mature and polished. She had cut her hair in a short bob and was wearing contacts instead of her usual black-rimmed glasses. Her complexion was usually evened out with a little bit of foundation but today she had a full-face beat. Sculpted eyebrows, a dusting of eyeshadow and highlighter.

"Thank you! You look great, as usual. How have you been?" she asked.

"Good, good. Finally got a minute to breathe. How about you?" I asked.

She sighed. "It's actually been a little challenging but I've been holding my own,"

"The work or-?" I questioned her. She was more than capable of handling her current role, so I wondered if something else was going on.

"I guess certain people feel I skipped the line or something and are wondering how an assistant got that position," she rolled her eyes.

I raised an eyebrow. "Anything I need to alert Alex about?" I questioned. Alex was her new boss.

She took a sip from her bottled water before waving her hands in front of her. "Oh no, I'm fine. More than fine. Thank you again for putting in a good word for me," she smiled.

"You're welcome and you deserve it. I don't care what anyone says." I said and remembered the same advice Rodney had given me.

"Thanks,"

After we ordered, I decided to test the water to see if I needed to get that extra backstage pass for Greg.

"So, how are things with Greg?" I asked carefully.

She shrugged. "Things are good. Really good. But I'm ready to take that next step, you know. I want to get married and have kids and he says he wants the same thing but after almost six years I'm still single and without a ring." She said in a frustrated tone.

I tried to think of something inspiring or encouraging to say but since I didn't actually know if I wanted to get married or have kids, I let the moment pass and instead asked, "Do the two of you have plans for New Year's Eve?"

She gave me a strange look before responding, "Yeah, we're going to his brother's house. He has a party every year,"

"Do you think Greg would want to go see Soul Skylight instead and maybe meet Xavier Ross?" I smiled.

Christina's eyes doubled in size. "Shut up!" she yelled.

"I mean if you'd rather go to the New Year's Eve party," I shrugged.

"Are you serious? Seriously Angela? Don't tease me," she sounded like she was about to start hyperventilating.

"Xavier is going to send me tickets with backstage passes for the New Year's Eve show at Radio City, you want to go?" I smiled.

"Yes! Yes!" she jumped up from her chair and hugged me. As she prattled on about the upcoming show, it would have been the perfect time to mention that Xavier and I were seeing each other but I didn't say anything. I'm not sure why. I think because it would've ruined her image of him as a fantasy guy– her celebrity crush who was almost unreal, unapproachable and unattainable.

It was kind of how I felt about Blair Underwood. He was married with kids in real life, and I had no idea what type of person he *really* was but my fantasy idea of Blair Underwood was how he'd appeared in the movie, *Set It Off*. Professional, funny, considerate, kind and of course sexy as hell! I would never want to be friends with his wife, that would totally ruin the image for me to find out he was a regular guy who left the toilet seat up.

But I knew Xavier as a real person. He was more than his Soul Skylight persona. And I cherished what we had together even if it was brief and infrequent.

Christina and I finished our lunch and walked back to the office together. We said our goodbyes in the elevator as she got off on the 10th floor and I kept going to the 25th. I hadn't realized how much I missed her. I didn't have any female friends, the last female friend I had was Sharon and we'd lost touch. It was good to have a woman to talk to about work, life, politics, shoes, relationships or whatever and share a female perspective.

I just wished I could be honest about my relationship with Xavier. She had asked me about Rodney on the way back to the office and I could tell she was hopeful that we were back together.

I told her I hadn't heard from him in a while, which was true. I actually hadn't heard from Rodney since he walked out on me at lunch last month, which was probably for the best. Xavier and I already faced a challenge with the distance, I definitely didn't want my ex to become an issue as well.

But my connection to Rodney just didn't seem to be going away for good– the week before Christmas, I received a delivery at my apartment. It was actually addressed to Rodney. The apartment I was currently leasing was where Rodney and I had lived together.

The only reason I hadn't moved was because apartments in Manhattan, especially spacious, rent-controlled apartments were extremely hard to come by.

Once I signed for the box, I sent him a text.

You got a box delivered here today.

He didn't answer for almost an hour.

RA: A box? What's in it?

AB: No idea. I didn't open it.

RA: Well can you at least tell me who it's from?

AB: Amazon

RA: They must have my old address on file. I'll pick it up tomorrow if that's okay.

AB: I'll be home after 6.

The next day when Rodney arrived, he wouldn't make eye contact with me. "So, where's the box?" he asked at the doorway.

"It's too heavy for me to lift." I lied. "You can come in and get it, Rodney."

"I don't want to cause any problems," he said.

I stepped aside and allowed him to enter the apartment. He still wouldn't look at me. I sighed and closed the door.

"Rodney are you really not even going to look at me?" I asked angrily.

He sighed heavily. "Where's the box Angela- never mind," he said as he spotted it in the corner of the living room near the small Christmas tree that I'd started decorating.

He walked towards the box and I hurried in front of him and blocked it.

"Rodney please, I don't want us to-,"

He looked at me then. "There is no *us*."

"I didn't mean it like that and you're right there is no us. There hasn't been an *us* for over ten months, so I don't understand why you're so angry with me."

"You told me that you weren't interested in a long-distance relationship and I believed you. I thought I had brought our relationship to an end when I moved to Houston. But it turns out you just didn't want a long-distance relationship with *me*. But I guess I shouldn't be surprised that you lied." He grunted.

"I never lied-," I started weakly.

"You lied about not wanting a long-distance relationship!" he shouted.

"Okay, now that's not fair. You accepted that assignment without even discussing it with me and then you just expected me to follow you blindly-,"

"I wanted you to go because I thought you loved me-,"

"I did love you!" I shot back.

"Really? It's been less than a year since we officially broke up and after three years together and an engagement you've already moved on like I meant nothing to you!"

My eyes widened. "So how much time am I supposed to let pass before I move on? Huh? If the tables were turned and you met someone two days after you moved out, you'd probably be inviting me to your wedding!"

He looked at me like I'd slapped him. "You don't know how wrong you are but you know what, it's your life and you have the right to do whatever you want. Let me get my box, and I'll be out of your way. Sorry for the inconvenience," he said, his tone was hard.

I'd never seen Rodney this way. It was obvious that he was angry and hurt but he'd never been cold.

"Rodney, will you please just talk to me?" I asked calmly. I didn't want things to end this way.

"What do you want from me, Angela? I can't lie and say I'm not hurt because deep down I was hoping that we would find our way back to each other. I meant what I said about wanting you to be happy. But I also know myself and I can't just be friends with you, it was foolish of me to even try. I need to make a clean break. I'm going to take the box and go," he picked up the box and left my apartment without a backward glance.

I don't know why Rodney's departure upset me so much. I guess because I'd come to count on him sending a random text or calling me to check in. Even though at times it could be annoying, it made me feel good to know that he was still a part of my life in some way. Having that connection to him had given me a sense of security.

But he was right we both needed a clean break and I needed to start depending more on Xavier, which was going to be difficult since he wasn't always available. However, he would be available and all mine for four whole days! Soul Skylight was performing at Radio City Music Hall on New Year's Eve and they would be taking a one week break after the beginning of the year. For the first time, I was looking forward to New Year's Eve more than Christmas.

I spent Christmas Eve and Christmas day in Philadelphia with my family. We had a rule about getting each other gifts– well, Mama had a rule. She wasn't a big fan of organized religion but she did have a strong belief and faith in God. As kids, we always got one or two things we wanted for Christmas but she never went overboard. She was fond of saying, "Jesus is the reason for the season." Even now she insisted gifts we purchased for each other had to be something fun or funny and under twenty dollars.

My mom's gift to us this year were matching green-striped pajamas. She made us take pictures wearing them, which she then posted on her Facebook page. She was thrilled when she got fifty-three likes from her sixty-five Facebook friends.

AJ's kids came over on Christmas Eve for a little while but spent Christmas day with Paula's family. I'd given each of them a hundred-dollar gift card to Toys "R" Us and they got a ton of presents from my parents, which AJ and I pointed out was hypocritical since they never bought us that many presents when we were growing up.

"The rules are different for grandkids," Mama shrugged and my dad agreed with her. I just shook my head and snapped pictures of my nephews tearing into all of their gifts. They got so much stuff they couldn't focus on one thing for more than a few minutes.

I watched their interaction with my brother– the sheer excitement, innocence and unconditional love they displayed made me think about what having kids of my own would be like. . .but the fantasy didn't last long. I realized I was only seeing one side of the picture. What was it like when there were no presents? What was it like day in and day out taking care of them? Feeding them, cleaning up their messes, wiping their snotty noses, and sitting out in the cold or heat all day watching their little uncoordinated asses play soccer. No, thank you!

Christmas Day was pretty low-key without the kids. We ate, played Spades and watched *A Christmas Story*. Xavier and I had been exchanging texts for most of the day but he called me when the movie was over.

"Merry Christmas!" he bellowed into the phone.

I laughed at his enthusiasm.

"Merry Christmas to you too!"

"So, when are you leaving Philadelphia?" he asked.

"Tomorrow evening."

"And then in four days, I get to see you!" His excitement was palpable and made me smile.

"I can't wait!" I said.

"Me either! I'm actually flying to Houston in a few of hours. We have a show there tomorrow night and then Dallas the night after."

Houston made me think of Rodney. I wondered if he was in San Diego visiting his mother.

"You got a cowboy hat?" I teased.

"Yeah, and some boots," he laughed.

And suddenly my mind was filled with images of Xavier as a rugged ranch hand wearing a cowboy hat, boots and a pair of chaps. And nothing else.

"I'd pay good money to see that," I whispered.

He gasped. "You are so bad," he chuckled. "I love it."

"I have no idea what you're talking about," I said innocently.

"Yeah, right. I might have to buy a cowboy hat before I leave Texas. Maybe you'll get to see it Friday night," he breathed into the phone.

I could see this quickly turning into a phone sex conversation and I couldn't risk it at my mother's house.

"Okay, we better stop," I laughed.

"I have no idea what you're talking about," Now it was his turn to feign innocence.

"Whatever!"

He laughed loudly. "Well, I won't hold you since I know you're with your family. I just wanted to hear your voice and let you know I can't wait to see you next week,"

"Me too,"

"Tell your family I said, Merry Christmas!"

"Will do, bye."

When I got off the phone, I turned around and my mother was staring at me.

"Aah! Mama, you scared me! Were you eavesdropping on my call?" I frowned. I was glad I'd ended the sexy talk with Xavier.

"Yes, I was. That was a quick conversation. Where is he?" she asked.

I rolled my eyes and walked past her to the kitchen. "He's in L.A."

"Why didn't he spend Christmas with you?" she questioned.

"Ma, I told you we're spending New Year's Eve together." I opened the refrigerator and took out her homemade cheesecake. My dad and AJ had both fallen asleep during the movie.

"Ooh, what do you think he got you for Christmas?" she asked taking a couple of plates from the cabinet. "A Lamborghini?"

I laughed and looked at her. "Really, Mama? What would I do with a Lamborghini?"

She shrugged. "I don't know, that just seems like the kind of gift these young rich, rappers buy for their girlfriends," she giggled.

After cutting the cheesecake, I placed a slice on each plate.

"Mama, he's not a rapper. And he's not buying me a Lamborghini."

"Well, maybe it's a Rolex," she grinned taking a bite of her cheesecake.

I shook my head and shoved a piece of cheesecake in my mouth.

"We decided not to get each other gifts this year," I swallowed. "This is so good!" I moaned.

Mama placed a hand on her hip and looked at me like I was crazy. "You told a man, who is probably a millionaire, not to get you anything for Christmas?" she frowned.

"I thought Jesus was the reason for the season. Isn't that what you've always taught us?" I raised an eyebrow.

She chuckled. "Jesus would want you to get a gift from a millionaire."

I laughed so hard I had tears in my eyes. Fortunately, she let the subject drop and didn't say anything else about Xavier. Not that it would have mattered nothing could've spoiled my mood, I would be seeing him in less than a week and that was the best gift he could give me.

On the way back to New York, I'd gotten a call from Greg, Christina's boyfriend.

"Hello,"

"Hi, Angela, this is Greg Hadnott, Christina's boyfriend."

"Greg? Hey, oh my god, is everything okay? Is Christina okay?" I asked immediately assuming his phone call meant bad news.

"Oh no, she's great- everything is fine."

I exhaled a sigh of relief. "Good, well what's up? How can I help you?" I asked. I had only met Greg in person twice and had never talked to him on the phone.

"I have a really big favor to ask and you can tell me no, I've just been trying to think of a creative way to do this and when Chrissy told me about the concert, I tried to come up with a Plan B but I didn't know if-," he rambled on.

"What is it Greg?" I asked with a hint of impatience.

"Okay, this is top secret, so please don't say anything to ruin it but I'm going to ask Chrissy to marry me. I was going to do it on Christmas Day, just leave the ring under the tree as a Santa gift, but then I thought maybe it would be romantic to do it on New Year's Eve and give it to her at midnight but now that we're going to the concert-,"

I smiled. I was happy for Christina because I knew this was something she really wanted.

"That's wonderful, I'm so happy for you guys! What can I do to help Greg?" I asked excitedly.

"Do you think- she mentioned you personally knew Xavier Ross, the lead singer of Soul Skylight. I know it's her favorite band and I thought maybe it would be cool to propose during the concert. Or what do you think? Would that even be possible? Do you think she'd like that?" he asked hesitantly.

"Oh wow, that's a huge gesture. Hmm, I tell you what. Let me call Xavier and find out and I'll let you know what he says."

"Great, thank you so much! Chrissy speaks so highly of you, she's always saying how amazing you are,"

"She's pretty amazing too, you're a lucky guy."

"I know, thanks!"

I sent Xavier a text and figured he would probably say no, since the show was in three days and it was such short notice. But he told me he'd run it by the rest of the band. He called me about thirty minutes later and said, yes! The band was excited because this would be the first Soul Skylight concert proposal and with it being New Year's Eve they thought it would be a cool thing for the fans to witness and the band's latest single would be the perfect song to serenade them afterward.

On the day of the concert, I met Christina and Greg at a bar near Radio City.

"Hey, Angela!" Christina waved at me when I entered, she and Greg sat near the door.

"Hey, how long have you guys been here?" I asked noticing Christina's nearly empty wine glass.

Greg smiled and waved but he looked like he was going to be sick. His brown skin looked ashen and beads of sweat rested on his forehead. His nerves were probably getting the best of him considering he was about to propose in front of six thousand people.

"Not long," Christina smiled. She leaned in for a hug and whispered in my ear. "Greg is being a buzz kill. I should have left him at home," she sighed and then pulled away.

"Are you okay?" I asked him.

"Yeah, yeah, excited about the show," he said unconvincingly.

Christina shook her head and took and a sip of her wine.

"Well, we should probably head over now. I told Xavier we'd get there a little early,"

Christina was vibrating in her seat. She stood and reached for her coat but Greg beat her to it and helped her put it on. "Are you sure you're okay?" she asked him in an exasperated tone.

"I'm good, I promise," he smiled weakly before looking over at me. I gave him what I hoped was a reassuring smile. We walked across the street to the venue and when we entered, I showed our tickets to a member of the security team and we were immediately escorted backstage.

"Oh my god! I can't believe we got backstage passes for Soul Skylight! I think I might faint." Christina shrieked as we followed security to the dressing rooms. "Please, don't let me faint." She held on to my arm. I looked at her and her honey complexion had completely reddened.

"Deep breaths Christina, deep breaths." I smiled. I looked back at Greg who was muttering to himself.

We walked down a narrow hallway until we came to a door with Xavier's name on it.

"Oh my god, this is Xavier's dressing room. Am I really about to meet Xavier Ross?" she asked bewildered.

My heart beat wildly realizing that I was also about to come face to face with Xavier.

The security guard knocked a couple of times before a voice said, "Come in,"

When the door opened Xavier stood on the other side wearing jeans, a gray t-shirt, and no shoes. He'd started to grow out his beard since I last saw him. He smiled widely, walked towards us and grabbed me around the waist. He then kissed me soundly on the lips.

Christina gasped loudly. So, I guess the secret was out!

Xavier turned to acknowledge her. She had an astonished look on her face but she wasn't looking at Xavier. She was looking at me.

"Hello, you must be Christina." He smiled.

She turned her attention to him and turned even redder. "You know my name?" she asked.

"Yes, Angie talks about you all the time." He smiled. He let go of me and put an arm around Christina. "I feel like I know you. Thanks for coming to the show." He was such a charmer!

"And you must be Greg, Christina's boyfriend." Xavier smiled and shook his hand.

Christina was still gaping at me. She was obviously shocked and probably upset that I had never mentioned Xavier and I were more than friends.

To take the focus off of me, I cleared my throat and spoke up, "Hey Christina, do you have your phone? Xavier, do you mind taking a few pictures?" I asked.

"Of course," he smiled.

Christina took her phone from her purse and I took a few shots of the three of them and then just her and Xavier.

"Hey, Tony!" Xavier called to the guard outside the door. "Can you ask the rest of the guys to come over for a minute? Tell them our special guest is here," he announced.

While we waited for Tony to return, Xavier planted himself next to me. He whispered in my ear and told me how beautiful I was and how happy he was to see me. I tried to keep my face blank but his mood was infectious and I found myself laughing and smiling along with him. Christina continued to gawk at us.

The rest of the guys came over a few minutes later and introduced themselves to Christina and Greg and of course, they acted as if they'd known me forever, which shocked Christina even more. After a few more photo's Xavier kissed me again and then had someone escort us to our front row seats.

"No way. No *fucking* way," Christina said after we settled in our seats. I'd never heard her use the f-word. My eyes widened.

"You and Xavier Ross? For how long? Why didn't you tell me?"

she asked and I could tell her feelings were hurt. Fortunately, before I had a chance to answer the lights went out and the band was being introduced.

They did an opening similar to the one I'd witnessed in Denver and the screams from the crowd were even louder. After performing a medley of their up-tempo hits, Xavier removed his guitar and grabbed the microphone from the mic stand.

"New York, New York big city of dreams!" he said into the microphone and the crowd ate it up. This was his signal for Greg to make his way to the side of the stage. I reached behind Christina and tapped him on the shoulder. He whispered something in her ear and she shrugged before turning her attention back to the stage as Greg walked off.

"How is everybody feeling tonight?" Xavier asked amid more screams. "Can you believe we are about to celebrate a New Year? Anybody making any resolutions? Who's going on a diet, changing jobs or getting married?" he asked. The women around us screamed, 'I'll marry you!'

Christina looked at me as if she expected a reaction. I rolled my eyes and smiled at her. I wasn't jealous of Xavier's fans because that's all they were– *fans*. He was a sexy man and I knew I wasn't the only woman who thought so.

"Well, I know somebody who has found the woman he wants to spend the rest of his life with-," Xavier started.

Christina grabbed my arm. "Oh no, he's going to propose to you!" she said.

I wasn't sure why she'd said, 'oh no' but I decided to file that for later as I kept my eyes glued on the stage.

"New York, help me welcome Greg to the stage," Xavier announced and the crowd cheered despite not knowing Greg.

I looked at Christina and she stared at me with a confused expression. I smiled at her.

Greg shuffled out towards the center of the stage and Xavier whispered something in his ear. Greg smiled and stood up straighter as Xavier passed him the microphone. Christina let go of my arm and covered her mouth with both hands.

"Chrissy, can you come up here, please,"

One of the security guys helped Christina over the barricade and on to the stage. The crowd cheered for her too. I was so excited for her.

"Christina when I first met you in college seven years ago, I remember asking you out and you laughed at me. You told me that you were there to get your education and not let some college player try to run game on you," he smiled and the crowd laughed.

She hung her head in embarrassment.

"Well, I have never been a player. I never wanted to be. I only wanted to find a girl who I could laugh with, grow with, learn with and love."

The audience said a collective, "Aw".

"You are a smart, beautiful, funny woman and your positive outlook on life inspires me. I want to spend the rest of my life with you," Greg got down on one knee and pulled a ring from his pocket.

Before he even asked Christina nodded her head vigorously.

"Wait, you got to let him ask before you say yes, make sure it counts!" Johnny chimed in and the crowd agreed.

"Christina, will you do me the extreme honor of becoming my wife?"

Christina nodded again before leaning down into the microphone and saying, "Yes," the crowd erupted as Greg placed the ring on her finger and stood to embrace her. He kissed her deeply and pulled away smiling wider than I'd ever seen him smile before.

Xavier walked over and took the mic from Greg.

"From Soul Skylight and the entire Soul Skylight family, we congratulate you guys and hope you have a long, happy life together. Fellas, don't you just love, love?" Xavier asked the band.

They responded by launching into their latest ballad, *From Here to Forever*. I got the feeling a lot of people would be getting married to that song.

Instead of paying attention to the band or listening to Xavier belt out the words, I found myself thinking back to when Rodney proposed to me.

****

We had gone to San Francisco and it was my first time, so Rodney made sure I did all of the sightseeing stuff like Fisherman's Wharf, Ghirardelli's, Lombard Street, traipsing across the Golden Gate bridge and even taking a tour of Alcatraz. I'd actually found the tour of Alcatraz to be terrifying. It was getting dark and I kept thinking we were going to miss the ferry back to the wharf and get trapped there. Otherwise, we'd had a blast and ended the night by eating at the incredible 5-star restaurant, Gary Danko.

The next morning, I was exhausted but Rodney was up and excited about our trip to Napa Valley.

"No, let's just stay here and cuddle. This bed is amazing." I whined. But he convinced me to get up with the promise of amazing wine and scenery.

We drove for about two hours to Napa, actually, Rodney drove and I went back to sleep. When I woke up we had arrived at the Brown Estate, a black-owned vineyard in Napa. We took the tour with a group of about ten but then a man who worked for the vineyard approached us and asked if we'd like to see the reserve barrel room. It hadn't been part of the tour, so Rodney eagerly said yes.

The man led us down a dark hallway and I started to get nervous, I grabbed Rodney's hand and whispered, "Are you sure he works here?"

He turned, looked and me and instead of saying anything, he smiled and kissed me. A few seconds later, we came to the end of a hallway that opened up into another room. There were barrels of wine all around us but I was more focused on the small table for two in the middle of the room. It was covered with a white linen tablecloth, there were two place settings and a vase of red roses sat in the center of the table.

"Rodney, what is all of this?" I asked.

"I thought I'd surprise you with a private tasting," he said. At that exact moment two people, who worked at the vineyard, appeared with bottles of wine and a silver platter of cheese, fruit, and prosciutto, which they placed on the table. It was the most romantic thing anyone had ever done for me.

"This is so sweet. This entire trip has been amazing! Thank you," I reached up and kissed him.

He grabbed my hand and looked into my eyes. "I want to give you the world Angela. I love you, so much,"

"I love you too," I said as tears filled my eyes.

Then he kneeled in front of me. "You're my best friend and I want to experience the rest of what this life has to offer with you. Angela Nicole Barnes, will you marry me?"

I was shocked. I loved Rodney and couldn't imagine spending my life with anyone else but I wasn't sure about marriage. At the time, I'd actually thought he deserved better. I was too ambitious, stubborn and conflicted. But I'd said yes anyway and I wore his four-carat ring with pride for six months before our relationship came to an end.

****

I'd been lost in thought until Christina and Greg returned to their seats.

"Oh my god! You knew, didn't you? You knew!" she squealed when she returned. I nodded guiltily.

I hugged her, "Congratulations! I'm so happy for you! Let me see this rock!" I teased.

It was a beautiful princess cut diamond surrounded by small sapphires.

"You did good!" I said to Greg giving him a hug as well.

"Thank you so much!" he replied.

After the concert ended, we headed backstage again and the band joined us in Xavier's dressing room for a champagne toast to Greg and Christina. It was only a little past ten o'clock but Greg and Christina left immediately following the toast to try and make it to Greg's brother's party to share the news with their family.

"You know what I've always wanted to do?" Xavier said after he'd showered and the two of us were alone.

I wrapped my arms around his waist feeling more comfortable now that there were no prying eyes around. "Does it involve being naked?" I pressed myself against him.

"Oh, there are a lot of things I want to do naked with you, trust me. But first I was thinking we could walk over and watch the ball drop," he smiled.

"What? Are you serious?" I wasn't expecting him to say that, it was such a touristy thing to do. I didn't know many native New

Yorkers who'd actually been to Times Square on New Year's Eve, myself included.

"Yeah! Come on, it'll be fun and then we can scratch it off our bucket list," he smiled down at me.

"That's not on my bucket list. Xavier, there are a million people out there and it's cold!" I whined.

I thought after the concert we'd head to my apartment and stay there until his flight left next week.

"I promise afterwards I'm all yours," he said reading my mind.

"How would we even do that? Aren't you on one of the Times Square billboards right now?" I reminded him. I'd seen a picture announcing the band's show tonight at Radio City. Not to mention people started lining up for a spot almost twelve hours ago.

"I'll be incognito," he winked. "And I have a security guy that has a spot for us,"

That's how I found myself wedged between a million people in thirty-degree weather counting down to a new year.

Xavier stood behind me with his arms around my waist, softly counting down with the rest of the crowd.

"Five, four, three, two, one" he whispered. Then he turned me towards him and raised the bandana that covered most of his face. "Happy New Year," he said against my mouth before dipping me back to kiss me long and slow.

When the ball drop and fireworks ended, we walked a mile to my apartment building in the freezing cold because getting a cab was pretty much impossible. We made it back to my building just as it started to snow. Once inside my apartment, I immediately turned up the heater a few degrees.

Xavier laughed and removed the black bandana and wool beanie he'd worn. "Haven't you lived in New York state your entire life? You'd think you'd be used to the cold by now."

"Never." I shuddered. It was quite ridiculous that I had been born and raised in the state of New York and had such a low tolerance for the cold weather, which was all but guaranteed during the winter months. I guess in my defense I'd never really spent much time outside, so I never got acclimated to the winter temperatures.

"Malibu is a bright, beautiful, sunny place if you ever want to visit," he said referring to his home.

"Hmm, I might have to check it out someday," I smiled. We started removing our coats, scarves, gloves and boots as our bodies began to thaw. "Well, let me give you the grand tour," I motioned around my apartment.

"This is my living room, which has a fabulous view of the Hudson in the far, far distance during the daytime," I laughed. "Here is the kitchen where I make the best cup of coffee at 4am. This is my office space," I walked down the short hallway.

I turned on the light in the space that was about as big as a walk-in closet but served as an office and gym since that's where I also kept my fold away treadmill. I was glad I'd remembered to organize last night. There had been papers and files all over the desk and filing cabinet. I glanced up at the painting that I'd gotten from Rodney. I'd had it framed and hung it over my desk. I felt a slight twinge of guilt but took a deep breath, shook off those feelings and turned off the light.

"The bathroom is next door and just there at the end of the hall is my bedroom,"

"I don't get to look at the bedroom?" he smirked.

I shrugged. "You've seen one bedroom, you've seen them all," I teased.

He leaned towards me like he was about to kiss me but instead slid past me and headed straight for my bedroom door. I actually didn't have a problem with him seeing my bedroom, it was my favorite room in the entire apartment. Besides, I'd planned on us spending the majority of our time there during his visit.

"Wow," he said entering the room and I smiled.

I had to admit, it was pretty impressive. I'd gotten rid of the traditional sleigh style bed that I'd shared with Rodney and replaced it with a queen size platform bed with a pale blue, suede tufted headboard. I chose cream and pale blue bedding; my sheets were Egyptian cotton topped with a chenille coverlet. All the pillows were gel fiber and a large white fur rug covered the hardwood floor under the bed.

I'd purchased two distressed side tables from an antiques store in SoHo and put silver lamps with crystal details on top of them. Finally, a pewter chandelier with crystals hung over the bed adding an extra touch of glam.

"This looks like something from an upscale hotel," he commented.

"I'll take that as a compliment," I smiled.

He turned and looked at me. "It's a shame though. . .," his voice trailed off and he sighed.

"What?"

"That it will all be such a mess soon," he grinned and grabbed me around the waist. He kissed me firmly on the lips and we fell back on the bed making the pillows crash down around us.

He grabbed my wrists and forced my arms over my head, holding them in place with one hand while he kissed me fiercely. He pushed his tongue inside my mouth and I moaned. Xavier's possessiveness during sex was such a turn on.

He rolled over on top of me and I felt his erection through his jeans. He rocked his body against mine creating friction that was almost unbearable. I desperately wanted to be free of my clothes, so that I could feel his skin. His lips left my mouth and he suckled along my neck.

"Too many clothes," he breathed on my shoulder.

"I agree," I panted.

We grabbed at each other's clothing– unbuttoning, unzipping and peeling away fabric until we were both completely naked. He resumed his previous position but this time his lips explored further down my body and when his fingers slipped inside of me and curled toward my G-spot, I couldn't stop myself from erupting.

As I convulsed under him, he reached over with his free hand and pulled a condom from his wallet. Even though I was coming down from a mind-blowing climax, I wanted more. He rolled on the condom and I took him in and squeezed him tighter and tighter until he was screaming my name. Afterwards, our respective days caught up with us and we both fell asleep from exhaustion.

The next morning, I got up early took a shower and called the bistro on the corner for a breakfast delivery. Right before the delivery guy arrived, someone from the Soul Skylight camp showed up with Xavier's luggage.

"Hey sleepyhead, are you hungry? I've got breakfast," I kissed his forehead. He yawned and stretched before opening one eye.

"Hey, what time is it?" he cleared his throat.

"A little after ten,"

"Man, I don't think I've slept this late in a long time. I need to call and see where my bags are,"

"They actually arrived about ten minutes ago," I pointed to the corner of the room where I'd placed his suitcase and duffle bag.

"Cool. Okay, let me freshen up and take care of this morning breath right quick, and I'll come out and eat. Did you eat?" he sat up in the bed. I'd noticed last night that he looked like he'd lost a few pounds. Now it was more apparent in the morning light. He was probably missing meals on the road.

"Nope, the food just got here,"

He side-eyed me. "I thought I'd be waking up to a big homemade breakfast." He said and for a minute he sounded serious.

"That was just a dream." I winked as I left him alone.

Although I loved a good meal, I wasn't a good cook. Rodney had cooked most of our meals but we'd both loved eating out, so it was never a big deal.

I'd ordered whole grain pancakes, turkey bacon (because Xavier didn't eat pork), eggs, and fruit. I took some plates from the cabinet and set the containers on the dining table.

"Can you cook?" Xavier asked after we sat down to eat. He had a playful smile on his face but it was still an annoying question. Did he expect me to know how to cook because I was a woman?

"Is that a deal breaker?" I asked pouring cream into my coffee.

"Nope. You make up for it in other ways," he waggled his eyebrows.

I rolled my eyes. As we started to eat, I couldn't help but think that maybe all Xavier wanted from me was a physical relationship. Was that all I wanted from him? I was about to ask him where he saw the relationship going but he beat me to the punch with a question of the blue.

"Tell me about your ex-fiancé," he quizzed.

I took a sip from my coffee and frowned. "Rodney?"

"So, his name was Rodney," he smiled.

I glanced at him over my mug. "Why do you want to know about my ex?"

He shrugged. "I want to make sure I don't make the same mistakes he did,"

I laughed. "Trust me, the two of you are nothing alike,"

"I bet. I'm just wondering what kind of man would let a woman like you get away,"

"I told you– he left to work in another city but in the end, it was a mutual decision. We both realized we wanted different things from a relationship."

"Well, his loss is definitely my gain," he smiled.

I returned the smile and took another sip of coffee. "What are your plans after the tour is over?" I asked hoping to gain some clarity on his expectations.

"I wish I could say we're taking a break but we're probably headed back to the studio. But we'll more than likely take a break before the next tour,"

"The next tour?" I asked surprised.

"Yeah, but that's at least a year or two away," he looked up at me and shoved a piece of bacon in his mouth.

"Oh, so what about in the meantime? I mean, what about you and I? Do you ever think that far ahead or do you think we'll be together a year from now?" I asked with a bit more frustration than I'd intended. It's not that I was expecting a commitment such as marriage but if I was going to be in a relationship with someone I at least wanted them a cab ride or driving distance away. I didn't want to be in a long-distance relationship forever.

He raised an eyebrow. "Where is this coming from? Sure, we'll be together- at least that's what *I* want. What about you?" he asked softly.

I sighed. "Yeah, I do. But at some point, I thought we'd at least end up in the same city,"

He placed his hand on top of mine and squeezed. "We will be. That's why I'm doing all this now, I don't want to be touring when I'm sixty. I should have us pretty much set up with another couple of albums and another tour. And we can move into the house in Malibu and-,"

I slid my hand away from his. "I-I can't move to Malibu,"

"I know, not now. I meant in a year or so. Or we can find a place in New York or maybe commute between both? I just want us-,"

His phone started ringing and interrupted the conversation. "Hold on," he walked over to get his phone out of his jacket pocket.

"Hello? Yeah, what's up?" he asked the caller.

I tuned out his conversation and stared down at my coffee. For the first time, I felt like things with Xavier might not work out. I had a life, a career, and family on the east coast. I wasn't prepared to just leave it all behind to follow Xavier to Malibu. And I didn't appreciate his comment about how he was working to get 'us' set up. I had my own money and career.

Or maybe I was looking at things all wrong, maybe it was time for me to stop being so self-absorbed and make a sacrifice for someone I loved. But did I love Xavier enough to follow him blindly to California?

We really needed to have a heart to heart talk and get on the same page. I was glad we had almost a week together to find out what it was we both wanted from the relationship.

"Ang-Angie?" I heard his voice as it brought me from my thoughts.

I looked up at him, he had a weird expression on his face. "Hey, you okay?"

"Huh- yeah, yeah. I'm good. Everything okay with you?" I motioned to the phone in his hand.

He sighed heavily. "I know this is horrible timing but we just got a call, last minute. . . they've asked us to perform at a White House event on Saturday. They had another band scheduled but something happened and they aren't able to make it." He smiled faintly and I could tell he was trying to suppress his excitement.

"The White House? That is huge! Wow, congratulations!" I said genuinely excited for him. I stood to hug him and then pulled away. "Wait- Saturday? This Saturday?" It was Thursday.

"I know it sucks, but this is a really big deal for us." He said pleading for me to understand.

"When would you have to leave?" I asked.

"Tonight. We're taking a private jet out at seven o'clock. We have a meeting and then rehearsals." He said sadly. "I am *so* sorry. If this was-,"

I held up a hand to stop him. "I get it. I understand." The band came first. Not me.

January

2014

I tried my best to be happy for Xavier. Performing at a White House event was a big deal for the band, however, I didn't like taking a backseat. But Soul Skylight was on fire and despite Xavier saying they would only do one more album and tour, I didn't believe it. None of the guys were even forty yet. What else would they do? He'd never mentioned anything else to me besides playing music.

In all fairness, we hadn't really talked about future plans. That conversation was supposed to take place during our long weekend together, which had been cut short. He'd offered to come back to New York on Monday after the White House performance but that would only give us a day together, so I told him not to worry about it and that I'd come to see him at the last U.S. stop in a few weeks.

"I promise things won't be this way forever. Don't give up on me okay?" he said as he lingered at my front door saying goodbye.

"I know. And I'm not giving up. I just miss you so much and wanted to spend time with you this weekend," I said. "But this is an incredible opportunity. Don't worry about me, go rehearse and give a kick-ass performance Saturday. Tell Barack and Michelle I said hi," I joked.

"Thank you. You mean a lot to me, Angie, you really do. I'll call you when I get to D.C." he promised as he kissed me gently and then with a deep, fiery passion that left me breathless.

"You can't kiss me like that and then leave," I grabbed his shirt as he rested his forehead against mine.

He bit his lip and smiled. "Just giving you something to think about until I see you again,"

After Xavier left, I moped around my apartment thinking about that kiss and wished it could have ended with us naked again instead of me all alone. I decided to stop feeling sorry for myself and fixed a mug of Chai tea and watched a documentary on the Nature Channel about penguins. For the first time in weeks, I thought about Rodney and wondered what he was doing.

I'd cut my vacation short and returned to work on Monday since Xavier was no longer in town. It made more sense to save the days for another time in case I wanted to surprise him on tour. I was so sick of that damned tour and it only been three months. I seriously didn't know if I'd be able to hang on for another three months.

When I returned to work Christina stopped by my office to chat during the afternoon. She was glowing and had gotten her nails painted a bright red color to no doubt highlight the beautiful, sparkling ring on her finger.

"How does it feel to be newly engaged?" I asked.

"Amazing!" she smiled. "I still don't know how Greg pulled that off. I mean I know he called you but I would have never expected him to do something so major. He can barely talk in front of a group of six let alone six thousand," she chuckled.

"When you really care about someone you find the courage to do things you never thought possible," I smiled and thought about my situation with Xavier.

It was as if Christina read my mind. "So. . . .you and Xavier, huh? How long have you guys been seeing each other?" she asked and I could tell by her tone, her feelings were definitely hurt.

I sighed. "Since the reunion."

She shook her head in disbelief and sat back in the chair and stared at me.

"I'm so sorry, I know I should have told you. I felt like such a hypocrite after saying all that stuff about not wanting a long-distance relationship with Rodney. And plus, he's an international celebrity, I just wanted to keep a piece of him to myself," I said quietly.

Her expression softened. "I get it. You don't owe me an apology. So, is this just a fling or are you guys serious?" she asked. I thought it was an odd question and made me remember her comment at the concert when she thought Xavier was about to propose to me.

"Why?" I asked. Surely Christina wasn't jealous of my relationship with Xavier. To be a fangirl was one thing but I was in a real relationship with him.

She shrugged. "Just make sure the two of you are on the same page, I don't want to see you get hurt,"

My eyes widened and I was about to ask her to elaborate but she stood suddenly and said she had a meeting to get to.

"We're thinking of either a traditional June wedding or waiting until August. As soon as I have a date, I'll let you know." She smiled but it didn't reach her eyes. She gave me a little wave before she left my office.

I was distracted for the rest of the day after Christina's visit. I turned her words over in my mind, I knew she was probably referring to Xavier and other women. He had some really forward female fans but I wasn't jealous or intimidated by them. I'd never been the kind of woman who tried to keep tabs on a man. I was only concerned with how you treated me when we were together. Of course, if I ever had solid evidence that there was another woman then it would definitely be over. I wasn't going to share him.

But after the cryptic conversation with Christina, I considered Googling Xavier. One of the reasons I'd never Googled him was because I hadn't wanted to read stories about him or his past. I guess

I'd wanted to keep our relationship in a bubble or maybe I was in denial. I decided I wouldn't Google him. We'd have a conversation and I'd let him tell me in his own words what he wanted and what he was prepared to do.

When I made it home later that evening my mom called.

"Hey Mama," I smiled into the phone. I hadn't talked to her in almost a week.

"Hey baby, how are you? Can you talk right now?"

"Yeah, I'm good, what's up?"

"I was just calling to gossip," she chuckled.

"Oh my, who have you got the goods on today?" I laughed.

"Your ex,"

"My ex? Who?" I don't know why I asked 'who', it wasn't like I had a bunch of exes but I couldn't think of anyone that my mom would have seen.

"Who? Why are you acting like you have a bunch of exes?" she cackled.

"Mmph, whatever, who Mama?"

"Rodney! I hadn't seen him in almost a year. He looks good. I was shocked to see him at your brother's house,"

"Wait, Rodney was at Allen's house? When was this? Why?"

"Well, you know Allen still goes to those poker games once a month, which is why Paula probably really left him, speaking of Paula- she dropped the kids off at his house right as the game was starting. And it wasn't even his weekend to have them, I mean I know she's angry but that's just too petty and to keep putting the kids in the middle of that mess. I don't know why-,"

"Mama! Focus! What was Rodney doing there?" I yelled to get

her attention.

"Oh. Well, last night was your brother's turn to host the game, so I went by to pick up the boys to watch them and your daddy was there too. He was supposed to watch the kids but decided his ass was going to stay and play cards, he made me so damn mad! Anyway, Rodney was there playing poker. It was so good to see him. I still don't understand why the two of you couldn't have worked things out. I love me some Rodney."

"First of all, we couldn't work things out because he moved to another state. Second, we broke up so that means he broke up with my family too. I can't believe Allen invited him to play poker. How are we supposed to have a clean break if he won't move on!"

"Calm down, it was just a poker game! And he told me he moved back to New York, probably to be with you,"

"Did he say that?" I asked. "And do I need to remind you that I'm seeing someone?"

"Oh yeah, this mystery musician. You didn't want a long-distance relationship with Rodney but you have one with this guy? The sex must be the bomb dot com," she snickered.

I was annoyed but couldn't help but laugh. "Mama, will you stop. I can't believe Rodney is spending time with my family. What if I wanted my new man to start playing poker with my brother?"

"I guess that would be pretty awkward. When are we going to meet your new man? Are you thinking about marriage, I mean I'm not telling you to rush into anything but if you want a baby, you don't want to be an old mother like my mama was- that's why her nerves were so damn bad!" Mama complained.

I wanted to tell her Grandma Hattie's nerves weren't bad, she was just mean. God rest her soul.

"Ma- I'm only thirty-four, I think I have some time to have

children,"

I'd never told my mom that I might not want children. I knew how much she adored AJ's kids and she probably couldn't wait for me to have kids as well. After listening to her tell me about how her sister, my Aunt Shirley had a hard time conceiving because she'd waited so late to get pregnant, I decided to end the conversation.

As soon as I disconnected the call with my mom, I called my brother.

"Hey Sis," Allen said into the phone.

"Hey, so why didn't you tell me that Rodney still plays poker with you?" I said diving right into my reason for calling.

"Because I'm just now talking to you and I already knew your gossiping mama was going to tell you,"

"I talked to you last week,"

"The game was just this past Saturday, what's the big deal? Rod is cool people, this ain't got nothing to do with you and him," he said annoyed.

I sighed harshly. "That is *not* the point! What if me and Paula were hanging out? That wouldn't piss you off?"

"Not at all, why you so pressed? Don't you have a new man?" he questioned.

"Yes, I have a new man. And that's my point, what if you wanted to invite him to the game? It would be inappropriate for Rodney to be playing poker with you,"

"Whatever. When are we going to meet this dude? Mama said he's a musician and she bet twenty dollars that it's Drake," he laughed.

"Your mama is a nut! Why in the hell would I be dating Drake? I'm almost ten years older than him," I chuckled.

"I don't think you're that much older than him and age ain't nothing but a number. If it's not Drake, who is it, is he famous or just some local?" Allen asked.

"He's pretty famous," I said vaguely.

"Aw, how you gone play me like that? I thought we were better than that,"

I sighed. "It's Xavier Ross," I admitted quietly. Allen had already graduated when I transferred to Drew High, so he never knew Xavier.

"Okay, should I know who that is?" he asked genuinely confused.

He was worse than me. Allen only listened to old school rap music. He probably still had a cassette player.

"Soul Skylight," I said thinking maybe it would ring a bell.

"Soul Sky- oh, yeah they sing *Time to Leave* and *I Wonder?*"

"Yep, that's them." I smiled despite myself. I didn't tell him *I Wonder* had been written about me.

"I can't do too much of this new music but they're actually talented. Where did you meet him?"

"We went to high school together. I saw him at our class reunion a few months ago and we just kind of clicked," I remarked.

"Cool- how is that working out dating a musician. Doesn't he travel a lot? I thought that's why you and Rod broke up," I could detect the judgment in his tone.

"There was more to the break up with Rodney. And yes, Xavier is on tour right now," I sighed and decided to be honest with my brother. "And it kind of sucks. I flew out to see him in October and he was at Radio City on New Year's Eve, so I saw him last week but we've been mostly talking on the phone, texting, and Skyping for three months,"

"That does sound like it sucks. Well, why are you with him? You're smart, pretty, got a great career and could probably have any guy you want. Don't sell yourself short, Sis you deserve somebody that's going to put you first,"

My eyes filled with tears. "I know- when we're together it's like we're the only two people in the world. It's just the time in between that's hard."

"Yeah, that's tough," was all he offered, so I changed the subject.

"What about you and Paula? She still refusing to sign the divorce papers?"

"Yep. But that's okay, the longer she waits the more I'm thinking of filing for custody of the boys. She's unstable and I don't think it's a good environment for them. Plus, I'm talking to another lawyer right now regarding the business. I'm going to try and buy her out and if she doesn't go for it then after this lease is up, I'll just have to find another place on my own. This spot is prime real estate but I think my clients would follow me if I left and went somewhere else,"

"I didn't know things were that bad. Yeah, your main priority should be the boys." I remarked. "I'm curious, how did you know when it was time to move on? Do you not love her anymore?"

"Whenever I look at my kids there will be some feeling of love for their mother since she is the one who brought them into this world but I don't feel any other connection with her past that. To be honest though, it was never a butterfly and firework type situation with Paula. The only reason we got married is because she got pregnant."

I hadn't expected him to say that. I thought about my relationship with Xavier. I definitely felt butterflies and fireworks with him. But I'd also felt that way about Rodney. I wondered what that said about me. Once my call ended with Allen, I started thinking about Rodney's connection to my family. He'd said he wanted a clean break, so as far as I was concerned that meant no more spending time with my brother.

I went to his office Monday afternoon right before lunch to see him in person and let him know my family was off limits. I felt this would also be an opportunity to see him again since it had been over a month. I supposed a part of me missed him.

When we came face to face, he wasn't happy to see me.

"Angela what are you doing here?" He frowned and stood from his desk.

"We need to talk," I said plainly.

He looked at his watch. "I only have about five minutes before I need to head into a meeting. What's wrong?" he walked around the desk and closed his office door.

"I thought the last time we talked you said you were going to move on," I reminded him.

"I have no idea what you're talking about," he was visibly annoyed.

"My mom said she saw you at my brother's house Saturday."

He stared at me and shrugged his shoulders. "And?"

"Don't you think it's a little inappropriate since we are no longer together to keep hanging out with my family?"

He rolled his eyes. "I'm not *hanging out* with your family. It was a poker game. I played poker with your brother before we met, remember?"

"But now that we're no longer together-,"

"We haven't been together for a while and guess what- I've played poker with your brother at least four times since we broke up." He went back to his desk and looked down at his computer screen.

"What? Why- my mother never mentioned-,"

"The games are at a different house each time. The only time I missed the games is when I lived in Houston."

"I don't want you playing poker with my brother," I said firmly.

"Why? You think we talk about you? Trust me, neither one of us ever brings up your name. I'm friends with the guys in that group and your brother just happens to be a part of it. I'm not giving up my poker games because you can't handle it." He grabbed a notepad from his desk. "My meeting is about to start. You know your way out?" he said dismissing me.

I hesitated and then sighed harshly as I turned to leave his office. I was so irritated, he was doing that shit on purpose– trying to keep the door open. A door that I admittedly was also finding hard to close.

I was so deep in thought that I'd overlooked the gap in the elevator floor when it opened to the lobby and my heel got caught. I tried to catch myself before I fell and ended up twisting my ankle. The security guard came over to help me up before calling the building manager.

I'd argued with the building manager that I didn't need medical attention. But he insisted that anyone injured in the building had to be taken to the nearest medical center (by ambulance!) to be checked out. They were probably afraid I would sue.

I honestly just wanted to leave and not make a scene. I needed to go home, take some Advil and put ice on my throbbing ankle. I hadn't wanted Rodney to find out but of course, they asked who I'd been visiting in the building and I had to tell them.

Rodney looked horrified when he came downstairs as I was being placed on the stretcher. He was probably angry that I'd embarrassed him at work.

"Oh my god, Angela are you okay?"

"I think I sprained my ankle, I fell coming off the elevator. I told them this wasn't necessary but they said it's a liability thing. I'm so sorry about this-," I muttered.

He grabbed my hand. "There's nothing to apologize for- where are you taking her?" he asked the paramedic.

"Presbyterian,"

"Okay, listen I'm going back upstairs to get my phone and I'll meet you there,"

"You don't have to do that," I squeezed his hand.

He gave me a strange look. "Is your um- is your *boyfriend* in town?" he asked like it pained him to say the word. "Will he be able to make sure you get home?"

"No, I'm just going to call Christina," The paramedics started rolling me away and Rodney walked alongside the gurney.

"Shit. Christina's off today." I remembered she said she'd be out of the office for a couple of days. "I can get a cab or call an Uber, seriously it's no big deal," I grimaced.

"I'll be there in fifteen minutes," he gave my hand a final squeeze before letting go.

I started crying once the doors of the ambulance closed. I'd never been in the back of an ambulance and although it wasn't a serious injury, I thought about how awful it would have been if I did have a serious emergency and had to be taken to the hospital. I'd be all alone. Even though Xavier was technically my man, I wouldn't be able to count on him.

"Are you okay, is the pain worsening?" the EMT asked concerned.

"No, it's okay- I'm okay," I stuttered wiping my tears.

After we arrived at the hospital emergency room, a doctor examined me and took x-rays of my ankle. I didn't have any broken bones and he confirmed it was just a sprain. I received a cortisone shot for the swelling and a dose of hydrocodone for the pain. The doctor told me to ice my ankle and elevate my foot. He also told me to stay off my feet for twenty-four hours. I already knew that wouldn't be possible, I had a staff meeting the next day. So, he gave me a short orthopedic boot and when we were done a nurse came in with a wheelchair.

I rolled my eyes. "Is this really necessary?" I asked.

"Yes, ma'am," she shrugged.

I sighed and stood as she helped me into the chair. After I signed the release paperwork, she wheeled me out to the front waiting room where Rodney was looking through a magazine. When he saw me, he stood and walked towards us. I smiled at him, happy that he was there.

"Hey, I actually drove in today, so I have my car outside," he motioned over his shoulder. Rodney was the only New Yorker I knew personally, who owned a car. He'd purchased it when he lived in Houston and instead of selling it, he had it shipped back to New York. It stayed in a storage garage most of the time.

"I have to take her to the car, hospital protocol," the nurse remarked. "You can pull around to the front door," she instructed.

"Okay, I'll be right back," he said leaving the two of us alone.

When I saw Rodney's silver Tesla pull into the circle drive, I informed the nurse, so that she could wheel me outside.

I buckled my seatbelt after I was in the car and Rodney closed the door. I watched as he exchanged a few words with the nurse and then crossed over to the driver's door. When he entered the car, he looked at me.

"You okay?" he asked concerned.

I nodded my head and burst into tears at the same time. I was so overwhelmed because despite everything that had happened between us, and the fact that I was in a relationship with another man, Rodney still cared about me and wanted to make sure I was okay.

"Hey, Angela, don't cry- are you in pain? Did they give you a prescription?" he put an arm around my back.

"I'm good, I'm being ridiculous. I'm okay," I sniffed and took a tissue from my purse.

"Are you sure?" he looked at me like I might crack at any moment.

I laughed. "Yes, stop looking at me like that! It's just- it's been a long day," I sighed.

"Yes, it has," he said quietly before buckling his seatbelt and driving away from the hospital.

Rodney parked in the fifteen-minute unloading zone in front of my apartment building to help me from the car.

"I got it," I winced as I moved away from him and tried to walk normally with the boot on my foot.

Rodney looked at me and shook his head before taking my oversized bag and hooking it over his shoulder.

"Lean on me," he grabbed me around the waist and allowed me to put the majority of my weight on him.

"Lean on me, when you're not strong, I'll be your friend, I'll help you carry on!" I sang and then laughed. I'd started feeling the effects of the medicine the doctor had given me. Hydrocodone always made me a little loopy.

"We got you home just in time," he chuckled as he helped me

through the front door of the building.

"Whoa, Ms. Barnes everything okay?" the security guard, Carlos asked.

"She sprained her ankle," Rodney answered.

"I'm clumsy, so clumsy," I said to Carlos.

"Well, you call down if you need anything," he replied.

It seemed to take the elevator forever to reach the 8th floor. Rodney and I stared at each other and I wanted to scream, "Will you be my friend, will you *please* be my friend," but I kept my mouth clamped shut.

Or at least I thought I did.

"Angela, we've already been over this," he sighed.

Once we were in my apartment, Rodney helped me to my room and on to my bed. He propped a pillow under my leg and took off my other shoe.

"Rodney, I can't thank you enough- look I- I don't have any bad feelings towards you- you're a good man and-,"

He held up a hand. "Save the speech, Angela, I'm not trying to rekindle our relationship-," he started angrily.

"That's not what I was about to say. Rodney, I care about you, a part of me always will but I don't want to hurt you or lead you on. I value you as a friend and I wish- we could- if things- I don't know- shit this medicine is making me delirious," My words started to get jumbled.

"I thought we agreed to a clean break Angela, I feel like you're sending me mixed signals," he frowned.

I reached for his hand and he reluctantly placed his hand in mine and I squeezed it.

HERE YOU COME AGAIN

"I'm sorry. I miss you, Rodney," I admitted. "Our friendship. You were my best friend," I yawned and my eyes closed.

A couple of hours later I woke up and called out for Rodney but he didn't answer. My phone started ringing and vibrating on my nightstand. I reached over to answer it and saw a Post-It note:

Had to get back to work. Call me if you need anything. –R

I smiled at the note and then frowned at my ringing phone, it was Xavier.

I'd talked to him briefly before and after the White House performance but we still hadn't had a conversation about the future of our relationship. He'd mentioned wanting to settle down one day but I didn't know what that meant to him. Maybe he meant being with just one woman.

After seeing Rodney again, I wasn't sure what I wanted or if I wanted that type of future with Xavier.

"Hello," I cleared my throat after answering.

"Hey Angie, I've been calling you- everything okay?"

"I sprained my ankle," I said into the phone.

There were loud noises in the background and what sounded like hammering.

"What did you say? Sorry, I can barely hear you- hold on, let me move to another location– that's better, what were you saying?"

I sighed. "I sprained my ankle." It sounded so trivial and not the big deal it had been earlier.

"Ouch. Are you okay? What happened?"

"I'm fine. Being a klutz. What is that noise?"

"They're putting together the stage for our show tonight. I can't believe we're more than halfway done."

"Me either. It will be so good to be together in the same city when the tour is over." I said without thinking.

He exhaled slowly. "Yeah, I guess we still need to talk about that. Any chance you want to leave cold, dark, drab New York for the California sunshine?" I could hear the teasing in his voice.

"New York is not drab!" I laughed.

"You know New York is drab and it's cold. You can barely stand the winter there. You definitely wouldn't have to worry about that in California."

I sighed. "I know, it's just- my entire life is here. My career, my family is right up the highway, my friends-," I thought about Rodney. "Everything I know is in New York,"

"I understand and I'm not talking anytime soon I mean we've only been together a few months."

When he said it like that, it made it seem wrong for me to have any expectations. And we'd actually been together *four* months. It's not like I wanted to marry him or anything but I did want him in the same city.

"But time flies and it's in my nature to be prepared. To have a sense of direction, it gives me a measure of comfort to know that we're on the same page," I said trying to tamp down my frustration.

"Comfort or control?" he asked.

"Maybe both," I answered honestly.

"Well, sometimes you have to let things unfold naturally and if things are meant to be, which I feel they are, it's going to happen the way it should. We don't have to force or plan anything, just continue being there for each other."

Like how he was there for me when I'd sprained my ankle, oh right, he wasn't.

"I guess," I said quietly.

"Come on don't do that, don't shut down- you don't agree?"

"I do, I guess I'm just a little frustrated. I knew going into this that there would be this distance between us but it's hard," I said and I hated how my voice sounded. Weak and needy.

"Baby, I know it's not easy and I'm willing to do whatever I can to ease your mind, I'd love to have you here with me for every show,"

"Ease my mind? It's not about not trusting you Xavier," I wondered what had made him make that comment.

"I know. I trust you too. Listen, we leave for Amsterdam next week and we'll be overseas for almost two months. Do you think you can take a leave of absence at work and maybe come on the road with me for a few weeks?" he asked hopefully.

I couldn't believe he was serious. Not about me coming on the road but about me just up and taking a leave of absence from work where I was recently promoted into a new position never held by a black woman before in the history of the company. It occurred to me that Xavier had no idea what I really did. He probably thought I walked through the mall spritzing people with perfume.

"Are you serious?" I asked in disbelief.

"Yeah, it'll be fun! You think you could get the time off?" he asked. He apparently thought I was excited about his invitation.

"Um- I don't know, you know I just got a new position, so it's weird timing but I'll ask," I said with a hint of sarcasm.

"Cool! Man, it would be so great to have you waiting for me when I got off stage. Then we could tour the cities and see the sights," he said and he sounded so thrilled at the thought of me 'waiting for him'.

"Yeah, that sounds like fun," I lied. "Ow," I winced when I moved my foot.

"You okay? Did you go to the doctor for your foot?" he asked.

"Yeah, it's just superficial but what a way to start my birthday week," I whined.

"Birthday week- aw, I feel so stupid. I remembered your birthday being in January, I forgot the date though," he said sadly.

"It's Thursday, January 15th the same as Martin Luther King Jr.," I recited. I'd always been so proud of being born on Dr. King's birthday, God bless his soul.

"That's right, I'm sorry I didn't remember,"

I laughed. "It's okay, you didn't miss it."

"I know but I should have known that. You remember my birthday?" he asked.

I did remember his birthday. June 4th. The fact that he didn't remember mine wasn't a big deal but it was a big deal that we'd never even had a conversation about birthdays or favorite colors or anything.

"June 3rd," I said intentionally misstating it by a day. I didn't want him to feel bad.

"June 4th," he said.

"Man, I was off by one day." I pretended to be upset.

He laughed and I could tell he felt a bit of relief that he wasn't the only one who had forgotten.

"What's your favorite color?" I asked.

"Grey," he responded.

"Grey? Is that considered a color?" I laughed.

We continued to talk and play twenty questions, which is

something we probably should have done months ago. Although we hadn't resolved anything about the future, at least it was part of our conversation now. We both agreed that we wanted to end up in the same city but beyond that, we hadn't really defined what the future would look like for us as a couple.

While on the phone with Xavier, Rodney sent me a text:

Hey, it's Rodney. Just checking on you. How are you doing?

I put Xavier on speaker so that I could respond to Rodney.

AB: I'm fine. Better. Thanks again for everything today. I really appreciate it!

RA: No problem. Take care.

The next day at work, everyone treated me like I'd had open heart surgery.

"Oh my god, what are you doing here. We could have rescheduled the meeting," my new assistant, Alice exclaimed. She was the polar opposite of Christina. A pale, redhead from Hoboken with a touch of obsessive-compulsive disorder, which made her super neurotic but also *extremely* thorough.

"I'm fine. It's just a sprain."

It actually felt much better. So much better that after three days of wearing the boot to work, I got it removed on my birthday. When I returned from the doctor's office that afternoon, I pretended not to know why Alice insisted I go to the conference room. As expected, my team had assembled in the conference room with balloons, presents, and cake to celebrate my birthday.

"You got a couple of deliveries that I put in your office," Alice whispered while I indulged in the best red velvet cake I'd ever eaten.

After I'd thanked everyone, I took another slice of cake and all the gifts I'd received to my office. There was a huge bouquet of lilies on my desk and an edible arrangement box. I immediately started to sneeze. Stargazer lilies were my least favorite flower; the scent was so overpowering that it caused me to sneeze constantly.

"Alice-achoo!" I called and sneezed at the same time.

"Yes?" she appeared at my door smiling. "Isn't that the most beautiful arrangement?"

"It's beauti-achoo!" I sneezed. "Can you take it to the conference room. Lilies make me sneeze," I sniffed.

"Oh no! Here, take the card," she removed the card and handed it to me before picking up the vase.

On her way out, I sneezed again as she closed the door. I walked over and opened it to get rid of the smell. I took a tissue from my desk, wiped my teary eyes and scowled at the card before opening it. Who would have sent me stargazers? Everyone knew they were my least favorite flower.

I hope you're having an amazing day. I wish I was there to celebrate with you. But we will be together soon. Love, Xavier.

I threw my head back and groaned. It was a sweet gesture but I wish he would've just sent roses.

I put the card down next to the slice of red velvet cake and opened the Edible Arrangements box. It was the dipped strawberries and pineapple arrangement. My favorite! I already knew who had sent it. I opened the attached card and smiled.

The best kind of arrangement is one you can eat. Happy birthday, Angela. –Rodney

I'd said that to Rodney after he sent me a huge arrangement of roses for my birthday when we first started dating. I told him it was a waste of money and that the best kind of arrangement was one you could eat and proceeded to school him on Edible Arrangements. He'd sent me one every year for my birthday since then.

I pressed the card close to my chest and smiled as I took one of the pineapples from the box and devoured it. I pulled my phone from my purse and sent Rodney a text.

AB: Thanks for the arrangement. I think I made myself sick eating it all in one sitting. I lied.

RA: You're welcome. I sent it to your office so you would share.

AB: You should know me better than that. Lol. Thanks again, it was very thoughtful.

RA: Happy Birthday, Angela.

I put away my phone and responded to a few emails. Later that evening after work, I met Christina and Greg for happy hour. I hadn't talked to Christina since our conversation about Xavier and she'd never mentioned him again. I assumed she was just respecting my boundaries. Not to mention, she had started planning her wedding, which took up most of the conversation.

After two drinks, I ended up calling it a night. I'd lied and said I would be seeing Xavier the upcoming weekend. I don't know why I'd lied. I think because Christina seemed to think it was just a fling. She probably didn't believe Xavier valued me and much as Greg valued her. I knew that wasn't the case but I still didn't want her to think things weren't serious between us. Even if I had doubts myself.

When I got home my mom called with my brother and dad on the line. They sang the most off-key rendition of happy birthday I'd ever heard.

"Wow, I don't know what to say," I laughed. "Thank you,"

"If you moved closer, I could've made you a carrot cake for your birthday. When are you coming back to visit?"

"I don't know Ma, maybe next weekend. But I can't eat any more sweets. I practically ate half a red velvet cake by myself today and Rodney sent me an edible arrangement. . .I think I'm falling into a sugar coma," I groaned.

"Rodney? I thought you broke up with him," AJ said.

"You and Rodney broke up?" My dad asked and sounded shocked.

"Al, get off the phone, you know they broke up! Do you have Alzheimer's?" my mom asked annoyed.

"If I had Alzheimer's I wouldn't be able to tell you I had it because I wouldn't know," my dad chuckled.

I rolled my eyes at my dad's comment but was glad he had interrupted. I thought I wouldn't have to answer until my mom spoke up, "Are you gonna answer your brother's question?"

I sighed harshly. "Rodney and I aren't back together. We're just friends." I hoped that would end the conversation.

"He told me the two of you weren't friends," my brother announced.

"What? And you said you don't talk about me," I remarked angrily.

"What happened to the musician Xavier?" AJ asked ignoring my response.

"Who is Xavier?" my dad asked.

"Her new boyfriend," my mom replied. "I was hoping it was Drake," she giggled.

"You know what- I've got to go. Thank you so much for the lovely birthday song. Goodbye." I hung before they could continue to interrogate me.

A few minutes later I got a text from my brother:

AJ: Sorry. I shouldn't have called you out like that.

I sighed.

Angie: No, you shouldn't have.

AJ: Just thought it was over. Surprised he sent you a gift.

Not sure why it surprised him. Rodney and I were engaged to be married at one point, we weren't just casually dating. And it was just an Edible Arrangement.

Angie: Not that big of a deal.

AJ: Okay. Sorry. Happy Birthday. Love you & hope to see you soon.

His 'hope to see you soon' reminded me of Xavier.

I took a long hot shower and afterward I stood in front of the bathroom mirror staring at my reflection. I couldn't believe I was thirty-five. It seemed like I'd just graduated from college a couple of years ago.

I distinctly remembered the five-year plan I'd made in college. I'd wanted to move to Manhattan. *Check.* Have a fabulous career in the cosmetics or fashion industry. *Check.* Travel the world. *Half check.* I'd traveled around but there were still places on my bucket list. And I'd wanted to meet the man of my dreams, fall in love and get married. I'd envisioned a big wedding in the Hamptons. A honeymoon in the South of France. *Definitely no checks.*

I'd never really defined the man of my dreams as far as qualifications. Maybe that's where I'd gone wrong. I should have been more specific. Or maybe finding a man shouldn't have even been a part of my plan. I hated when women felt somehow incomplete if they didn't have a man or weren't married. It wasn't that I thought a man would complete me, I just enjoyed the companionship. I liked having someone around to snuggle with, to debate movies, go out to restaurants and travel with, and someone to kill spiders!

I supposed I could find a female friend to do those things but being a heterosexual woman, the bonus of having a male partner was you'd also have someone to have sex with– preferably amazing, monogamous sex.

While examining my body, my phone rang in the other room. I grabbed my robe from the back of the bathroom door and ran to answer it.

I smiled and tried to make my voice sound upbeat. "Hello?"

I looked at the time on the microwave clock. It was a little after ten o'clock Eastern time.

"Happy birthday to you, happy birthday to you- happy birthday my beautiful Angie. Happy birthday to you!" Xavier sang into the phone and I ended up with a genuine smile on my face.

"Thank you, that was beautiful," I said.

"You're welcome. Sorry, I'm just now calling, we have a little time before our next set,"

"Where are you again?" I asked. They usually didn't do two shows a night.

"Vegas,"

"That's right," I recalled.

He had begged me to fly out to Vegas to see the band and to celebrate my birthday but at the time I had the orthopedic boot and didn't know how long I would have to wear it. Not to mention, I wasn't a big fan of Las Vegas. I lived in New York. If I wanted bright lights I could walk to Times Square. If I wanted to see a show, Broadway was a cab ride away. And I didn't gamble, so it just didn't have any appeal.

"Did you get my flowers?" he asked.

"Oh yeah- thanks! They were beautiful," I said and my nose itched remembering the strong smell from earlier.

"So, what did you do today?" he asked.

"Went to work, ate too much cake, had drinks with Christina and Greg and then my family sang happy birthday to me on the phone but their version was tragic in comparison to yours," I laughed.

"That sounds- actually it sounds sad. I wish I could have been there to take you out." He sighed.

I was sick of focusing on his lack of availability.

"It won't be this way forever, right?" I said echoing his words.

"Right, I got you something but I'm going to give it to you in person."

"Ooh, what is it?"

"A surprise." He laughed.

"Can I get a hint?" I asked. I thought about the flowers from earlier and decided not to hold my breath.

"No. But I'll see you real soon," he said with a hint of mystery.

"That sounds promising," I smiled into the phone.

Someone speaking over a PA system cut our call short.

"Sorry, I've got to run but I wanted to make sure I told you happy birthday and let you know I'm thinking about you. Always."

"Me too," I said.

"Talk to you later," he said disconnecting the line.

I lay awake in bed that night staring at the ceiling wondering if Xavier and I would still be together on my birthday next year and if so, would I still be spending it alone.

February

Mother's Day, Christmas and Valentine's Day were our busiest holidays and I was glad that I'd be preoccupied with work instead of focused on spending Valentine's Day by myself. But as it turned out, I wouldn't actually spend Valentine's Day alone because Xavier surprised me by coming to town. Soul Skylight had a couple of Canadian dates and then they would be heading overseas to start wrapping up the tour. I'd expected a call, maybe some Facetime sexiness but I never expected to see him face to face.

Just when I felt like the distance was too much, he did something sweet to renew my faith in him.

He'd called earlier in the day to tell me Happy Valentine's Day and then he called back at four o'clock. "Hey, I know the work day is winding down and I'm just wondering what you're doing after work,"

I chuckled. "I don't work a traditional nine to five, so the workday isn't quite over for me yet."

"What if you had an incentive to leave early?" he asked.

"I'm listening," I was only half listening. I was also reviewing our latest commercial script.

"There is a famous musician downstairs in front of your work building and he said if you don't come down right now, he's going to start serenading random women on the sidewalk,"

"Really. Wait, what?" I asked confused.

He laughed. "I'm opening the door. Oh, there's nice lady, maybe she'll want me to sing to her,"

"Xavier, what are you- are you here- *in New York?*"

"Only one way to find out," he hung up the phone.

At first, I thought he couldn't possibly be downstairs and then I thought, it's Xavier, of course, it was something he would do. I quickly saved my files and powered down my laptop before removing it from the docking station.

I said my goodbyes to my team and rushed towards the elevator. It seemed everybody had the same idea because it took forever to make it down to the lobby. When the revolving glass door came into view, I saw a Lincoln Town Car limousine parked out front. I slowly walked through the door and tried not to stare just in case it was a coincidence.

Then the back window went down.

"Hey pretty lady, you need a ride?" Xavier grinned at me.

I tried to play it cool but when I saw him, I squealed.

He opened the door and I slid inside. I let my bag fall to the floor before closing the door. Once it closed I launched myself into his lap and kissed him.

"What are you doing here?" I asked unable to contain my smile.

"I came to ask you to be my Valentine," he grinned and kissed me like our lives depended on it and I moaned loudly.

"Excuse me, Mr. Ross are we ready?" A voice came from the driver.

"Oh my god," I muttered trying to remove myself from Xavier's lap. I was so embarrassed but Xavier laughed and held me in place.

"Yes, Arthur we're ready,"

I buried my face in Xavier's shoulder and laughed. "You see what you do to me?"

He thrust his hips up towards me and I could feel him hard beneath me. "You feel what you do to me?" he kissed my neck.

After a while, I realized I had no idea where we were going.

"Wait, so what's the plan? Where are we going?" I pulled away breathless. I removed my coat and scarf because we had generated so much heat that I'd started to sweat.

"I thought maybe we'd get something to eat, drink and see the city,"

I hated to be a buzz kill but there was no way were getting into a restaurant on Valentine's Day in New York without a reservation. But before I could say anything the car came to a stop.

"Excuse me," Xavier smiled and crossed over to the right side of the car. I looked out the window and saw a man walking towards the car holding a champagne bucket.

Xavier let down the window.

"Hey Jake, thanks so much, I really appreciate it,"

"No problem Mr. Ross," the guy passed a champagne bucket covered with a white linen napkin through the window.

Xavier put the bucket on the bar and removed the napkin revealing a bottle of Krug Grand Cuvee and two champagne glasses.

"What are you doing?" I giggled. I was delighted at how the Valentine's date was starting off.

As the car pulled away into traffic again, Xavier popped the cork on the Krug and poured me a glass.

"Cheers," he raised his glass and I raised mine in response before gently touching his glass and making a clinking sound in the quiet of the car.

I took a sip of champagne and smiled as the bubbles tickled my tongue. I sat back in the seat, kicked off my shoes and got comfortable.

The next stop came almost ten minutes later, we were out front of Carmine's. There was already a line formed outside but similar to what happened at the last stop, a waiter appeared at the window with a large to-go bag.

Xavier lowered the window and people tried to get a peek of who was inside the car. As soon as the food exchanged hands the car started to smell of pasta and bread. He'd gotten an order of Pomodoro, garlic bread and veal parmigiana along with chocolate covered strawberries.

We chatted and fed each other pasta before I asked, "Is there a reason why we're riding around eating in a limo? I mean as long as you're here it's cool, definitely a first for me but I'm just curious,"

His expression fell as he swallowed a bite of pasta. "I'm only here for a few hours before I have to head to Montreal. Then next week we leave for the European leg." He said sadly. But before I could reply, he asked: "Did you get a chance to ask your boss for some time off?"

I didn't know what it said about our so-called relationship that Xavier still didn't know *I* was the boss.

"No, I need to look at the dates again," I lied.

"Sorry for ruining the mood but I guess since I'm on a roll– they asked us add more international dates to the tour. I was outvoted and so we've added six more dates which means another month or so on tour."

"What? Are you serious?" I snapped.

"I know and believe me it's the last thing I want to do. I mean I could probably pull a diva mood and tell them I'm not doing it but I don't want to start any shit between the fellas. That's why I'm really hoping you can get the time off,"

So, he had known about this the last time he talked to me but intentionally didn't tell me. We drove around the city for a while before I spoke up.

"Well, for what it's worth this was a really sweet gesture. Thanks for making my Valentine's Day special." I smiled.

He smiled brightly. "I have something else for you. A belated birthday gift," he pulled a small turquoise box from under the seat.

"Oh my," I smiled.

"Just a little something," he shrugged.

It was a diamond tennis bracelet from Tiffany's. The universal gift men bought for women when they had no clue what to get or if they were trying to apologize for doing something wrong. It wasn't that I was ungrateful but I'd gotten a similar bracelet from Rodney after a big fight we had two years ago.

"It's beautiful," I managed to say as I removed it from the box. I extended my arm for him to put it on my wrist.

"Do you really like it? I noticed you don't wear a lot of jewelry, so I wanted something a little understated," he said as he clasped the bracelet around my wrist.

Understated? The bracelet had to be at least two carats more in weight than the one Rodney had given me.

I looked at him and smirked.

"But I also wanted you to have some bling," he laughed.

I placed a hand on his face and kissed his lips. "Thank you," I smiled.

He returned the kiss gently at first and then it became heated and hungry. I'd thought about dry humping him but before I could even get aroused, our date came to an end. The driver dropped me off at my apartment and then drove away to take Xavier to the airport after we'd said our goodbyes. As I rode up in the elevator with the leftover pasta, I thought about his news. He'd be gone an additional month or two. I hadn't signed up for that and I honestly didn't know if I wanted to wait for him. That night I removed the tennis bracelet Xavier had given me, placed it back in the box and put it in the bottom of my underwear drawer next to Rodney's.

The rest of the weekend was quiet and uneventful. I was actually excited to return to work. My excitement multiplied when a courier delivered a gift from one of our media partners that afternoon– two tickets to *A Time to Kill* on Broadway. I couldn't believe a play had been adapted from one of my favorite books. It was also me and Rodney's favorite movie. I didn't even think twice before calling him at work.

"Rodney Anderson," he answered.

"You will never believe what I got tickets to!" I said excitedly.

"Angela?" he asked. And my heart dropped a little. He didn't recognize my voice on the phone anymore.

"Yeah, sorry. I guess I should have said it was me. I got two tickets to see *A Time to Kill* on Broadway! Did you even know they'd adapted a play?" I asked.

"No, I did not,"

"So, do you want to go? The tickets are for the Saturday matinee,"

He was quiet and then cleared his throat. "Why are you asking *me* to go?"

I realized how inappropriate it must have appeared to him since I was seeing someone, not to mention I had accused *him* of not making a clean break.

"I don't know, when I got the tickets I immediately thought of you. Since that's one of your favorite movies," I said quietly. "And

I guess I really wanted to go and thought it would be fun to go with you," I admitted. Besides it's not like Xavier could go, he had a show Saturday in Canada.

"And what does your boyfriend have to say about this?" he asked.

"He's in Montreal or Toronto or somewhere. And he doesn't control me or who I choose to be friends with," I said strongly.

"Huh. Okay, so we're back to this friend thing," he sighed harshly.

"Rodney-," I groaned and regretted that I had called him.

"No, it's fine. Actually, that does sound like fun. Count me in," he said but his voice sounded strange, almost mocking.

"Are you sure? I mean you don't have to feel obligated,"

"I don't feel obligated," he assured me.

The rest of the week flew by and when Saturday afternoon rolled around, I waited out front of the John Golden theater for Rodney in the cold. I thought he was going to stand me up but after about five minutes he showed up.

"Hey, why are you out here? You're going to catch pneumonia," he scolded.

"I was waiting for you," I said and at that moment my teeth chattered.

"You could have stepped into the lobby," he said. "Here, let's go inside," he opened the door for me.

I gave Rodney the tickets and he showed them to the usher and we were escorted to our seats. As I followed behind Rodney, I smiled and couldn't help think how familiar it all felt. Being there with Rodney felt like old times but I had to remember it wasn't old times and that Xavier and I were together.

Before the show started I'd seen Rodney sending a text; he had a big smile on his face. He turned the phone off and then put it in his pocket.

The show was good but not nearly as gripping as the book or the movie for that matter. The actor that played Carl Lee on stage did a fine job but no one could top Samuel L. Jackson when he screamed from the witness stand, *"Yes, they deserve to die and I hope they burn in hell,"* That scene from the movie still gave me chills.

After we left the theater, I pulled my scarf tighter around my neck and up over my ears as we walked down the sidewalk. I remembered the big smile on Rodney's face earlier and decided to ask what had been on my mind:

"So, have you started seeing anyone yet?" I asked carefully. We had agreed not to talk about our personal lives but I was curious.

He stopped walking and eyed me. "I thought our personal lives were off limits,"

I shrugged. "Just making conversation."

He sighed harshly. "Conversation, huh? What happened to discussing the weather." He laughed and started walking again.

I looked up at the sky, it was a typical February day in New York. "Clear skies, no sun, freezing. Not much else to say,"

"How about those Knicks?" he put his gloved hands in his pockets.

"Oh wow, diversion– that definitely means you've found someone,"

"It is absolutely none of your business and a conversation that we should not be having but yes, I've met someone. I'm too busy to get serious right now but there is a lady I've taken on a few dates," he smiled.

"A lady, hmmm," I said intrigued by his term for her. I wondered if they were having sex and instantly felt jealous, which made no sense. I'd had sex with Xavier multiple times, so I don't know why I'd expected Rodney to be celibate. I guess that would officially close the chapter on our life together once he started getting serious about someone.

"Why'd you say it like that?" he laughed.

"No reason. Well good for you," I tried to sound sincere.

"So, what's your status? You and the rock star still dating?" he asked and made a face.

"Yeah, it's starting to get complicated though," I said honestly.

His pace slowed and he turned his head towards me. When I looked up I couldn't read his expression.

"Well, nobody said relationships were easy. Okay, I'm about to turn into a popsicle. I will never adjust to these New York winters. Let's get you a cab," he ended the conversation and walked to the corner to hail a cab.

"You don't want to ride?" I asked as a taxi approached us.

"I'm only ten minutes from here, I'll make it," he said and shivered at the same time.

"Really? You take one more step in this weather and you're going to get frostbite,"

He opened the door for me when the cab came to a stop.

"I'm only getting in if you get in," I challenged.

He rolled his eyes. "Fine,"

After dropping Rodney off, we continued on to my apartment and I gave the cabbie a ten-dollar tip before hurrying inside my building.

I immediately sent Rodney a text, per his instruction, when I made it inside.

AB: Made it home.

A few minutes later he replied.

RA: Good. Thanks again for inviting me to the show.

AB: No problem.

A few hours later, I got a call from Xavier. He sounded like he'd just awakened.

"Did you just wake up?" I asked. The time zone in Montreal was the same as New York. It was five o'clock in the evening.

"Yeah, late night last night," he cleared his throat but he didn't elaborate.

"Is that what they mean by partying like a rock star? Hanging out late and sleeping until – what time is it there?" I asked.

"It's the same time it is there, *mom*," he said sarcastically. I'd never heard that tone from him.

"I was just kidding Xavier," I said and a frown instantly appeared on my face. Maybe he thought I was trying to check-up on him or judge him for sleeping the entire day away.

He sighed and offered up a half-ass apology. "I know, sorry. How was your day?" he tried to make his voice sound a bit more cheerful but it was too late. He'd already pissed me off.

"I went to a play," I said. I wanted to tell him that I'd gone with Rodney but decided against it only because it wasn't fair to put Rodney in the middle of my relationship drama.

"What did you go see?" he asked and yawned.

"*A Time to Kill*," I said flatly.

"I never heard of that one, you went by yourself?" His tone sounded slightly suspicious.

I smiled smugly although he couldn't see me. "I went with a

friend," I said and decided not to toy with him although I definitely could. "A lady from work," I lied.

"Oh so, how was it?" he asked with a hint of relief.

I told him it was based on the movie, which he hadn't seen so I was sure he hadn't read the book. We made small talk before he said he had to go and for the first time I was glad to get off the phone with him.

Over the past few weeks, it seemed little things Xavier did or said had started to annoy me. I think it all stemmed from the fact that their tour had been extended. I don't know why I didn't just end the relationship, it wasn't like I didn't have a choice. I could have walked away at any time. But I didn't want to do it over the phone or when he had to go off and perform. If and when I decided I'd had enough, I'd tell him face to face.

That night I settled in to watch my favorite show, a show that Rodney had actually gotten me hooked on. I was watching episodes from the previous season, in preparation for the upcoming new season, because I was behind a few shows. After an intense scene, I sent Rodney a text.

AB: Oh my God, are you watching GOT right now?

RA: GOT?

AB: Game of Thrones.

RA: Oh. Nah. Stopped watching it.

AB: WHAT? Are you serious? You got me hooked and you stopped watching it?

He didn't answer right away. Meanwhile more mayhem played out across the TV. After a few minutes, my phone chimed and I looked down to see a text from Rodney:

RA: Dany just made her dragons burn the Good Masters! 😭

AB: You liar! I thought you didn't watch it anymore. 😒

RA: Are you serious? This is the best show on TV!

I smiled and was happy there was something we still shared. Xavier didn't watch much TV and he thought Game of Thrones was a video game. I didn't even bother explaining it to him.

I'd invited Rodney to lunch the following week and he declined. I thought we'd turned a corner and would actually be able to be friends but he was still a little wary. But I wasn't giving up, I knew we could make a friendship work. I called him Thursday evening just to say hi and could tell he didn't really want to talk to me. But I asked him about his mentoring program with E&Y and got him to open up.

The program called for executives at Rodney's level and higher to not only mentor lower level management employees but also recent college graduates who were working at the associate level.

"The tricky part is going to be getting the partners to tailor the program for minorities. I think they may be afraid that it sends the wrong message." Rodney commented.

I frowned. "The wrong message? That it's okay to help disenfranchised people get a little equity in Corporate America?" I asked sarcastically.

Rodney chuckled. "I might have to use that if they shoot me down. No, I'm sure the initial response will be that we should accept *any* employee into the program who possesses the potential to be successful."

"Oh. Well, I can see why they would use that as a rebuttal but I'm sure most of the White employees who qualify have already sought out a mentor. They have a level of comfort in asking for help and guidance where as black or brown employees work three times as hard and just *hope* somebody will take notice."

"This is true. What do you think about this– what if on the back end of the agreement there is a clause that outlines the diversity requirements of the mentees accepted?" he asked unsure.

"So, they would have to accept a certain percentage of minorities?" I asked for clarification.

"Yeah, or is that too much like affirmative action?"

"A little," I said honestly. "The key is making sure the potential is there and that these mentees not only add value but they are given an opportunity to be successful. As long as the Company knows it isn't about charity, it's about equity and leveling the playing field,"

"Exactly! I knew you'd get this!" he said excitedly. "Okay, I'm going to rework some of the language ahead of my meeting next week. Thanks for your help and support Angela. I know you don't have any reason to-," he started and I cut him off.

I didn't want him to think this was a burden or a favor, I would always support him in any way that I could because he would do the same for me.

"Thank you for seeking my feedback, I'm very flattered. And I know this program will be a success! And if E&Y doesn't want to implement the program, I think you should look into starting a non-profit on your own. You have the connections to make it happen. And you can do exactly what you want without corporate restrictions." I suggested.

"Plan B in the making, I like how you think," he praised. I could tell by his tone he was grinning from ear to ear and so was I.

One of the main things that I'd cherished about my relationship with Rodney was how he also appreciated my mind. He would occasionally ask my opinion on big decisions and always valued my input.

I talked to Rodney for a few minutes longer before we ended the call. A couple of hours later, I was looking through my closet for a pair of Chanel boots I'd purchased last season when I got a call from my brother.

"Hey AJ? What's up?" I asked distractedly.

"Hey, uh- I just called to let you know dad is in the hospital," he said quietly.

I stopped and gave him my full attention.

"What happened?" I asked.

"He had a heart attack- he has to have surgery, there are some blockages," I heard something in my brother's voice that I hadn't heard often– fear.

"Oh my god, when is he having surgery? Should I come- I should come. How's mama doing?" I asked sitting on the edge of my bed.

"She's freaking out. It was kind of scary- she said he was slumped over in the chair when she came out of the bathroom and she thought he was dead. She called me screaming on the phone, shit, I never really thought of anything bad happening to him. This is-,"

I stood and cut him off. "Oh my god. I'm coming- what hospital?"

AJ gave me the information and I started packing a bag and I realized I needed to rent a car otherwise I'd have to wait until tomorrow for a flight or train. I was completely frazzled. My dad and I didn't have a close relationship after he and my mom divorced, even after he started coming around again, I still wasn't close to him. But the idea of him dying made my heart feel like it was breaking. We'd wasted so much time not talking and would never get that time back. I didn't even know him as a person, I'd never given him a chance. I'd spent so much time just seeing him as the man who hurt my mother.

I was about to log on to my computer to figure out transportation to Philly when my phone rang. It was Rodney.

I didn't have time to talk to him but he knew my father and I wanted to let him know what had happened.

"Hey Rodney," I said anxiously.

"I just got off the phone with Allen. He told me about your dad, I can take you to Philly to see him." He said gently and I immediately started to sob.

"Hey, don't cry, Angela. Are you okay?" he asked concerned.

"Yes. No. I don't know– what if, what if he dies?" I cried.

"Don't talk like that, your dad is a strong guy. He's not going to die. I'm on my way over to your apartment. I'll take you to him,"

Rodney drove us to Ardmore in the middle of the night to get me to the hospital to see my father. We were quiet for most of the ride and soon two hours had passed. After Rodney took the exit to the hospital, I started to hyperventilate.

"Oh my god, oh my god," I tried to calm myself. Rodney reached over and grabbed my hand and gave it a gentle squeeze.

"Angela, just take a deep breath,"

By the time we made it to the hospital it was past visiting hours but the nurse allowed Rodney and I to see my dad. My brother wasn't there but my mom was asleep next to his bed. My dad was also asleep. I sent my brother a quick text to let him know we'd arrived and he said he'd be back in the morning.

I whispered to let Rodney know what Allen had texted when my mom woke up.

"Angie?" she asked groggily.

"Hey, Mama," I whispered.

She stood and hugged me tightly. "I didn't know you were coming tonight. Hey, Rodney," she said hugging him as well.

We stepped out into the hallway. "What happened? How is he?"

"Earlier this evening he was sitting up watching TV and I went to the bathroom and when I came out I found him slumped over in the chair clutching his chest. They say he has a blocked valve– something called stenosis. They want to do a procedure tomorrow to clear it with a balloon-," she waved her hand. "A bunch of technical stuff. Your brother understood it more than I did."

"But is he going to be okay?" I asked.

She shrugged. "They say sometimes they go in and find other blockages that you can't see from the x-rays and plus when messing with the heart- there's just-," she covered her mouth. Rodney put an arm around her and she leaned into him.

"Al Barnes is a strong man, he's going to get through this," he said and I wanted to believe him.

Rodney walked my mother to the cafeteria to get a cup of coffee while I stayed with my dad. I'd gotten a text from Xavier on the way to Pennsylvania but didn't respond since I was in the car with Rodney. I pulled out my phone after Rodney left with my mom.

Hey, I'm in Philly. My dad had a heart attack. At Bryn Mawr hospital, surgery tomorrow.

Xavier called a couple of minutes later and I stepped back into the hallway to answer the call.

"Hey, Angie- how are you? Is your dad okay?" he asked.

"I honestly don't know. My mom said he has to have surgery tomorrow, it's late here and I haven't talked to a doctor yet." I said as my voice cracked.

"Oh wow, baby I'm sorry. How are you holding up?"

"I'm okay- he's at a good hospital. Just trying to stay positive," I said. I looked over at my dad's door and saw him move around and then heard him call out for my mom.

"Oh, oh- my dad just woke up. I'll call you back," I said hanging up the phone.

"Glo- Gloria?" My father's voice sounded scratchy and scared.

"Hey daddy, she's getting coffee. You okay, do you need me to get the nurse?" I asked.

He just stared at me for a minute before exhaling. "Nah, I'm good. I'm good." He lay back on the bed and closed his eyes.

"When did you get here, what time is it? You shouldn't be driving on the road so late by yourself," he cautioned. I couldn't believe he was the one laying in the hospital but he was worried about me.

"I didn't, Rodney drove me," I announced as I sat next to the bed. "How are you feeling?"

He closed his eyes and sighed. I thought he'd say it was a dumb question or that he was fine but he turned and looked at me and I'd never seen him look so fragile in my entire life.

"Scared. I'm scared. I'm only sixty-two. I ain't ready to die," he took a shaky breath.

Tears filled my eyes and I grabbed his hand. "You're not going to die,"

"Maybe not today but one day, we all will. This just makes it more real, you know."

I squeezed his hand.

"I want to tell you in case I don't ever get another chance that I love you Angie and I'm proud of you. I know you've blamed me for our family breaking up and I didn't do much to try and fix things between us. I figured you and your brother were grown and nothing

I could do or say would make a difference,"

"Stop talking like you won't be around," I said at a loss for words.

"You never know, kiddo," he said calling me a name he hadn't called me since I was a child.

I let out a shaky breath. "I love you too,"

I hadn't realized how late it was until Rodney and my mom returned from the cafeteria, it was almost two o'clock in the morning. My dad's surgery was scheduled for tomorrow afternoon, so Rodney and I decided to get a room at the hotel across the street and my mom stayed at the hospital.

He automatically booked two rooms before I could tell him one would be fine.

"I know it's going to be hard, but try to get some sleep," he said as he walked me to my room.

"I will. I can't even-," I started. "Thank you so much for coming, for bringing me here. It means so much to me," I said sincerely.

He smiled faintly and squeezed my shoulder. I moved closer to him and hugged him tightly. He hesitated but hugged me back.

"Get some sleep. Call me in the morning and let me know when you're ready to go back to the hospital,"

"Okay,"

I tossed and turned most of the night, and it seemed as soon as I closed my eyes, the sun was coming up. After taking a shower, I called Rodney and we walked back over to the hospital together. When we arrived, my dad was being prepped for surgery and we were directed to a private waiting room down the hall.

When we entered the room, my brother was already seated.

"Hey," AJ looked up from his phone and then stood to embrace me. He hugged me for a long time before letting go and kissing the top of my head.

"Thanks, man," he gave Rodney a hug as well.

My mother joined us after they took my dad into surgery and Rodney left to get some bottles of water from the gift shop. A minute later someone entered the private waiting area. I raised my head and my mouth fell open.

It was Xavier.

He was dressed casually in black jeans, a grey sweater, and black leather jacket. He looked tired like he hadn't gotten much sleep.

"Xavier?" I whispered.

"What the hell?" AJ murmured.

My mom had nodded off and she sat up when she heard the door open. "Hey. What's going on- who's that?"

I stood and went to him. "What are you doing here?" I asked confused. "Aren't you supposed to be in Amsterdam?"

He hugged me. "You didn't sound too good on the phone. I wanted to come and check on you. How's your dad?"

Tears filled my eyes. I couldn't believe he'd come to check on me and my dad, a man he'd never even met. Perhaps I had been too quick to discount our relationship and maybe he wasn't so selfish after all.

I hugged him tighter. "Thank you for coming. My dad is in surgery right now,"

I heard my brother clear his throat.

"Oh- sorry- this is my brother, Allen and my mom, Gloria Barnes," I said introducing him. "This is Xavier Ross."

"Hello, nice to meet you. Sorry to be meeting under the circumstances," Xavier shook Allen's hand and then my mom who stared at him wide-eyed.

"Maybe Xavier can walk you to the cafeteria to get some coffee," my brother said in a firm tone. I frowned at him and then realized why he was trying to get rid of us. *Rodney.*

"Yeah, okay we'll be right back," As I turned to grab my purse, Rodney entered the waiting area with a bag of bottled of waters.

I froze in place. I'd never expected the two of them to come face to face. Especially not now.

"Hey, you okay?" Rodney asked looking from me to Xavier.

"Uh- yeah- I- uh," I swallowed. "Rodney, this is Xavier Ross,"

"Hi, Rodney Anderson," Rodney shook Xavier's hand. He seemed confused until Xavier put an arm around me.

"Angie, you ready to get some coffee, babe?" Xavier smiled sweetly and kissed my cheek. He was definitely being extra possessive on purpose. He'd never called me 'babe' before.

Rodney's eyes widened in recognition but he quickly recovered as Xavier and I left the waiting room.

When we got to the cafeteria we ordered two coffees and sat next to each other in one of the vinyl covered booths.

"Rodney. Rodney? Where do I know that name from?" Xavier asked as he opened a packet of sugar and poured it into his coffee.

I didn't know if he was serious or trying to catch me in a lie.

"Rodney's my ex, he and my brother are still friends," I said by way of explanation.

Xavier nodded slowly but didn't say anything.

"He brought me here – he drove, so I rode with him," I continued to explain.

He took a sip of coffee.

"When exactly did the two you break up?"

"There's nothing going on between me and Rodney," I said defensively.

"I didn't accuse you of anything but I could see it all over Rodney's face. He's not over you,"

I shook my head. "You saw him for all of twenty seconds. Rodney and I have been over for almost a year." I said annoyed. It sounded like he was accusing me of something or maybe I felt guilty because Rodney was still in my life.

He held up his hands in front of him indicating he wasn't trying to start anything.

I sighed. "I'm sorry- I'm just I'm really worried about my dad,"

"I know, come here," he put an arm around me and tucked me into his side.

I held on to him for a few minutes and felt awful that Rodney had seen us together. After we finished our coffee I suggested we head back to the waiting room, I wanted to be there in case there was news about my dad. He locked his hand with mine and his fingers felt like sandpaper. I almost made a comment about it but I was too focused on coming face to face with Rodney again. Before we walked into the waiting room I'd planned to let go of Xavier's hand but I think he could sense it, so he held on even tighter.

When we entered the waiting room Rodney wasn't there.

"Any news?" I asked sitting next to my mom. Xavier sat down next to me.

"Not yet- I'm praying that no news is good news," Mama said patting my knee.

"Xavier, Angie said your band is on tour. Were you playing in Philly?" Allen asked. I sat back in my chair and Xavier leaned forward.

"Nah- we were in Montreal. The rest of the guys are headed to Amsterdam. I'll take a later flight. I'll probably make it there in the afternoon and catch a few hours of sleep before the show starts,"

I still couldn't believe he'd gone through all that trouble for me. For my dad. I instinctively grabbed his hand and gave it a squeeze. I was a little saddened by the fact that Xavier was a stranger to my family. I'd only mentioned him to AJ and my mom a few times but I'd never really talked about my family to Xavier.

"Well, thanks for being here for Angie." My brother said but something was off about his tone.

"Yes, it was very kind of you," my mom echoed.

I wanted so badly to ask where Rodney had gone but it probably would have made Xavier even more suspicious.

A few minutes passed and Xavier pulled his phone from his pocket. I'd felt it vibrating against my leg.

"I need to take this. I'll be right back," he said to me.

After he left, I looked over at my brother. "Where'd Rodney go?" I asked.

"Back to the hotel. He told me to call him when dad came out of surgery. Angie, that's foul to have your man show up with Rod being here," he frowned.

"So tacky," my mother agreed.

My eyes widened. "Give me some credit, please," I whispered harshly. "I had no idea he was coming!"

My brother just shook his head. I knew he didn't believe me.

"He's cute though," Mama smiled.

"It's been over two hours. When are they-," my brother started when the doctor entered the room.

"Hello, hello!" she smiled broadly. "We just finished up and Mr. Barnes did great, the angioplasty was a success and we were able to clear the blockage!"

"Praise God!" my mother said as she clasped her hands together.

My brother stood and shook the doctor's hand. "Thank you, thank you,"

I hugged my mom.

"He'll be moved to recovery in the ICU for monitoring but we'll let you see him. He may still be under anesthesia but you can go in," the doctor said before she disappeared.

My brother came over and embraced me and my mom.

"Listen, I know the two of you have had issues with your daddy but he loves you both so much. And I appreciate you being here for him," my mother said as tears streamed her face. She wasn't usually an emotional person and I never recalled her being a crier. I knew then that she was still in love with my dad.

"Oh Mama, of course. We've had our issues but we care about daddy too," I assured her.

"Yeah- he was a good provider growing up, and he makes you happy," My brother agreed.

My mother kissed his cheek.

"Is everything okay?" Xavier asked entering the waiting room. He seemed apprehensive.

I smiled and went to him. "Yes, my dad is out of surgery, it was a success!"

"Aw, baby that's great!" he hugged me tightly.

Xavier hung around for a little while and we ended up back in the cafeteria for lunch. When we sat down my phone chimed indicating I had a text from AJ:

Rod wants to know if you have a ride back home. He's going to head back to NYC

I tried to keep my expression blank. I would take the train back to the city. I wanted to stay one more day.

Angie: Tell him I'll take the train tomorrow. And thanks for everything.

AJ: Ok. Won't lecture you now since you're with your boyfriend. But we need to talk.

I rolled my eyes and put away my phone, when I looked up Xavier was staring at me.

"You okay?" he asked.

"Yeah- that was my brother," I stirred my chicken noodle soup. I felt like shit for abandoning Rodney.

"I've never understood why hospital food is so terrible and it's supposed to be a place that takes care of sick people," he chuckled.

"I know," I said still thinking about Rodney.

"When did your parents get back together? I remember they divorced when we were in school, that's how you ended up at Drew, right?"

I sighed. "Yeah, they never remarried but they've recently gotten back together,"

He raised an eyebrow. "You sound like you don't approve."

"I don't. . . but I know she loves him and he loves her. I guess I've been carrying around my disappointment from the divorce when the truth is that had nothing to do with me. I don't want to see my mom hurt but I can't live her life any more than she can live mine," I shrugged.

"This is true. What's up with your brother? I don't think he likes me,"

"He doesn't know you. AJ is a typical overprotective big brother,"

"You sure? Or do you think he believes I'm the reason you broke up with his friend?"

I sat back in my chair and pushed the soup bowl away from me.

"Xavier, there is nothing going on between me and Rodney," I said angrily.

He stared down at his half-eaten sandwich. "I know. But there could be," he looked up at me. "He's available, he cares about you, he knows your family. He wanted to marry you,"

I folded my arms in front of my chest. "Well, maybe I didn't want to marry him,"

"Why?"

Because I was scared I'd be a horrible wife and he deserved better.

"I wasn't ready," I lied.

"You never want to get married?" he asked sounding shocked.

"I didn't say that,"

"Do you want to get married and have kids someday?"

"Where is all this coming from?"

"Isn't this the conversation you've been wanting to have with me? Trying to figure out the future?"

I wanted to have the conversation but not now. Not with my father recuperating from surgery. And not until I made sure Rodney was okay.

"Yeah, but I thought we agreed to wait until after the tour to-,"

"You don't have to wait until after the tour to tell me if you want to be married with kids," he said incredulously.

"I don't know. To be honest, I can see myself married but I don't know about kids,"

It may have been my imagination but he appeared to be relieved.

"What about you? Do you want to get married and have kids?" I asked turning the tables.

"I can see myself married but I don't know about kids," he smirked repeating my words.

I smiled. "I actually *can't* see you married. What about all your screaming, adoring female fans who like to sneak naked into your hotel room?"

He laughed. "They will still be there but I'll be home with my wife instead," he winked.

I didn't know if I could be the right wife for Xavier either. I just wanted us in the same city. But being married to him was another story. We didn't really have much in common other than fantastic physical chemistry and I wasn't sure that would be enough.

We chatted some more before going back to see my dad. He looked so fragile and helpless laying in the hospital bed with tubes in his nose. Since I was still booked at the hotel, I told my mom she could spend the night with me but she declined and stayed the night with my father again.

Xavier walked me across the street to the hotel and we managed to get in a quickie before his car picked him up to take him to the airport. I'd felt distracted and disconnected as we had sex against the bathroom counter with our pants down around our ankles. I think we'd only done it because it was expected, I didn't even have an orgasm.

As soon as Xavier was gone, I called Rodney but the call went to voicemail.

"Hey Rodney, just calling to check on you and make sure you made it back okay. Thank you again for bringing me to see my dad, I don't know what I would have done without you," I said. "I'm sorry about Xavier- I had absolutely no idea he was coming. I would have never done that to you- anyway, I hope you're okay. Talk to you soon,"

The next morning, I called my office and informed them that I would be taking a few personal days after my dad's surgery. He wouldn't be released for a few days and I wanted to be there to help my mom since he would be coming home with her.

I walked over to the hospital and ran into AJ in the parking lot.

"There she is! Where is your superstar boyfriend?" His tone dripped with sarcasm.

"He left because you were being rude," I lied.

"Man, whatever. Did you call Rodney?" he asked.

"Yes, but it went straight to voicemail. I left him a message,"

"That shit was foul, Angie," he said angrily.

"I told you I didn't know he was coming!"

"Yeah, but you just ghosted on Rodney after he got here!"

"What did you expect for me to do? You wanted the three of us sit down together and hold hands?" I yelled.

"Why are you even with that dude? Because he's famous and has green eyes?" he snorted.

"That is so stupid- I'm not even-," I refused to respond.

"Because you don't care about him not the way you still care for Rodney,"

"You don't know what you're talking about, okay? And why are you so interested in my life? Aren't you going through a divorce and custody battle?" I spat. And it was a low blow. He flinched and then looked at me in disgust.

"You're right, but at least I'm not pretending with anybody including myself," he pushed past me and entered the hospital.

We were both frowning when we walked into my dad's hospital room.

My mom looked back and forth between us. "Oh Lord, what happened?"

"Don't worry about it Ma- how are you doing dad?" AJ asked my father.

"Good, I'm good. But your mama is going to make me even better," he smiled goofily at my mom and I figured he was on some strong medicine.

She looked down at him and smiled before looking back at my brother and me.

"Me and your daddy are getting remarried!" she announced.

My brother and I glanced at each other, I don't think either of us expected that. But I'd meant what I said to Xavier. I only wanted my mom to be happy. They had apparently found their way back to each other again and who was I to stand in their way.

I smiled at them. "Congratulations! I'm happy for both of you," I hugged my mama and kissed my dad's cheek.

My brother stared at me like I was a traitor before he smiled and offered his congratulations as well.

After a couple of hours, I convinced mama to leave the hospital and go to Target to pick up some stuff for around the house in preparation for my dad's release.

"So, what happened between you and your brother?" she asked

pulling a basket from the stall.

I sighed harshly. "He makes me so sick! He thinks he knows everything. He was going on and on about me doing Rodney wrong, so I told him to mind his business and worry about divorcing his wife and getting custody of his kids,"

"Ooh, that was a low blow," she laughed as she pushed the cart into the store. We headed down the personal hygiene aisle after entering the store. Mama said she needed some soap and toothpaste.

"Mama, it's not funny. I shouldn't have said that. He just made me mad being all judgmental,"

"Well, what is going on with you and Mr. Green Eyes? I thought you and Rodney were back together?"

"Why does everyone keep saying that? Did Rodney tell you that?"

"No, but when you're with Rodney, I can't explain it. You're more relaxed, yourself- you seem on edge and unsure with this Xavier guy,"

"And you got all that from meeting him for like five minutes?" I argued.

She chuckled. "Something is going on because you're being really defensive right now,"

"I'm not being defensive! I just don't like people treating me like I don't know what I'm doing," I said in a frustrated tone.

"Do you know what you're doing?" she asked.

I stared at her for a minute. I'd never been able to lie to her.

I shook my head. "I don't know," I lowered my voice as a woman passed by us on the aisle.

"Did you leave Rodney for Xavier?"

"No! Rodney and I had already broken up when I reconnected with Xavier."

"Well, then why are you having trouble letting go of Rodney? Is it because he's available and Xavier's not? Do you want to be with both of them?" she questioned.

"No, it's not like that. Rodney and I were friends, really good friends before and during our relationship. I just miss him and sometimes when we're together, I do start to question why things ended."

"Why did they end?"

I shrugged. I wanted to tell her that I blamed her and my father for the dysfunctional example they'd set.

"Do you ever want to get married or have kids?" she asked.

"I don't know and I'm at that age where I need to make a decision and I don't want to choose wrong."

"You don't have to choose at all, you know. There's nothing wrong with being single. Don't force yourself into a situation because you feel desperate. Neither one of them might be the right man for you."

"I don't want to look around and I'm fifty and alone," I said tearfully.

"But you've got to be in it for the right reasons or things won't work out and you'll still find yourself fifty and alone."

I didn't reply, so she continued. "The only reason I said what I did about Xavier is because I don't think the distance is giving you a chance to really get to know each other. It's easy to have it all together when you know somebody is coming to town and how long they'll be there. You can have- what Chris Rock said- 'your representative' show up and avoid anything that might not seem appealing."

When my mom wasn't being over the top she was usually spot on with her assessments.

"I know it's only been a short while that we've been dating but I feel we're constantly starting over or playing catch up and we're not getting to the next level-,"

"So, you haven't had sex with him?" she asked a little too loudly.

"Ma! That's not what I meant, I mean whenever I see him it's basically 'how was the show', 'where are you going next', 'when will I see you again?' He never asks me about work or my family. I told him I got a promotion and he never even asked me about it. I don't even think he really gets what I do. He asked if I could take some time off to tour with him overseas, so that I could be waiting for him when he came off stage," I ranted. I still couldn't believe he'd said that. It made me feel so insignificant.

"Did you say anything?"

"No." I hung my head.

"You don't want to start letting stuff that's important to you take a back seat. Trust me. Anybody who knows you knows how important your career is to you. If this man is someone you're thinking of making a future with then he needs to know that too and there is nothing wrong with you telling him, 'I know you might want me to be waiting for you when you get off stage but I'd like the same thing because my work is just as important to me'," she advised.

She was right. I don't know why I acted like a lovesick teenager whenever Xavier came around.

"And if Rodney is really your friend, you need to call and apologize to him and then you need to let him go until you figure out what you want to do. I can tell he still loves you and you stringing him along is not right or kind," she scolded.

My eyes widened. "I am not stringing Rodney along and for the *last* time, I had no idea Xavier was coming here, if he would have told me he was coming, I would have told him not to,"

"Okay, but you still need to let Rodney go."

The idea of letting Rodney go, truly letting him go forever caused my heart to constrict. I didn't want to let him go. I didn't want him out of my life.

"Why can't we be friends? He told me he'd started dating someone, so he's moved on." I reasoned.

"Just because you date someone else doesn't mean you've moved on," she countered.

When we were done at Target, we stopped by the grocery store to pick up some healthier food options for my dad's recovery and then to my mom's house to clean up. The hospital didn't release my dad before I left Philly but he was doing well, so I felt okay about going back to New York.

I'd tried calling Rodney again when I made it back home, but he didn't answer. He was probably avoiding my calls. I needed to see him in person to make sure he was okay. That *we* were okay.

Wednesday afternoon I bought him lunch and took it to his office as a peace offering. But when I arrived his assistant told me he wasn't available.

"Did he tell you to flag my name?" I asked.

"Excuse me?" she asked and seemed both confused and agitated.

"I stopped by to say hello and drop off his lunch," I continued.

"Okay, well I don't show you on his calendar, so like I said, he's not available. You can leave the lunch with me and I'll make sure he gets it," she said in an authoritative tone.

I frowned at her. "I can give it to him myself, I don't need-,"

"Angela?" I turned around and Rodney stood behind me.

"Mr. Anderson, I tried telling Ms. Barnes you weren't available," she said in a sugary sweet voice. I wanted to slap her.

"Thank you, Charlotte. Please hold my calls for the next fifteen minutes," Rodney said turning towards his office. Although he didn't say anything, I followed him.

When we were inside, he closed the door.

I smiled at him. "I brought you a sandwich from-,"

"I don't want it. And I don't want you coming to my office anymore unannounced," he said firmly.

He stood near the door and didn't offer me a seat. It was obvious he was still angry.

"Rodney, I'm sorry about what happened at the hospital. I didn't know he was coming and-,"

He held up a hand. "I don't need your apology, Angela. He's your man, he has the right to be wherever you are– I'm the one who needs to leave the picture. You and I are no longer together, we have no kids together, no property- not even a dog. There is absolutely *no* reason for us to be in contact,"

I stared at him in disbelief. "How can you say that? Is that how you really feel?"

"It's not about how I feel. Those are facts." He said coldly.

"So that's it. We're not friends anymore?"

He barked a laugh. "You never wanted to be my friend, not really. You wanted me to fill in for your boyfriend when he's not available,"

"That is unfair and untrue," I wanted to ask him about his girlfriend but he continued his tirade.

"Really? I think it's pretty accurate. You want to have your cake and eat it too. Keep good old dependable Rodney on the side since he's always available and have fun with the wild and unpredictable Xavier whenever he comes to town."

"Where is all this coming from? Is this still about the what happened at the hospital?"

"Wow, you just don't get it. Let me ask you something," he folded his arms across his chest. "Did he know we had been in contact *before* the ride to Philadelphia? Had you ever mentioned that you and *your friend,* Rodney went to lunch or to a play or that we text and talk on the phone? Did he even know you sprained your ankle and where you were when it happened?"

I couldn't say anything, I'd either not told Xavier about any of it or I'd lied. I turned away from Rodney's smug expression.

"That's what I thought. I'm done being part of your little triangle Angela, it ends now!" He snapped.

I closed my eyes, swallowed back my tears as I opened the door and left quietly. I knew better than to argue with Rodney when he was angry, it would only make things worse. I took a cab back to my office and tossed the sandwich in the trash can in front of the building. I kept refreshing my email and checking my phone to see if Rodney had sent me an apology text. He hadn't. And he wouldn't because everything he'd said was true.

In the weeks following the confrontation at Rodney's office, I felt such a void in my life. You'd think I'd be sad because my boyfriend was overseas and I hadn't talked to him in almost two weeks but it wasn't him that I missed.

March

*T*he calls from Xavier decreased while he was overseas. But he called me when he'd flown back to the States for a meeting in L.A. As soon as I heard his ringtone, I answered and before I could say hello, he started talking.

"Hey, Angie, listen I don't have much time to talk but I wanted to let you know there is a story coming out on TMZ that is absolutely not true. I went out to dinner with a woman last night, it was a business meeting, and when we left the restaurant there were a few paparazzi taking pictures- Angie are you there?"

I'd only heard most of what he said. I zoned out a when he said he went to dinner with a woman.

I cleared my throat. "I'm here. Who does TMZ think she is?"

"Probably my girlfriend or someone I'm sleeping with. . .that's how it is in this business. You have dinner with someone then you're sleeping with them, if you see them more than once you're getting married. It's crazy and it's not true. I just wanted to make sure I talked to you before you saw it on the news or online."

"Oh, okay." I didn't even watch TMZ or follow celebrity gossip sites but now I was curious.

"You believe me, don't you?" he asked desperately.

"Yeah, sure- I believe you," I said and tried to make it sound true.

"Good. Look, I've got to run but I will call you tomorrow and hopefully, we'll get to Facetime before I head back overseas."

"Can't wait," I smiled to make my voice sound more enthusiastic.

For the first time since I'd found out Xavier was a member of Soul Skylight, I Googled him.

I hadn't needed to Google him initially because Christina had sent me a ton of links taking me directly to images and songs. Then after we'd reconnected I didn't want to Google him because I wanted to trust and believe him when he said I was the only woman in his life. There was also a small part of me that hadn't want to find out anything negative about him that would make me doubt my decision.

But he'd sounded off on the phone. So, I asked Google 'who is Xavier Ross'. I clicked on his Wikipedia page, which was just an overview of his music career and a rough edit of his early life in Buffalo. There was also a fun fact about how the group got its name; apparently, the guy who discovered them said he thought their music was like a skylight from the soul, and the group transformed that into their band name. I skimmed the rest of the article before pressing the back arrow.

Then I asked Google 'who is Xavier Ross dating' and several gossip sites popped up with old articles and images of him with a few different women and one famous actress. But the article that caught my eye and almost made me stop breathing was an article called a Blind Item. The person who wrote the article asked the reader to guess what famous male singer of an R&B band had a secret child and they'd italicized and capitalized it with the caption, *I WONDER*, which was a popular Soul Skylight song.

Several people in the comments had indicated they thought it was Xavier Ross. Then there was one detailed comment: *It's definitely Xavier Ross. I know the girl who had the baby for him. It's a boy with green eyes just like his. It was a one night stand before the band blew up. He paid her off and she signed an agreement to keep the baby out of the media, so it wouldn't mess up his rising sex symbol status.*

Then other people commented saying that it was 'sorry' and 'trifling' to pretend your child didn't exist for money and fame.

Lies! They had to be lies. There was no way Xavier had a child and hadn't told me. After I got my breathing under control, I'd tried to call him back but the call went straight to voicemail. I looked at the article again, it was dated June 3, 2010, which meant the child had to be four or five years old, *if* there was a child.

Christina was a huge Soul Skylight fan, surely, she'd know if the rumor was true. I called her and almost hung up before she answered. I was being ridiculous and I felt bad for not calling her before now. It had been a couple of weeks since I'd talked to her.

"Hi, Christina!" I said with fake excitement when she answered.

"Hey, Angela. How are doing?" she asked cheerfully.

"I'm good. Hey, I had a quick question for you," I hesitated and realized I was probably being paranoid.

"Sure, what's up?"

I laughed, "Nothing- I'm sure it's nothing."

"Is something wrong with you and Xavier?" she asked. I forgot Christina had worked for me long enough to tell my moods by the inflection in my voice.

"I heard a rumor," I lied. "Xavier never mentioned that he has a child, had you ever heard that rumor?"

She was silent for a moment. "Yes, I have, but I don't think it's true. I mean, if he's never mentioned it to *you* and no one has ever seen this alleged child, then it's more than likely just a rumor," she said quietly.

I laughed nervously. "Yeah, that's what I figured. I need to get off the Internet."

I didn't want Christina to think I'd only called to ask about Xavier although that *was* the only reason I'd called, so I decided to file the issue with Xavier away for later.

"So how are the wedding plans coming along?" I asked. She and Greg decided to have a June wedding, so she was in full-blown preparation mode.

She let out an exasperated sigh. "To be honest I think we should just go to Vegas alone and get married,"

She went on to tell me how both of their families were offering unsolicited advice and that Greg's mom had sent her a list of almost one hundred people to invite.

"Whoa, that's insane!" I remarked.

"I know! First of all, it's *my* wedding, not hers. Second, the venue can only accommodate one hundred fifty people. She and I had a pretty good relationship before the wedding plans started but now I can't stand to be in the same room with her!"

"Aw, that sounds frustrating. Hopefully, it's just the excitement of the event and once it's all said and done the two of you can have a nice lunch and laugh about it. Is Greg at least being supportive and telling his mom to chill out?"

"He's actually been great about reigning her in. When he looked at the list, he told her she didn't even like half the people on there and the other half didn't like her," Christina laughed.

She went on about the plans and having to change the colors and her dress and I injected the obligatory responses, 'that sounds amazing' and 'I bet it's going to be beautiful' but my mind had started to drift back to Xavier.

I couldn't believe we'd been together for almost five months and he'd never mentioned a kid. It had to be a lie. But I wondered if there were other omissions that Xavier had made or neglected to tell me about his life.

Who was I kidding? What we had wasn't a real relationship. And I guess that's what had attracted me to him and why I had willingly agreed to be with him because there was a lack of expectation. He wouldn't be around to really expect anything but sex when he came to town or when I visited him. We'd just have a good time. But then things changed. I realized that hooking up with him when he came to town wasn't enough for me. I wanted more. I wanted to be able to call and talk to him whenever I felt like it, I wanted to have dinner dates a few nights a week, I wanted to share a favorite television show, I wanted to discuss the state of the world, I wanted to talk about my career and I wanted someone to make a big deal about my promotion at work!

And I'd had that. I'd had all of that with Rodney and I let him go. I let him leave and go to Houston because I was a coward.

"Angela? Hello, are you still there?" Christina called over the line.

"Yeah, I'm here- sorry, so you were saying you didn't think it made sense to have a DJ and a band?" I tried to recall her last words.

She chuckled. "No. Are you okay? Is this about Xavier?" she asked.

I didn't want Christina to know just how screwed up things were, so I faked a yawn.

"No, I didn't get any sleep last night and I'm exhausted," I lied.

"It's seven fifteen," she said.

"I know. I'm such an old lady," I sighed.

"Angela, you know you can talk to me. We're friends," Christina said softly.

"I know and I'm fine. I'll talk to Xavier and get that whole mess straightened out but right now I think I'm going to shut down early,"

"Okay," she said hesitantly.

"Seriously, don't let your future mother-in-law ruin your wedding day. This is about you and Greg. I know it's going to be a beautiful ceremony. I can't wait to see you in your dress, I'll talk to you later."

After I hung up the phone with Christina, I looked out the window at the Hudson in the distance and the faint lights over the walkway. I needed to get my life back on track. I didn't want to become one of those women who made themselves sick because of the actions of a man. I didn't need or want that kind of drama in my life.

But what did I want?

I walked to my office and sat down at the desk. I took out a notepad and at the top, I wrote, **What I Want**. I scribbled the words: good health, good food, financial freedom, travel experiences, I wanted to be promoted to a regional leader for the Estee Lauder brand, then maybe a group president continuing on until I reached the pinnacle with a position on the executive team.

I sat back and looked at my list and realized two things: One, I was obsessed with my career. Two, I hadn't mentioned anything about a relationship.

That was part of my problem. I didn't honestly think I could have a successful career *and* a successful relationship. My mom had to choose. I didn't want to choose. I didn't want to end up sacrificing everything for a relationship and then if the person I was with decided to leave, I'd have nothing.

But I wasn't my mother. I had a college degree and a pretty nice retirement portfolio so far. I had options. I also had options for a relationship.

On a fresh sheet of paper, I drew a line down the middle of the page and made two columns.

On the left side, I wrote **Rodney** and one the right side, **Xavier**. I laughed grimly. Rodney had made it *very* clear that he and I were done. I wasn't sure why I considered him a viable option but I left his name anyway.

I started jotting down all the pros about Rodney: intelligent, smart, great sense of humor, handsome, financially sound, wonderful conversationalist, cared about me, loved me, respects me, dependable, fun, great personal hygiene

Xavier: smart, talented, handsome, romantic, sexy, financially sound (I guess), cares about me, fun, spontaneous

Then the cons, Rodney: can be too serious, inflexible, stubborn

Xavier: no solid foundation, unavailable, not honest (?), nothing in common (other than sex)

I looked down at the paper and then ripped it from the notepad and balled it up. I couldn't believe I was being so superficial. Neither of them was the perfect guy, there was no such thing.

Maybe what my mom had said was true and neither Rodney nor Xavier were right for me. Or maybe it was me. Confused and afraid. If I was being honest, I missed both of them. I missed Rodney's laughter and how being with him always made me feel comfortable and safe. I used to see that as a bad thing and now I longed for it. I missed being in Xavier's arms and feeling his warm lips against mine. When I was with him the world disappeared.

I took my phone from the charging dock and decided to call my brother. I hadn't talked to him since I left Philly a few weeks ago.

My dad was at home with my mom and officially moved in, although I think he was already living there before his heart attack. He was doing great and they'd planned a quick wedding ceremony at the justice of the peace in a couple of weeks and then a week-long trip to the Bahamas. Mama wanted me and my brother there as witnesses and I didn't want to ruin the day with unsaid words and anger simmering between us.

"Hello," he answered.

"Hey," I replied.

"What's up," he sighed. His tone filled with impatience but he probably felt obligated to talk to his only sibling.

"I was just calling to say hi and to apologize for the stuff I said about the divorce and custody. That was cruel. I really hate that you're going through that and I know it's not easy."

"Apology accepted. And I'm sorry for getting all in your business. You're a grown woman and what you do and who you do it with is none of my business." He said.

"Apology accepted, I know it came from a place of concern. I guess it pissed me off because I felt guilty and you were right about me still caring for Rodney, things are just complicated right now. But I never meant to hurt him," I said sincerely.

"I'm not the one you should be telling this,"

"I tried. He hates me," I said.

AJ laughed, "You're so dramatic. Rodney does not hate you. He's not even that kind of dude."

"I don't know, you didn't see him and hear how he talked to me," I argued.

"What you mean how he talked to you?" he asked on edge. I could hear the protective big brother about to make an appearance.

"He was really upset and told me not to come to his office unannounced anymore and that we weren't friends," When I said it out loud I got a lump in my throat.

"Yo! You went to his job? For what?" AJ shouted.

"A peace offering. I was trying to bring him lunch. He said I was keeping him around because Xavier was unavailable."

AJ was quiet.

"I don't want to end up alone but I don't think I'm cut out to be somebody's wife and mother," I said sadly.

"Is that something you even want?"

"I don't know. Isn't that crazy? Shouldn't I know that? And why wouldn't I want that? That makes no sense, does it?"

"I think you should talk to somebody to work through your issues,"

"I'm talking to you," I remarked.

He chuckled. "And I'm more screwed up than you are. I meant like a professional, a therapist."

"Oh, so now I'm crazy? Do you see a therapist?"

"Seeing a therapist doesn't make you crazy. And actually, I am seeing somebody," he admitted.

I gasped. "Really? Why?"

"I have a lot of shit that I need to work through– stuff with mama, daddy, Paula- stuff from when I was deployed. I don't want to be that guy who suppresses everything and drinks it away or sexes it away or is so angry and volatile all the time. I got two boys looking at me for a role model. I want to do right by them and myself," he said and he sounded so vulnerable.

"I know the divorce isn't even final yet, but do you think you'll ever get remarried?"

"I don't know. . . if the right woman came along I probably would,"

"How will you know if she's the right one?" I asked.

"I think marriage and relationships are a lot of work but I don't think it should *feel* like it. Making efforts to be there for someone, compromising on the minor things, being careful with someone's feelings and their heart should be a natural instinct and not something that you dread or feel forced to do. If I find someone who I wouldn't mind missing an Eagles game for– then she's a keeper," he laughed.

"But it has to be mutual. If only one person is making all the sacrifices and catering to the other person's needs and insecurities then that shit is doomed." He warned.

"That's my biggest fear that I'll end up with the short end of the stick. I'll get married and be expected to give up my career to stay at home with the kids and then I'll be resentful because my husband gets to leave the house every day and have a life,"

"Yeah, you definitely need to talk to somebody because that sounds like your mama's life, not yours,"

I groaned. "I know. It's stupid,"

"It's not stupid, it's just how you were raised,"

I sighed. I was sick of talking about my dysfunction, so I changed the topic.

"So, are you ready to be a witness at our parent's wedding?" I asked carefully.

He snorted. "I suppose. I just hope he's not pretending to have this life-changing moment because of his heart attack and then decides he doesn't want to be married anymore." AJ said. "The thing that pisses me off the most about him is that he never really took responsibility for his part in the entire thing and looking back, now that I'm an adult, I get that it was between the two of them as husband and wife, but you don't just bail on your kids,"

"He told me he figured we didn't need him anymore because we were practically grown,"

"What? Man, get outta here with that. Excuses! He was glad to be free in more ways than one. Shit, even when they were together we hardly ever saw him."

"I know but she's happy with him, so I think we should try and be happy for her. And give him a second chance since he will officially be her husband again."

AJ laughed. "All that sounds so crazy since he's always *officially* been our father,"

I talked to AJ for a few minutes longer and he promised he'd be nice and respectful at the ceremony.

I didn't hear back from Xavier for another week and during this time, TMZ had in fact published a video on their website of Xavier leaving a restaurant with a woman. But the story they ran along with the video claimed the woman was India White, a celebrity attorney who specialized in family law. They said it had been long speculated that Xavier, the front man for R&B band, Soul Skylight had a secret love child and his meeting with White was to rehash his child support agreement with the mother of his child.

I was stunned. I'd immediately opened another tab on the internet and searched for India White. Sure enough, the woman in the video was an attorney with a specialty in family law. But why would Xavier need a family law attorney? He was an only child and his mother died when he was eleven. He moved from Brooklyn to Buffalo to live with his grandmother, who had since passed away. I wondered if it had something to do with his father, he had been on drugs and in and out of jail.

Maybe he'd resurfaced after all these years trying to extort money from him. I sounded delusional and naïve. There was only one explanation and Xavier confirmed it when he'd called me at work the following week.

"Hey, I am so sorry for just now getting back to you. The time zone here is still messing me up. How you doing?"

"I'm fine," I said tightly.

He sighed, "You saw the TMZ thing, huh?"

"As a matter of fact, I did. And I believe you when you say there's nothing going on between you and that woman,"

"Good, because there isn't anything going on between us, you're the only woman I want. And I know these next few weeks are going to be the toughest for us but if we-,"

"Xavier, I have one question."

"Okay, what?" he asked and I could hear the apprehension in his voice.

"Do you have a son?" I asked.

He didn't respond.

"Hello?" I called.

"It's not what you think-,"

I laughed although there was absolutely nothing funny about the situation. *It's not what you think?* Maybe the child was adopted or one of those internationally sponsored children.

"Do you have a biological son?" I asked rephrasing the question.

He sighed. "Yes,"

I was speechless. I couldn't believe we'd been together for five months and he'd never mentioned having a child, which meant he was probably a deadbeat dad.

"I've got to go. I can't talk to you right now," I said.

"Please don't hang up!" he begged.

"I don't know what to say to you right now,"

"Listen, he's almost five years old and me and his mother weren't ever really together, my manager made her sign a non-disclosure agreement to keep him out of the media and-,"

"So, you're not in his life?" I asked feeling agitated. It was bad enough that he'd withheld information from me but the fact that he didn't see the child, who was innocent in all this, was worse.

"It's complicated,"

"It always is, I need a minute to process. I'll talk to you later," I hung up without giving him a chance to reply.

I stayed in my office working for the rest of the day trying to ignore the fact that my boyfriend just told me he had a five-year-old son. It made me question everything he'd ever told me. I didn't like being lied to or treated like I was gullible. But that's exactly how I'd behaved with Xavier when we were younger and he obviously thought I was still that girl. I wasn't. I was a grown ass woman and I wasn't going to tolerate disrespect from anyone including Xavier Ross, I didn't give a damn how many records he'd sold.

I wondered what he'd meant about it being complicated and why he'd made the mother sign an NDA. Was she also famous? Maybe she was married. Did the child have special needs? My mind raced from one scenario to the next. A part of me felt bad that I hadn't allowed him to explain and another part of me was pissed that I was in a situation with a man who had a secret love child.

I decided I at least wanted to know the entire story before I broke up with him because that was the only logical thing to do. The time and distance was too much. And now adding a child into the mix, I wasn't ready for that. That's probably why he said he didn't want children because he already had one. I tried to put the issue with Xavier and his son out of mind as I prepared for my parent's wedding that weekend. I didn't want my family knowing especially since they already weren't that fond of him.

Friday morning, I took the train to Philadelphia and my brother picked me up and we met our parents at the courthouse where they were getting married by a district judge.

My mother looked beautiful in her cream-colored silk shift dress. She wore a pearl hair clip in her short, curly hair that had started graying. Her makeup was always flawless, she had the ability to apply makeup like a professional. Even without makeup, she was still gorgeous and her skin practically wrinkle free. She also had a nice figure from walking each morning before work and cutting back on sweets. Although she was fifty-eight, she seemed to be aging in reverse.

My father, on the other hand, seemed to have aged faster over the years. He was four years older than my mom and at sixty-two, he looked closer to seventy. His chocolate skin tone had lost some luster over the years and he was almost completely gray, except for a few black strands scattered scarcely in the hair on his head and his beard.

For the ceremony, he had chosen a navy-blue suit with a white dress shirt and cream tie to compliment my mom's dress. They were smiling widely at each other like they were still the twenty-somethings that had met over thirty-seven years ago. My brother had a blank expression on his face but I knew he wanted to roll his eyes and groan out loud. I smiled at them, they both seemed genuinely happy. As the judge started the ceremony I recalled a not so happy time.

****

"I'm done! I'm not doing this shit anymore! I'm so sick of trying to please you all the damn time and it's still not enough! It's never enough. And you have the nerve to come in here acting like nothing happened!" my mom yelled at my dad after he hadn't been home for almost a week.

"I was working," he said simply.

"Bullshit! Tina said she saw you down in Atlantic City!" she yelled.

"Woman, are you for real? So, you gone take the word of your nosey, miserable ass cousin over me?"

I closed my door and turned up the music on my Walkman to drown out the arguing. That's all they ever did was argue; well, whenever my dad decided to come home. AJ was lucky that he had already graduated high school and was away in boot camp. The arguments had gotten worse and I couldn't wait to leave either.

Mama had surprised me two weeks later when she left him. She'd said they were getting a divorce, and she and I moved into a small apartment across town. She had been saving money in a separate account and had a plan for getting a job and living without my dad. She said she'd been planning it for over a year.

Back then she'd been so hurt and angry that she barely uttered my father's name and she never really encouraged me or my brother to keep in touch with him. She'd only said, "He's your dad but I can't make you have a relationship with him." So, I didn't. Even after the two of them were on speaking terms, I was cordial to him but we were never close. But I wasn't the one marrying him or the one that would have to live with him. My mother was a smart woman and usually had sound judgment, so I trusted she knew what she was doing.

****

After the ceremony, we went to Butcher and Singer restaurant for lunch. Halfway through lunch, my dad stood to make a toast.

"I can't tell you how happy I am to be here with my family– the only woman I've truly ever loved and our beautiful children, who I am so very proud of. Here's to what I hope is a new beginning for us all and that we grow closer in the years to come."

"Cheers!" My mom exclaimed clinking her glass with my

father's.

"Cheers," I tapped my glass against theirs and then turned to my brother.

He tipped his glass towards us before downing the entire glass of champagne. I pinched his arm.

He looked at me with wide eyes and kicked me under the table. To our parent's credit, they were so wrapped up in their own little bubble that they didn't even notice we were trying to maim each other. They would be leaving on a late-night flight for a week-long honeymoon, so after lunch, I hugged them both tight and gave them some parting words.

"Have a wonderful time and be safe," I smiled squeezing my mom's hands. "I'm so happy for you, for both of you, I hope that this time your marriage lasts and you treat each other well," I said as I looked into my dad's eyes.

He hugged me again. "Thank you, Angie, that means so much to me and I promise to do right by your mama until my dying day,"

My brother hugged my mom and whispered something in her ear that my father and I couldn't hear. It made her laugh out loud but when she pulled away she had tears in her eyes. My brother shook my father's hand and then we were off to the train station, so that I could catch the 4:45 train back to New York.

"Are you really supporting this marriage?" AJ asked me on the way to the train station.

"It doesn't matter if we support it or not. It's done. Besides I've got my own issues. I pray he treats Mama right because I think this time around she might kill him in his sleep," I laughed and so did AJ.

We rode in comfortable silence for the rest of the way.

When I made it back to my apartment later that evening, I took a shower, relaxed on my couch and was about to call Xavier when my phone rang. It was Christina.

"Hey, Christina can I-,"

"Turn your TV to channel 7," she said instead of hello.

The TV was already on but I had it muted, I quickly switched to channel 7. There was a news report saying Xavier had been rushed to a hospital in Berlin after collapsing on stage. Early reports said it was due to exhaustion although drugs and alcohol hadn't been ruled out. I sat down on the edge of my sofa and covered my mouth.

"Angela- hello- are you there? Are you okay? I'm on my way over there," Christina announced.

"No! No, I'm fine- I'm fine. Let me call you back," I disconnected the call and immediately dialed Xavier's number.

The news report had probably gotten it wrong. It more than likely wasn't Xavier that had collapsed but Eric, he was the one with a history of drug use. Xavier's phone went straight to voicemail and my body started to tremble.

"Hey, um- it's me, Angie. I just saw the news. Are you okay? I'm really worried. Call me," I ended the call and started to cry.

I waited for an hour and after I didn't hear back from Xavier, I called the hospital where they reported he'd been taken. Obviously, they wouldn't tell me anything or that he was even admitted there, I'm sure I sounded like a crazy fan when I tried to explain that I was his girlfriend.

I didn't even have the phone number of anyone in the band or his management team. I opened the email that I'd received with the Denver itinerary and hit 'reply'. I reminded the person who I was and asked about the incident in Berlin. It came back undeliverable. I felt so desperate that I almost looked up crazy Brenda on social media to see if she knew anything. I kept refreshing the Google search in case new information got posted but there was nothing, meanwhile, Christina had sent me a text:

Just checking on you. Are you okay? Have you talked to him or anyone from his team?

I'd planned on ignoring the text because I didn't want her to know I didn't even know anyone on his team.

Instead, I texted back:

Not yet.

April

*T*he next day I finally got more news about Xavier's condition when his manager called me.

"Hello, may I speak to Angela Barnes?" an unfamiliar voice asked after I answered the phone. I hoped it wasn't a telemarketer. I wasn't in the mood and would probably take my frustrations out on the poor unsuspecting soul.

"Hello Ms. Barnes, my name is Phil Dyson and I'm Xavier Ross' business manager,"

"Hello, yes, oh my god thank you so much for calling! I saw a report on the news, how is Xavier doing?"

"He is still in the hospital in Berlin but should be released tomorrow. He will be flying home to California to recuperate for a few weeks and asked that I let you know."

"Okay, well what happened is he-," I started. I wondered what kind of condition Xavier was in that he couldn't contact me himself.

"I'm sorry, Ms. Barnes that's all I have to say. I'm sure Xavier will be in touch with you soon and the two of you can talk at that time. Have a good day," he said and the line went dead.

"Hello? Hello? Seriously?"

So, he was fine but he couldn't do me the courtesy of calling me himself? Instead, he'd had his manager call and talk to me like I was a random associate. I'd had it! Once he made it back to California I would go see him to make sure he was okay and then I would end this stupid relationship.

I went to the small wine rack Rodney had installed before he moved and pulled out a bottle of Merlot. After opening it, I poured myself a generous glass.

"This is such bullshit!" I yelled taking a long swallow.

I was so angry. We weren't in high school anymore and this cloak and dagger shit was not attractive and I wasn't putting up with it. If he wanted to be with me there would have to be some major changes on his part.

"What the fuck? What am I talking about? I don't want to be with him. I don't want to be with a man who has a child that he doesn't even claim!" I said out loud. I took another swallow of wine and the glass was empty.

I gave myself a refill and continued talking aloud. My filter and demeanor totally changed after a few glasses of wine, which is why I didn't drink that often. And if I drank when I was angry, I was like a Molotov cocktail.

"And furthermore, do you even know my zodiac sign or favorite book? All you know is my favorite position! I mean the sex is good. It's *very* good," I giggled as I took another sip. "But not good enough for me to just hang on to you like a damned groupie!"

That's how his manager had talked to me like I was an inconvenience that he had to deal with on Xavier's behalf.

"Fucking men, they think the sun revolves around them! Am I supposed to be happy that Xavier Ross is giving me the time of day? I didn't even know who Soul Skylight was…I don't give a shit about any of that!" I gulped the remaining wine and should have stopped but instead, I poured another glass. This is the moment in which I would look back and wish I could get a do-over.

"I should be married now. If Rodney would have never moved his ass to Houston, we'd be married and living happily ever after and Xavier wouldn't even be an issue. This is all Rodney's fault!" I slurred.

It was a huge lie to say it was Rodney's fault or to assume we would be living happily ever after. But I needed someone to share in the responsibility for this current hot ass mess I was in! I thought back to when Rodney and I first met, I would have never even imagined that we would become romantically involved. He just wasn't my type.

✱✱✱✱✱✱✱✱✱✱✱✱✱✱

I visited my mom over the long Memorial Day weekend and she'd made some of her famous buffalo wings for my brother's monthly poker game. He was hosting at my mom's house because his ten-month-old son Kyle was sick and his wife, Paula didn't want the game at their house interrupting Kyle's sleep. She had told him to cancel the game but he insisted on having it and Mama had volunteered her basement. If I had known my brother and five of his rowdy friends were playing poker at my mom's house, I would have visited another weekend.

"Oh, it'll be fun. We can be hostesses like in Las Vegas. Did you bring your fishnets and bustier?" she cackled.

"I'd rather get ten root canals at the same time than wait on AJ and his friends," I'd declared. Because if the tables were turned, AJ would not be serving me and my friends drinks and chicken wings!

"Listen to Miss Feminism, girl stop acting like somebody wants to make you an indentured servant and put some more wings on that platter. Smile and show a little cleavage, you might get some good tips," She giggled leaving the kitchen to answer the front door.

I rolled my eyes and tossed the wings angrily on to the platter. I walked down to the basement and put the platter in middle of the food table Mama set up for the guys.

When I turned around a tall guy had entered the room. He had skin the color of milk chocolate, a tapered haircut, wore glasses, and had on a pair of faded jeans with a burgundy polo shirt. There was nothing remarkable about him at first glance.

"Hey Poindexter, what's with the glasses?" AJ laughed.

"Ha ha, I've never heard that one before. I tore my last contact," he shook his head and went around the table giving the rest of the guys high fives. When he looked over at me, he smiled and I noticed he had one dimple in his left cheek and his teeth were perfect. His smile had completely transformed him.

"Hi, I'm Rodney are you Allen's wife?"

A few of the guys laughed but AJ howled.

"Hell no! That's my sister, Angie."

"Angela," I corrected. Nobody called me Angie but my family. "And why are you laughing like that? You think I'm not wife material?" I placed my hands on my hip and looked at AJ.

AJ took a swig of beer. "You're not *my* wife material. That's gross."

"Whatever. If you gentlemen need anything else. . .tell AJ to call his mama," I smiled prettily and Rodney chuckled.

"I see it runs in the family," he laughed as I left the room.

I had tried to convince Mama to go see a movie or something since AJ and his friends were being loud and obnoxious. Truth be told I just wanted out of the house. I felt claustrophobic.

"You were this way as a child, could never sit still always getting bored and moving on to the next thing before you finished what you were working on. I think you may have had ADD but never got diagnosed," she said. We sat at the table in the kitchen because she said she wanted to talk but I knew she wanted to be close by in case AJ needed something. Some things never changed.

The guy I'd met in the basement– Rodney, stuck his head in the kitchen door. "Hey, Mrs. Barnes, I'm headed on a beer run. Do you need anything?"

"Hey, Rodney. No, I'm good I don't need anything," she smiled at him and then looked at me. "Hold on, can you do me a big favor?"

I gave her a warning glare.

"Can you take Angela with you? She's bored out of her mind and needs some fresh air."

I stared at her in disbelief. I couldn't believe she was trying to pawn me off on some strange guy. I was about to tell him, no thanks, but then he said, "I need some fresh air too. You're more than welcome to come along,"

I'd thought about it for a second. "Hold on a minute," He seemed nice enough but just in case I went back to the basement to talk to AJ first.

"I'm going to the store with your friend, if he tries anything I have mace and a stun gun in my purse, and I will leave his body on the side of the road," I whispered.

"Shit, hold on fellas," AJ followed me upstairs.

I grabbed my purse and joined Rodney and my mom in the kitchen. Not sure what AJ said to Rodney but he looked a little scared. AJ also assured me that Rodney hadn't been drinking, which is why he had been chosen to make the beer run. The ride to the store was a little awkward at first but then Rodney's grip on the steering wheel loosened and he'd started making small talk.

"So, you live in Manhattan?"

I was about to answer when he started back peddling.

"Not that I'm trying to find out where you live or anything, just making conversation,"

I snickered. "I'm actually in East Village,"

"I'm in Chelsea."

"You don't sound like a New Yorker," I observed.

"I'm originally from California. Sacramento,"

"How long have you been in the city?"

"About two years. After grad school, I worked as an expat in London for three years, then did some work in D.C. for a year before moving to New York,"

I was impressed.

"What kind of work do you do?" I asked.

"Corporate tax and audits. I'm a tax manager with Ernst & Young."

A corporate man. Correction, a *black* corporate man with a master's degree, expat experience that lived less than twenty minutes away from me. I smiled as I thought of him as a future possibility.

"What?" he asked.

"Huh?" I asked confused. I hadn't said anything.

He smiled at me. "What's that look for?"

"What look?" Had he caught me glazed over thinking about him? I hoped I wasn't blushing.

He shook his head and focused back on the road. I could see the store in the distance.

"What do you do? If you don't mind me asking?" he'd asked when we stopped at a red light.

"I'm an Assistant Marketing Manager for Estee Lauder,"

"Oh, what brand or do you work for the main division of Estee Lauder?"

My eyes widened. No one had ever asked that as a follow-up question when I told them where I worked. Most people thought I worked at the makeup counter in the mall.

He smirked at me. "What? Are you surprised I know that Estee Lauder owns other cosmetic brands?" he laughed.

"A little," I smiled. "I work for Clinique,"

"Cosmetics or fragrance?"

I laughed. "Shut up! Why do you know so much about the breakdown of a beauty business?" I was becoming more intrigued by him.

He glanced at me before moving through the green light and pulling over to the parking lot of the grocery store.

"I briefly worked on an E&Y account audit for Estee Lauder. It was an internship,"

"What a crazy coincidence!"

Rodney parked the car and instead of getting out, we ended up talking. We were gone so long my brother called Rodney and threatened his life if anything had happened to me. Before Rodney left we'd exchanged phone numbers and made vague plans to grab lunch one day since we discovered we were both foodies who loved trying new restaurants in the city.

I didn't talk to Rodney again for almost a month. Then one day we met for lunch and were pretty much inseparable after that. Going to openings of restaurants, bars, art galleries and Broadway shows. Rodney had some connections who were always getting us on an exclusive list. However, we were strictly friends, who enjoyed each other's company.

It was nice having a platonic male friend. It's not that I didn't find him attractive, he was incredibly smart, handsome, had an amazing smile and he always smelled so damn good! I'd just assumed we were only meant to be friends or that he was gay since he hadn't made the first move. I was cool with our friendship status until a woman who worked with Rodney asked him out on date. He'd told me about their conversation because he wanted to get my opinion on the situation. He didn't know if he should go out with her because they worked together.

The thought of another woman taking him away from me had opened my eyes in a major way, I realized I wanted him for myself.

"I think you should tell her 'thanks, but no thanks' you already have someone you can take on a date," I'd said nonchalantly as we sat drinking coffee at a sidewalk café.

He raised an eyebrow. "I do?"

I looked at him in disbelief. "Seriously? So, what am I, chopped liver?"

He laughed. "No, but I thought- I mean, you and I are just friends. Aren't we?" he asked confused.

I'd felt like such a fool for trying to make a move on him that he hadn't reciprocated or even acknowledged. He apparently wasn't interested in me in that way.

I shrugged. "Well, if you like her then you should go out with her," My mouth went dry after the words left my mouth. "I should probably go, I've actually got some reports to look over for work tomorrow," I lied as I grabbed my purse from the chair next to me.

"Hey, are you okay?" he asked. I nodded my head but refused to look him in the eye.

"Yeah, I'll talk to you later," I left the café not sure if I'd ever talk to him again. I knew once he started dating another woman she was not going to like the two of us hanging out so much.

By the time I made it back to my apartment I'd gone from being hurt and confused to pissed off. Who did Rodney Anderson think he was? Did he think I wasn't good enough for him?

I took bottle of water from my refrigerator just as someone knocked at my door. I hoped it wasn't my neighbor, Mrs. Goldstein. She was a lonely widow. She baked cookies at least twice a week and invited me over to have tea, and she'd tell me all about how the neighborhood had changed and what life was like when she and her husband, Marty first moved in forty years ago.

When I looked through the peephole I was surprised to see Rodney. I stood stock still and wondered if I should pretend I wasn't home.

"Angela, I saw your shadow fill the peephole," he said.

I sighed. These old buildings made it hard to be stealthy.

I opened the door and plastered a smile on my face. "Hey, what's up? What are you doing here?" I asked leaning against the doorway.

"I came to make sure you were okay," he eyed me curiously.

"Yeah, I'm fine. Why wouldn't I be?" I titled my head and stared at him. Did he think I would slit my wrists because he'd told me we were just friends?

"I don't know, I– can I come in? I'm sure Mrs. Goldstein is listening?" he whispered pointing at my neighbor's door.

I moved aside to allow him into my small studio apartment. Once he was inside, I leaned back against the door and folded my arms across my chest.

He turned to look at me. "Earlier, you seemed upset when I said we were just friends,"

I waved him off. "What? No, I must have been distracted about work." I said strongly.

"You're lying and you're not even doing a good job," he said softly. I loved and hated that he knew me so well.

I decided to lead him down another path. "I was just thinking how once you start dating this woman, she's not going to like you having female friends and I guess that will probably be the end of our friendship." I said sadly.

"Dating? I haven't even responded to her and you've got us dating?" he asked incredulously.

I shrugged in response. "It will happen eventually. If not her, someone else will come along,"

He mimicked my pose. "What about you? What happens to me when you start dating some guy?"

I actually hadn't thought of that. "I'm not- there is no guy,"

He dropped his arms to his sides and walked towards me. I looked away.

"And there is no woman, only you," he said softly.

I dropped my gaze to the floor before looking up at him. "What is that supposed to mean?" I didn't want to make any assumptions.

"Come on, Angela, you know what it means. We've been hanging out, having fun and getting to know each other but I do want more with you. I honestly only asked you about that woman to see what you would say." He reached for my hands and threaded our fingers together.

I cleared my throat. "So, nobody asked you out?" I squeezed his fingers tightly.

"Ow," he laughed. "Yes, there is actually a woman who wants to go out with me. But I don't want her. I want you," he said and his voice was filled with hope that I wanted the same.

I'd smiled and pretended to be thinking about it. "I guess I want you too," I shrugged.

"You guess?" he smirked as he leaned in close to me until our lips were a few inches apart.

"I want you too," I stared at his full lips as I leaned forward.

And then he leaned in the rest of the way, closing the gap between us and kissed me. It was a gentle peck at first and then a long pull before he wrapped his arms around my waist and kissed me deeply. I was breathless when it was over.

He rested his forehead against mine, "So should I tell the lady at work I have a woman?" he smiled.

I nodded and kissed him again. And that's how our relationship had begun.

****

The sound of my upstairs neighbors dragging something across the floor brought my thoughts back to the present. I stared at my wine selection and contemplated opening another bottle even though I was reeling from the bottle that I'd just drank. Staring into the cabinet, I spotted the Cabernet that Rodney and I had gotten from the Brown Estate. We had agreed to open it on our one year wedding anniversary. We'd only been engaged six months before we broke up. I took the bottle from the cabinet and had the brilliant idea to take it to Rodney. He could have it because I didn't want any reminders of my life with him.

I stumbled over to the table and picked up my phone to call an Uber. Once I got a confirmation, I put my phone in my pocket and grabbed my purse and the bottle of wine.

The woman who picked me up tried to talk me out of going to Rodney's apartment after I'd told her my life story.

"Sis, I don't know you but it's obvious you're drunk. Are you sure you want to show up at your ex's like this? What if he has a woman over there?" she asked.

"Good! That would be perfect! They can drink this bottle of lies together!" I shouted.

"Yo, but if you're drunk and she tries to fight you, then what? She might beat your ass,"

"I have mace and a stun gun in my bag. I will make sure to blind that bitch!" I said angrily.

"If you say so," She laughed and proceeded to drive me to my destination near Columbus Circle.

When I arrived at Rodney's building, there was a burly, dark skinned security guard at the desk in the lobby.

"Can I help you?" he asked.

I held on tighter to the wine bottle. "Special delivery for Rodney Anderson,"

He raised an eyebrow. "Is Mr. Anderson expecting you?"

"Not at all," I answered honestly. "But I have something for him." I tried to wink at the guard but started blinking uncontrollably.

"O. . .k, let me give him a call," he picked up the phone and dialed a number. "Hello, Mr. Anderson there is a woman here, what's your name ma'am?"

"Lola Falana," I giggled.

Rodney's mom had idolized Lola Falana; he was surprised that I'd known who she was when we first started dating.

"Yeah, I would say so. Yes. Okay, will do. Thanks," the guard hung up the phone and came around to where I stood.

"Right this way, ma'am," I thought he was about to throw me out of the building but instead he led me to the elevator. Once I was inside he reached over and pressed the sixth floor. Or it could have been the ninth. Things were a little fuzzy.

When the elevator doors dinged and opened on the sixth (or ninth) floor, Rodney was there with a frown on his face. I had missed his face so much.

"Have you lost your mind?" he chastised under breath. He grabbed my arm tightly and pulled me down the hallway.

"Ouch!" I complained.

He pulled me inside what I assumed was his apartment before he closed the door. I'd never been inside his new apartment. It was nice really nice, Rodney had excellent taste.

"What are you doing here?" he asked angrily.

I held the bottle of wine towards him. "Here, I bought this for you,"

He scowled at me and then looked at the bottle. "I bought that bottle in Napa,"

"I meant I bought- brought, that's the past tense of bring, right? Anyway, it's yours and you can have it,"

"Angela, how much have you had to drink?" he asked.

"That's beyond the point- I mean besides,"

"And what exactly is the point of you showing up at my apartment, drunk, at ten o'clock at night?" he folded his arms across his chest and stared down at me like he always did when he thought he had made such an amazing point or won an argument.

"The point is– this bottle is full of lies!" I said shaking it. His eyes widened and he stepped forward and grabbed it just as I lost my grip.

He sighed as he saved it from crashing to the floor and placed it on a nearby table.

"I really don't have time for this, whatever this is you're doing." He exhaled and pinched the bridge of his nose.

"Whatever I'm doing? I'll tell you exactly what I'm doing!" I said dropping my bag to the floor. "I'm taking back my life the way it was before I met anybody. Taking it back to when I was alone and could always count on myself. Back to before *you* made believe in love," I accused as I pointed a shaky finger at him.

He wiped his hands over his face. "Did you and your boyfriend break up or something?" he asked annoyed.

"This has nothing to do with that liar. This is about the liar in front of me- *you*!"

"Me? What did I ever lie to you about? You were the one good at telling lies in our relationship," he reminded.

"You said you'd love me no matter what! And you didn't!" I yelled. "You asked me to be honest with you and I did and things were never the same," I said as my voice cracked.

"Angela, you are going to regret this in the morning," he shook his head.

"You think I don't regret it now? My personal life is in shambles and it's your fault! If we would have gotten married-,"

"We would have been miserable! And you're right after you *finally* told me you didn't think you ever wanted kids, it did change things. Only because for three years you pretended you did! You knew how important having a family was to me and you just said what I wanted to hear-,"

"Because I loved you and I knew you'd leave me and you did! You ended up going to Houston and leaving me!" I cried and he didn't deny it. "You never even told me you were looking for a transfer."

"Because I wanted to escape!" He confessed and that shocked me.

"I didn't know how to leave you and I guess a part of me didn't want to, I wanted to get away for a while and thought some space would be good for both of us but I was so unhappy without you. I missed you so much, just seeing your face every day and hearing your voice. So, when I got the opportunity to come back to New

York, I jumped on it."

I smiled and sniffed as I felt the effects of the alcohol wearing me down, I was really sleepy. I sat down on his couch and laid my head back against the soft cushions.

"The only reason I don't know if I want kids is because I don't think I'll be a good mother," I said and a yawn escaped. "Not to mention I figured a child would slow me down and force me to make sacrifices. Or you would expect me to give up my career. I'm selfish and scared," I sighed as my eyes fluttered. I cleared my throat and tried to wake up.

I smiled dreamily at him. "But you and I, we were *so* good together. And as much as I tried to blame you for hanging on, I admit it's been me– all me, afraid to really lose you for good." I said and my eyes closed to the darkness.

The next time I opened my eyes, light flooded the room. I sat up and swore I could feel my brain sloshing around in my skull. I put a hand to my forehead and realized I was covered in a blanket.

"Ow, oh," I groaned and my mouth felt like it was stuffed with cotton balls. I started to focus in on my surroundings, I wasn't in my apartment. I looked down and there was a glass of water and packet of hangover herbs on the table. I had to be at Rodney's, he was the one who had introduced me to the magic pack of hangover eraser.

Just as I downed the packet and swallowed the tepid water, he appeared. "How are you feeling?"

"Like absolute shit," I croaked out.

He smirked at me and shook his head.

"I was hoping it was all a dream and I didn't actually come over to your apartment drunk last night," I sighed.

"It wasn't a dream,"

I closed my eyes and threw my head back against his couch. "I am *so* sorry," I apologized.

When he didn't say anything, I opened my eyes and looked up at him. He sighed and sat down next to me. I covered my mouth because I was sure my breath smelled like rotting grapes.

"No apologies necessary this time, it was a long overdue conversation. Just wish you could have been sober for it," he smiled. "Do you remember anything?"

Unfortunately, I wasn't like most people who had no recollection of what they had said or done when intoxicated. I remembered everything including ignoring my Uber driver's advice.

"I remember all of it," I said behind my hand.

"I've smelled your bad breath before," he chuckled.

"Whatever," I dropped my hand.

"What happened with Xavier?" he asked.

I held my head down. I didn't really want to talk about Xavier but I'd opened this entire can of worms, so there was no point in holding back now.

"Turns out he has a secret love child. I found out from TMZ. And he also recently passed out at a concert. The news says it's from exhaustion or drugs. But because he had his manager call me, I don't really have all the details," I sighed.

"Are you serious?" Rodney asked in disbelief.

I nodded my head.

"Wow,"

"Wow is right," I stretched my arms over my head. "What time is it?" I asked.

"A few minutes after seven," Rodney said looking at his watch.

"I guess I should get going. It's bad enough I messed up your night, I don't want to ruin your morning,"

"I'm about to make a couple of bacon, egg, cheese croissants. If you're interested," he offered.

I hadn't had one of Rodney's bacon, egg, cheese croissants since we broke up. He knew it was my favorite breakfast. I wasn't certain what the gesture meant but decided not overthink it. I would just look at it as a peace offering and an opportunity to spend another hour with him. Besides, the greasy bacon would probably help my hangover as well.

After we ate, we made small talk about work and then I decided to leave. I could tell there had been a shift between us but I was still confused. Were we back to being friends? I didn't question his motives, I just thanked him and left.

Once I returned home, I took a shower, brushed my teeth and did a co-wash on my hair. I also realized I didn't have my phone. I assumed I'd left it at Rodney's. I had a few errands to run, so once I got dressed I took a cab back to his apartment.

I was glad the security guard from last night wasn't there.

"Hi, I'm here to see Rodney Anderson. I actually left my phone at his apartment and just need to get it,"

This guard was an overweight white guy with a bored expression. He looked at me like I'd given him entirely too much information.

He called Rodney but he didn't answer. I waited about five minutes and asked him to call again. He acted as if I'd asked him to pull a ten-ton steel bar across the lobby.

"Hello, Mr. Anderson there's a lady here who said she forgot something at your apartment – okay, yeah, will do," he said before looking at me. "You can go up Ms. Smith,"

Ms. Smith? I was about to correct him but it occurred to me that

Rodney was probably expecting someone. A female visitor. My feelings were hurt but I had no right to be upset or jealous.

I hurried to the elevator and pressed the sixth floor. I went to the unit at the end of the hall and knocked. Rodney opened the door wearing only a towel around his waist. He looked like he'd just gotten out of the shower.

"Did you forget something Jan-? Angela? What are you doing here?" he glanced past me down the hallway.

"I am so sorry, that was me calling downstairs. I think I left my phone," I winced. "Did you see it?"

"No, I didn't,"

"Well, can you call it and see if it rings? I don't want to cause any problems or confusion so the sooner-," I pointed towards his living room. I would get my phone and leave quickly before his guest arrived.

"Huh? Oh, okay, let me get my phone." He allowed me inside and I closed the door. I tried not to stare at the planes of his muscular back. His body was familiar and foreign at the same time. I hadn't seen Rodney not fully clothed in almost a year.

He picked up his phone from the docking station on the kitchen counter and pressed a button on the screen. I heard a faint buzzing and followed the sound to his couch. My phone had fallen in between the cushions.

"Got it!" I said avoiding eye contact with him.

"You good?" he asked.

"Yeah, I knew you'd moved on, you told me you were dating someone- I mean we both- you know,"

"Oh, yeah," he said softly. I looked at him with the realization that it could be my last time seeing him.

My eyes roamed over his body. His chest was broader and more defined, he had a perfect six-pack ab situation going on and the towel hung low on his waist giving me the perfect view of the muscled 'V' around his hips. I rubbed my neck and turned away blushing.

"I should go, I know you're expecting someone," I said

"Actually, I'm not. There was someone here a little while ago, we worked out together," he said absently.

I clamped my mouth shut and just nodded my head as I tried to force away the image of Rodney 'working out' with some woman.

His eyes widened, "No! I meant *actually* working out, me and a friend worked out in the gym upstairs," he laughed lightly.

I covered my face. "Bye," I laughed as I walked past him.

"Do you think I'd be bold enough to say something like that?" he licked his lips and it was innocent but also very erotic at the same time.

I shrugged. "I don't know? Maybe that's something you picked up in Houston. You've changed since you been back."

He gave me a curious glance before smirking at me. "Is that good or bad?" he placed his hands on his hips and it could have been my imagination but it seemed he was intentionally flexing his muscles.

"I haven't decided yet," I bit my lip and smiled at him. And I realized a few things. One, we were flirting with each other. Two, Rodney was still only wearing a towel, which had slipped even lower on his hips. Three, we were standing face to face.

He exhaled harshly. "Angela," he cautioned. Because he knew before I did what was about to happen. I stepped forward, took a shaky breath and kissed him.

His sighed harshly.

"No- you, you belong to someone else, Angela. This isn't right," he said firmly but he grabbed me around the waist.

I shook my head. "I belong to myself. He and I haven't- I haven't seen him in person in over two months. That was a mistake. It was a mistake," I kissed him again.

This time he pulled me closer and kissed me in a way that he'd never kissed me before. It was filled with so much longing and need. Whenever I tried to pull away to catch my breath he recaptured my mouth not wanting to let me go. I gently placed a hand on his chest and he stopped as we both tried to catch our breath.

"What are we doing?" he asked and he sounded so distressed.

"I've missed you so much," I said instead of answering his question. This was where my heart belonged. I kissed him again and reached down to undo his towel.

His hand covered mine and stopped me. He used his other hand to tilt my chin, forcing me to look in his eyes. I smiled at him and tried to convey with every muscle in my face that I wanted him just as much as he wanted me.

He stepped away from me and my smile faded. But then he reached out, grabbed my hand and led me to his bedroom. I kicked off my sandals and followed him wordlessly.

Rodney's room was incredibly modern with an understated touch of masculinity. He had a king size, platform bed in the middle of the room, which was decorated in a monochromatic palette of taupe's and browns.

He kissed me again before pulling my maxi dress over my head in one quick motion. He stared down at me in my cotton underwear, which was mismatched.

"I guess I should have worn something sexier," I said trying to lighten the mood but Rodney's expression remained intense.

"You don't need to wear anything to be sexy, you just are," he said hoarsely. His words made my entire body flush. "You don't know how much I've missed you." He pulled me against him and unhooked my bra letting it fall to the floor. He gently ran his fingertips over my breasts and kissed me slowly and sweetly.

Sex with Rodney was always a slow burn and he was the master of foreplay. He would touch and tease my body to the point that when we finally had sex I was a melting, blubbering mess. But tonight, his touch was at times tentative and then rushed like he expected me to stop him at any moment.

I gently placed a hand on his face. "I'm not going anywhere," I promised.

I removed my underwear after undoing his towel and we lay down on the bed together. We allowed our hands and lips to reconnect with bodies that had once been exclusively ours. We touched, tasted and teased each other until we were both worked up into a frenzy. There was no talking, no need for explanation or direction, our bodies had always been attuned to each other. We knew what the other liked, wanted and needed just as much as we knew our own desires.

Rodney kissed me and moved so deep inside of me that all my nerve endings came alive! I wrapped my legs around him and forced him in deeper. I'd never felt as connected to anyone during sex as I did with Rodney, including Xavier. Being with Rodney was about more than a release or fulfilling a sexual fantasy. Our lovemaking connected our souls.

I could feel myself about to reach my climax and then he whispered, "I love you, Angela, I love you," and I completely exploded around him. Tears filled my eyes and I clung to him never wanting to let go.

He came a few seconds later, gathered me in his arms and held me close. It was like gravity ceased to exist. Holding on to each other was the only thing keeping us anchored to the Earth. As we lay there basking in the aftermath of that incredible love making experience, I thought about what had just happened and although I felt bad about cheating on Xavier, I'd had an epiphany. I could see myself married to Rodney and starting a family. Rodney would be an amazing father and he would never treat me the way my father had treated my mother. Rodney *was* my destiny.

I nodded off and woke up to the smell of Chinese takeout. I looked at the clock. It was a little past four o'clock in the afternoon. I used his bathroom to freshen up, then got dressed. When I entered his living room, I saw him in the kitchen. He looked over his shoulder and smiled at me.

"I ordered some Pad Thai," he announced.

I walked to the kitchen and we sat down and ate together in silence. Afterwards, I took a bottle of water to the living room and sat on the couch trying to think of how to approach what had happened between us earlier that afternoon.

"I guess we should talk about what happened?" Rodney sat next to me on the couch.

I sighed. He was right, we definitely needed to talk but I didn't know what to say. I was still in love with Rodney but I felt I at least owed Xavier a chance to explain plus didn't want to end things over the phone.

"Rodney last night was beautiful and I still obviously have strong feelings for you-," he was smiling tenderly at me. "But I need to talk to Xavier and get-," I was about to say 'closure' but he went ballistic before I could finish.

"Are you fucking serious right now, Angela? So, after everything–you made love to me and you're going back to *him*?" He frowned and stood.

I stood to face him. "Rodney, calm down. I'm just saying I need to hear him out, I owe him that,"

"You don't owe him shit! This is- I can't believe you!" He ran his hands over his head and turned his back to me.

I touched his back and he shrugged away.

"Don't. I can't keep doing this! I can't. I'm not willing to keep waiting for you anymore! I love you, Angela, I want a life with you. I've made that more than clear. I'm sick of the games-,"

"I'm not playing games!" I exclaimed.

"Bullshit! I've always said you want your cake and eat it too!" he accused as he turned to face me.

"That's not true,"

"Prove it. Call him right now and tell him it's over." He demanded.

My eyes widened. "You want me to do it over the phone?"

"Isn't that how you find out everything from him? Over the phone?"

Ouch. I flinched.

"I'm not calling him, Rodney. I can't even get in touch with him right now. You don't understand what-," I wanted closure with Xavier, so there weren't any misunderstandings.

"No, I don't understand and I'm done pretending I do! I'm going to take a shower, when I get out I want you gone." He said leaving the room.

I watched as Rodney disappeared to the back of his apartment. I stood motionless as he walked away from me. When I heard the water from the shower, I walked towards his room. I wanted to go in and tell him that I was just going to end things with Xavier. But before I made any promises I wanted to be one hundred percent sure things were over between Xavier and I. Rodney deserved that. So, I grabbed my bag, put on my shoes and left his apartment. I would come back to him completely free and we would start over.

May

*T*he following Saturday was the beginning of a new month. I flew to Los Angeles and then drove to Malibu to see Xavier. It was my first time at his house and would more than likely be my last. Xavier's house resembled something out of *Architectural Digest*. The entire back wall of the house was made up of glass windows that overlooked the Pacific Ocean. The living room was starkly decorated with two white couches in the center of a marble floor, a glass table, and a glass bookcase along the back wall that held a few trophies including a Grammy. An acoustic guitar rested in the corner of the room.

An older lady wearing a grey business suit had allowed me into the house and led me to the living room to wait for Xavier. I sat nervously like I was in the house of a stranger instead of the home of the man I'd been involved with for almost seven months. I sat alone for ten minutes before he appeared. I was shocked by his appearance; not only had he grown out his beard again but it was bushy and untrimmed, so was his hair. He also looked like he'd lost even more weight.

"I can't believe you're here." His head was lowered and he didn't look at me.

"I came to see you in person. I wanted to make sure you were okay and we need to talk," I stood and walked towards him.

"Are you okay?" I asked approaching him. I gently rubbed his face and he leaned into my touch.

He sighed deeply and closed his eyes. "This last leg of the tour has been rough with these additional dates. I'm just so tired,"

He opened his eyes but kept his gaze on the floor. He also seemed withdrawn and not as affectionate as he usually was with me.

"You seem different," I whispered.

Sorry, I didn't have time to shave," he laughed quietly.

"You won't even look at me," I grabbed his chin. I tried to make eye contact but he pulled my hand away from his face, and walked past me. I turned and watched him.

He slowly turned around and finally looked at me. His eyes were red and there were deep, dark circles around them. Tears filled my eyes. He was obviously experiencing something more than exhaustion.

"I've been really messed up. And I've missed you so fucking much," he said.

"What do you mean 'messed up'?" I asked not certain I wanted to know.

He smiled faintly and I saw a glimpse of the boy I'd fallen in love with all those years ago.

"You know, I never told you this but I volunteered the band to play at the reunion without pay, and ended up giving them my salary from the first stop on our tour."

I didn't understand why we were talking about this but I was curious.

"Why?" I asked.

He shrugged and pointed at me. "Because of you. When I got that first notice that the high school reunion committee looking for help for the reunion-," he took a deep breath and paused before continuing. "I had been in and out of rehab and was about three weeks sober when the letter came. I was so fucked up and even though I'd detoxed I was still in an empty place, I had lost a lot of weight and looked like I was losing the battle against a horrible disease. I was a fucking mess. I didn't want you to see me that way, so I started seeing a nutritionist, working out and seeing a counselor. But I wanted to make sure you would come, wanted to send you a message that I'd be there- not even knowing or caring, I guess, whether or not you were married. So, I volunteered the band to play three songs that night. The guys were pissed at me but I didn't give a shit because I had this feeling in my gut that you would be there,"

My eyes were still wide from hearing his confession.

"And there you were. I'm not going to lie, there have been a lot of women over the years but I never really cared for any of them or loved them- they were just there and willing. I've done some stuff that I'm not proud of but since September, it's just been you on my mind and in my bed. I've been tempted but I swear I've been faithful to you. Regarding my son– I actually have two children with two different women. I had somewhat of a relationship with one of them, the other it was just a one-night stand," he sighed.

My heart was in my throat.

"I wasn't prepared for how fast success came at us and having access to so much so soon, I was immature and didn't handle myself accordingly. After my second son was born I actually got a vasectomy because I didn't want any more children with random women," he confessed.

I thought I'd been transported to an alternate universe as the room slowly started to spin. I was so dumbfounded that I couldn't open my mouth to respond, so he kept talking.

"Sometimes I feel so lonely. Even with the guys- it's like- I want more and I feel so stupid for even saying that. I mean, I'm making all this money for singing and playing the guitar. I've been all over the world and I know I'm truly blessed. But it's not always what it's cracked up to be. When you were asking me about our future-,"

"Xavier, we don't-," I tried to cut him off. That wasn't a conversation I wanted to have with him anymore.

He walked over to me and grabbed my hands. "You deserve that, a future with someone who's available and wants to a commitment," tears filled his eyes. "And I'm a selfish bastard for even asking this but I want you to wait and give me a chance to get done with this tour, focus on staying sober and be that man because I love you."

This was not how I imagined things playing out at all.

"I slept with Rodney, my ex," I blurted out.

He let go of my hands and I closed my eyes.

"What?" he asked.

I opened my eyes and stared at him. A flurry of emotions from confusion to anger and finally hurt flashed across his face.

"When I found out about your son, I was blown away. I was so hurt that you never told me. And I wondered what else hadn't you told me and I questioned how well I really knew you. Then I had to find out on the news that you were rushed to the hospital in another country and I had no way to get in touch with you," I took a deep breath. "I went to talk to Rodney because he's there, he's always there and I've been able to count on him when you weren't available-,"

"Stop! Okay, just shut up! You knew I was going on tour- *you knew* it would be challenging but you said you understood and you'd try to make this work. And now you're making it my fault that you fucked your ex behind my back!" he yelled angrily.

"I'm not blaming you! It was all me, all my fault. And you're right, I agreed to the long-distance relationship and I never should have because I knew going into it, it wouldn't be enough. I guess seeing you at the reunion all the memories and feelings came rushing back and I thought that maybe, just maybe it was our chance to finish what we started as kids."

"It could've been- how could you do that to me?" he asked in a pained voice.

"I'm sorry. It was wrong and wasn't fair to you or Rodney. And I'm not trying to minimize what I did but Xavier…how could you omit so much about your life!" I shouted. "You have *two* children, you can't have kids, you were an addict and I'm willing to be that's not all and you never bothered to tell me *any* of this," I said angrily. "Would you have even told me if that TMZ video hadn't come out?"

"Well, I guess it wouldn't have mattered anyway since this was obviously a mistake you made," he said bitterly.

"Xavier, I don't regret our time together and getting to know you again. It was amazing but I'm not cut out for this. I need stability. I need honesty, trust, and reliability. And I'm not willing to compromise or wait for you to figure out your situation. I'm sorry," I said strongly.

He glared at me and left the room without a word. I sighed before picking up my bag from the couch and leaving his house.

I'd been able to change my flight and headed back to New York later that evening. I hated things had ended the way they did with Xavier but I couldn't remain in a relationship with him after his confessions not to mention the long distance, it had been over two months since I had even seen him. But most importantly I had to break up with him because I was still in love with Rodney.

I couldn't wait to get back home and back to Rodney. My flight landed at JFK a little after midnight, so I decided to wait and call him the next day. After a fitful night's sleep, I woke up late the next morning, showered and got dressed before walking a few blocks to hail a cab, I'd changed my mind and wanted to see Rodney in person.

When I arrived at his building a group of people were waiting for the elevator and the guard wasn't paying attention, so I blended in with them and got on the elevator. When I made it to Rodney's floor I smiled, we would finally be together and get our chance at a happy ending. However, it wasn't the fairytale reunion I'd imagined.

He scowled at me before stepping into the hallway and closing his door behind him. "What are you doing here?" he whispered harshly.

"I came to talk to you,"

"Talk about what? It's been a week since I've heard from you!" he snapped.

"I know, I've just been making sure-," I started but was interrupted when his door opened.

"Rodney? You're out of- oh, I'm sorry," A woman opened the door, she was barefoot. She gave me a questioning glare before apologizing and closing the door.

Rodney exhaled loudly and muttered, "Damn."

"I've got to go," he said in a clipped tone before going back inside his apartment and leaving me alone in the hallway.

Tears filled my eyes as I backed away from the door. I had apparently waited too long.

When I visited my mom that weekend for Mother's Day, I put on a brave face and pretended all was well but I kept replaying the scene at Rodney's apartment over and over in my head. I'd ended up cutting my visit short and told my mom I wasn't feeling well, which was true. For the rest of the month, I wandered aimlessly through my daily life and worked on autopilot. I couldn't believe things had taken such a drastic turn.

Rodney hadn't made any attempt to contact me but I wasn't over him. I'd even gone to his favorite restaurant to order one of their world famous Italian Crème cakes for his birthday. I'd planned on having it delivered with a letter of explanation. While waiting at the bakery counter, I looked in the restaurant dining room and saw him with the same woman from his apartment. I hurried from the building and walked almost eight blocks in the wrong direction before I'd realized it. For the first time, I considered leaving New York and transferring to another city.

I wouldn't be able to survive seeing Rodney around town with another woman. I imagined one day I'd run into him and they would be holding hands with their son or daughter as they laughed and walked through the city avoiding rain puddles. And it would destroy me.

June

I began to slip into a semi-depressed state and initially considered skipping Christina's wedding because I thought it might make me feel even worse about my situation. I lied and told her I would be out of town on business during her bridal shower but I'd put aside my selfish thoughts and attended the wedding ceremony. Her wedding was beautiful and it had actually made me feel better to witness her happiness. She wore a long white traditional lace gown and veil as she walked down a pink rose-strewn aisle to where Greg stood smiling affectionately at her. They had a small wedding party, which consisted of only two bridesmaids, two groomsmen, and a flower girl. The wedding was in upstate New York and there were over a hundred of she and Greg's family and friends in attendance.

I hadn't talked to Christina in a while, so she wasn't fully aware of everything that had taken place between me and Rodney or me and Xavier. I hadn't wanted to burden her with my drama in the midst of all her wedding planning or dampen her spirits, so when she'd asked, I lied and told her my standard response, "I'm fine."

"Oh my god, thank you so much for being here Angela! I know I have been a horrible friend but as soon as Greg and I get back from our honeymoon, we're having a girl's night to catch up, okay?" she hugged me tightly right before hurrying off to cut the five-tier wedding cake.

After Christina's wedding, I went back to being in a funk, I let calls from my family go to voicemail until my brother threatened to come to New York. So, the next time he called, I answered.

"Hey, why are you stalking me?" I asked playfully.

"What's up with you? Mama's worried about you. You haven't called and you missed Brandon's birthday party,"

"Aw shit, did I- I am so sorry, I'm going to send him something special. What is he into these days?"

"Ang, what's wrong?" he pushed.

"Nothing, I've just been crazy busy," I lied.

"Are you sure? You know you can talk to me," he encouraged.

He was right, I could talk to him about anything but I didn't want my brother to be disappointed in his little sister.

"How was the party?" I asked changing the subject.

I pretended to be listening as he recapped the party and I injected an 'oh really,' 'wow' and 'are you serious' to make it seem like I was paying attention.

"How are things with you and Xavier?" he asked when there was a lull in the conversation and I decided to be honest.

"We broke up," But I didn't say anything else.

"And you're okay with that?"

I laughed. "I'm the one who broke up with him, so yeah I'm good," I assured him.

"What about Rodney, have you talked to him?" he asked cautiously.

"Nope," I said and tried to keep the tremor from my voice. "Have you?" I asked anxiously.

"Nah. Angie, are you sure you okay?" he asked in a frustrated tone.

"I'm fine, everything is fine." I said.

Thankfully he was at work and couldn't talk long, but promised to call me back later.

I'd lied to my brother and told him I was fine, but everything was far from fine. I was so heartbroken that I'd started to get physically ill, unable to keep anything down and was off my game at work. I started spending the day locked in my office, so I wouldn't have to face anyone.

One day after coming from the deli downstairs, my vision started to blur and I felt myself falling. I had fainted at work. When I came to I was on a conference room couch and the company nurse was taking my vitals.

"Do you know what day it is?" she asked shining a penlight in my eye.

"Wednesday, June 16th," I squinted.

"What year?"

"2014," I said annoyed.

"What's your full name?"

"Angela Nicole Barnes and I am fine," I said. Mostly embarrassed than anything that I had fainted at work.

"Ms. Barnes are you on any medication for diabetes or other illnesses?"

"No,"

She started filling out a form and I sat up.

"When was your last period?"

That struck me as an odd question, I looked at her and she stared back at me expectantly.

"Uh-um," I actually couldn't remember. "I'm sure I probably wrote it down- had to be last month some time."

She eyed me before writing a note on the form. She put the clipboard down and grabbed my arm to take my blood pressure.

"You appear to be okay. I recommend following up with your primary care physician and make sure you're eating regularly. And just to be sure, you might want to take a pregnancy test,"

I rolled my eyes. "Sure thing," There was no way I could be pregnant, I thought to myself. Although, I hadn't been taking my birth control pills regularly; I'd been a little distracted by the drama going on with Xavier. Speaking of Xavier, he was sterile and Rodney had used a condom when we had sex. Hadn't he? I tried to think back to that day. I couldn't remember but I was sure Rodney had thought of that.

I didn't make a doctor's appointment but I did buy a pregnancy test from Duane Reade although I knew it would be a waste of money. The cashier raised an eyebrow as she scanned the test and a bag of Reese's mini peanut butter cups. I went back to my apartment and realized I hadn't eaten all day. I tore open the bag of Reese's and poured a handful into my mouth before opening the refrigerator to see if I had anything to eat. There was left over Bang Bang chicken from Café China that I hadn't finished at lunch yesterday. I poured the contents into a bowl and warmed them in the microwave.

I sat down in my office to sort through the nearly two hundred work emails I'd accumulated during the week and ate while I worked. Afterwards, I took a shower and when I emerged I looked at my body in the mirror. I'd actually lost weight from not having an appetite due to the stress of both breakups. I had a little pudge in my stomach, which was probably the result of the chocolate and chicken I'd eaten.

There was just no way I was pregnant. I decided not to take the test and instead arranged my pillows on my bed to watch TV before I went to sleep. At some point, I dozed off and had the strangest dream about being pregnant with twins and when they were born one of them looked like Rodney and the other one looked like Xavier.

I woke up startled and glanced at the clock on my bedside table, it was 3:38 am. I threw the covers back and decided to take the test. It took less than a minute for the bright red plus sign to come in to view. I picked up the box to see if plus meant I wasn't pregnant. My mouth fell open and my hand shook. A plus sign meant you *were* pregnant.

"No, no, oh my God," I said as I slid to the floor holding the stick in my hand.

I didn't know what to do or who to tell or if I should tell anyone. Rodney and I were no longer together and we'd had several conversations where he'd said he never wanted to be a 'baby daddy', regulated to paying child support and weekend visitations. I wouldn't be able to take care of a child alone. Sure, I was financially stable but who would watch the child while I was at work? Who would teach it to walk, talk and how to avoid strangers? I was not prepared or equipped to be a mother. I was terrified.

The right thing to do would probably be to terminate the pregnancy but the more I thought about it, I couldn't kill a baby I'd created with Rodney. Besides I knew he would never, *ever* forgive me if he found out. I'd tell him about the pregnancy but I wouldn't have any expectations. If he didn't want anything to do with the child, I wouldn't force him into a fatherhood role. When the child was old enough I'd just tell him or her their father was a war hero that had died during the war. Although there weren't any current wars going – thank God. Or maybe I'd tell them I'd gone to a sperm bank. But there was plenty of time to think about that later. The most pressing question was the due date? I needed to know how long I had before my life changed forever.

I made an appointment with my gynecologist for the following week to confirm the pregnancy and due date. Once I had all the information then I'd contact Rodney. I was still in shock and slightly panicked when I arrived at the doctor's office a week later.

"Hi Angela, how are you?" Dr. Chowdhury asked entering the exam room.

Dr. Chowdhury had only been my gynecologist for a year after my previous doctor had retired.

"I'm good, totally shocked- but all things considered, good," I said shakily.

"Okay, well let's take a look and see what's going on. This might be a little cold,"

She rubbed a clear jelly-like substance on my stomach. Then she explained she'd be using a fetal Doppler to try and find the baby's heartbeat. *My baby's heartbeat.* My own heart rate accelerated at the thought of hearing a life I was carrying. I desperately wished Rodney was there with me. I'd never planned on having children and I definitely didn't want to be a single mom. How could I have been so careless!

"Hmm," she murmured. She moved the apparatus around on my stomach but there was only the sound of static. She told the nurse that she was going to use another machine.

"Angela, we're going to step out, I need you to undress from the waist down."

"Is everything okay?" I asked as the nurse gave me one of those paper-thin blankets.

"I want to do another test, I'll be right back," she tried to smile comfortingly but I knew something was wrong.

When she returned she used a slim probe that she explained was a transvaginal Doppler, which she would insert into my vagina to detect fetal activity. She said she hadn't been able to locate the baby's heartbeat with the other machine because I was more than likely early in the first trimester, and the transvaginal Doppler would have a better chance at locating the fetus. She flipped a switch and a fuzzy screen came into view. I could feel the probe moving around inside me.

"Oh," she softly as she looked at the screen. I followed her line of sight but I couldn't make out anything.

"What?" I asked.

"I'm sorry Angela, there is no heartbeat. There was the beginning of fetal development but the pregnancy appears to be terminating itself," she pointed to a blob on the screen.

"I don't- I don't understand." I stared at the screen confused. I didn't see or hear anything.

"You're having a miscarriage," she said sadly.

"Well, can you stop it? How did that happen?" I wondered if the wine I'd drank a few days before taking the at home pregnancy test was to blame.

"No, there is no heartbeat or fetal activity. It is not uncommon for this to happen with first pregnancies. Sometimes the body just isn't ready, but it shouldn't affect your ability to conceive again. You can try again in a few months,"

Once I was able to process what she was telling me– I lay back on the table, covered my face and sobbed. I couldn't understand why I was so devastated by the loss of something I said I never wanted. I knew it was probably for the best because even God knew I'd be a horrible mother but it felt like I'd lost Rodney all over again.

"We'll give you a few minutes alone. Take your time and get dressed and when you're ready we'll go to my office and talk," Dr. Chowdhury offered me tissues before she and the nurse left the room.

I stayed in that position for at least another ten minutes before I stood to pull on my underwear and pants. I looked down at my stomach and gently rubbed it.

"I am so sorry." I cried.

A few minutes later as I sat in Dr. Chowdhury's office, she told me again that there was nothing I did or didn't do that had caused the miscarriage. It was just an anomaly that sometimes occurred during pregnancy. She said I had two options, stay at home and let the pregnancy continue to dissolve naturally and that it would be similar to a really heavy period with some cramping or I could come back Friday morning for a dilation and curettage (D&C), which would be an invasive procedure to open my cervix and scrape the uterine lining to remove any remaining pieces of the placenta.

Neither option sounded appealing but I couldn't imagine sitting at home waiting for the baby to be expelled as blood. So, I scheduled the appointment. She said it would be an outpatient procedure but I'd need someone to pick me up and stay with me for a few hours afterward.

I started to cry again at the realization I was all alone. There were really only two people I could call. My brother or Christina. But I didn't want my parents or AJ to know yet. *Or ever.* So, I called Christina.

"Hey, Angela! Oh my god, you must have ESP. I just told Greg I needed to call you now that we're back and settled in." she sounded more bubbly than usual.

"Oh yeah, how was the honeymoon?"

"Incredible! Bali is like paradise on Earth, I swear. We didn't want to leave," she gushed.

"I've heard it's pretty amazing. Well, I'm glad you guys had a good time. I can't wait to see the pictures,"

"We took a million of them. Getting them off the camera will probably take a week," she laughed.

"I um- I really hate to ask but I need a huge favor. I'm having a procedure on Friday and the doctor is insisting that I have someone take me home and stay with me for a couple of hours to make sure I'm okay and then that's it, you can be back at work by lunchtime." I said nervously.

"A procedure? Angela, what's wrong? Are you sick?" she asked concerned.

"No- ah- just some female stuff. They're removing fibroids," I lied and felt awful.

"Oh- okay, yeah my cousin had that done. No fun. What time Friday?"

"Eight o'clock. Mount Sinai,"

"I should be able to make that work, I'll let Alex know-,"

"Can you tell him you have some type of an appointment? I don't really want anyone knowing-,"

"Sure, sure- I'll tell him I have an appointment and I'll be back by lunch,"

"Perfect. Thank you so much, Christina, you're a lifesaver,"

Friday morning Christina met me at the hospital and chatted about her honeymoon while I waited to be called. After I'd been assigned a room, I changed into a hospital gown and signed a million forms releasing the hospital and doctors from liability.

The nurse started an IV and a few minutes later a tall, white man who looked like Brad Pitt entered the room.

"Hi, I'm Dr. Taylor and I will be administering your anesthesia today," he smiled. "Just relax take a few deep breaths."

He moved some items around on a tray and my eyes widened when I saw a huge needle. Dr. Taylor looked down at me and chuckled.

"I'm not going to give you a shot, I promise," he winked. "It's administered intravenously,"

I exhaled and started thinking about what would happen when it was all over. Nobody had to know I was ever pregnant. It would be my secret burden to bear. I imagined if I told Rodney I had been pregnant and had a miscarriage, he'd probably accuse me of making it happen on purpose.

A few seconds passed and I started feeling really drowsy.

"How are you doing?" Brad Pitt smiled at me. What was Brad Pitt doing in my room?

I smiled up at him. He was such a gorgeous white man. And I told him so.

He laughed and then said, "She's ready,"

I heard a loud noise and saw a bright light before I heard Brad Pitt's voice again. "Can you count backward from ten to one?" he asked as he put something over my face. Was he trying to see how long I could hold my breath?

"Ten, nine, twenty," I said and my eyes fluttered closed.

The next time I opened my eyes, Brad Pitt was gone but Dr. Chowdhury was there and she was smiling down at me.

"Hi Angela, how are you feeling?"

"Okay," I croaked out before clearing my throat. I wondered when the procedure would start. "When will you get started?" I asked.

She smiled faintly. "We're all done. You just lay here for a few minutes and let the anesthesia wear off and I'll be back to check on you and give you some instructions for home. Is there someone here to make sure you get home okay?" she asked.

I was stunned that the procedure was over and I hadn't remembered any of it.

"Yes, my friend Christina. She should be in the waiting room."

"Great, I'll have one of the nurses let her know your progress. It should only be another forty-five minutes to an hour and we can release you.'"

And just like that, I was no longer pregnant.

Christina had a Lyft driver waiting for us when I was released. She helped me to my apartment and made sure I was nice and comfortable on the couch. It was only a little past ten o'clock in the morning.

Christina was quiet but she kept giving me curious glances as she flipped through a magazine. We'd been back at my apartment for less than an hour when she finally said what was on her mind.

"Are you sure there's not something else going on Angela? You just seem different," she remarked sadly.

I adjusted the pillow under my head. "I'm good." I smiled faintly.

"You know when I got the position at Clinique, I was so excited that I wasn't at the makeup counter in Macy's. Instead, I got to work for the Estee Lauder corporate headquarters learning the business from the inside out. But when I got to work under you, it was like I'd hit the lottery. Working for one of the only black women at your level, having you as a mentor and eventually a friend meant more than you know. A lot of the other assistants talked about me saying I was doing too much or that I acted like I was a secretary from the 1940's because of the way I took care of you," she smiled. "But my goal was to make sure that you were successful because I knew without a doubt you would make sure I was successful as well, and you did. I am so extremely grateful for everything that you've done for me and-,"

"You deserve it, you worked hard for it Christina." I interrupted not sure where the conversation was headed.

She smiled. "I think that we've established an impenetrable work bond and I would never *ever* betray that but I also consider you a true friend. You can trust me. I know you didn't want me to know about you and Xavier, probably because of how I was fangirling but you-,"

"I was pregnant," I whispered.

"What?" she asked shocked.

"I was pregnant but I lost the baby– had a miscarriage. They did a D&C today to make sure everything was gone," I said softly.

Christina covered her mouth and started to cry. "I am so sorry. I don't know what else to say. Did you tell Xavier?" she asked angrily.

"It wasn't his baby,"

Her eyes widened and she sat back in the chair. "Wha- who?" she asked confused.

"Rodney," I said as a yawned escaped and I wiped my eyes. "He didn't know. We're not- he's seeing someone else," I sighed. "I'm sorry for not telling you, I feel like I'm supposed to be setting an example and I never wanted you to see me as someone whose personal life was such a mess," I sniffed.

"Oh Angela," she moved to sit on the edge of the couch and grabbed my hand. "You're only human and you're allowed to make some missteps."

I told her about me and Rodney and my breakup with Xavier before falling asleep.

When I woke up, I went to the restroom to pee and passed a blot clot and the mild cramping in my pelvic area stopped. After promising her one hundred times that I was okay Christina finally left and said she'd come back to check on me later.

After Christina left I flipped through the TV channels and settled on a marathon of *Diner's, Drive-Ins and Dives* on Food Network. I'd always thought about taking a road trip and going to some of the places Guy Fieri mentioned on the show.

I kept my mind numbed by watching TV for the next few hours but eventually started thinking about Rodney and Xavier. It still hurt that things were over between Rodney and I, but never in a million years did a think another woman would be the reason. If I wouldn't have lost the baby I'm sure Rodney would have been happy, he probably would've broken up with his girlfriend, so that we could be a family. But there definitely wasn't a chance of that happening now.

Speaking of babies, I still couldn't believe Xavier had *two* kids! Two kids that he never mentioned to me and he thought we would just be able to keep moving forward as if nothing happened. Of course, this would be after he went back to rehab *again.*

The best thing for me was to be by myself for a while. I wished both Rodney and Xavier well but my mind was made up– I was taking a sabbatical from men.

I took another nap and woke up to my ringing phone. Christina had called to ask what I wanted for dinner. I ended up ordering Fettucine Alfredo and orzo soup from Blossom Café. Christina dropped off my food but didn't stay long because she and Greg had plans, so she left me alone. Something I was getting used to.

A week passed and I had physically recovered from the D&C however, emotionally I was having a hard time. I continued to keep my head down and work hard; I needed to stay on top of my game so that I didn't end up unemployed.

During the day, my mind was occupied with work and I didn't have much time to think about the baby or Rodney but at home it would hit me like a ton of bricks. I cried myself to sleep most nights and after I fell asleep it would only be a few hours before I started dreaming; it was the same nightmare every time. I would hear a moaning sound and I'd walk to the bathroom and Rodney would be laying on the floor covered in blood asking why I killed our baby.

I realized I needed professional help but a part of me felt like I deserved the emotional punishment. That it was karma.

AJ called me a few days later and announced he would be in New

York over the upcoming weekend.

"Why?" I asked.

"I've got a meeting with a potential investor," he said. "And I want to see you."

That's how Friday evening I ended up face to face with my big brother.

"Have you lost weight?" he asked, his eyes bulging when I opened my apartment door.

"Well, hello to you too," I said offended.

"Sorry, hey Ang," he pulled me in for a hug and held me tightly. I tried to keep my emotions in check.

"So how was the meeting?" I asked after he was inside my apartment. "You want something to drink?"

"Nah- I'm good. The meeting was good, really good. I'm probably going to end up getting another location in Philly *and* New York. That way Paula can have the current shop and I can finally get her to sign those divorce papers."

"Two locations? How much of the business are these investors asking for? You're dealing with reputable people right, not loan sharks?" I asked.

He laughed. "You're funny. Hell no, you think I want somebody breaking my legs or threatening my kids?" he frowned. "It's actually a guy who owns a successful shop here and he's been trying to get something off the ground in Philly too, so we're talking about collaborating."

"Oh, okay. You know who you should have talked to first-,"

He groaned loudly. "I'm not asking our father for one dime."

"I'm just saying, you know he has a lot of money from all that offshore engineering work plus his pension,"

"Yeah, but the last thing I'm trying to do is go into business with family again." He said and then he looked at me. "What's going on with you?" he asked.

"What are you talking about?" I said not making eye contact with him.

"Don't try and play me, *Angela*. You and I both know something is up. Do I need to bring Mama here to get some answers out of you?" he asked angrily. He only called me 'Angela' when he'd had enough of my bullshit.

I sighed harshly.

"I'm worried about you. Does this have anything to do with Rodney living in London part-time?" he questioned.

My eyes widened and I sagged back against the couch.

"He's living in London?" I asked as my voice cracked.

"Shit, you didn't know?"

I couldn't stop the tears even if I wanted to. I started to cry and my brother pulled me into his embrace and rocked me.

"It's okay, it's okay. You're not alone, Angie, talk to me." And so, I did. I told him everything.

He was upset with me for not calling him or Mama to take care of me after the miscarriage but he also said he understood.

"Please, please whatever you do, don't tell Rodney. If I ever see him again, I should be the one to tell him,"

"I agree," he said.

"What about Mama? Are you going to tell her?"

"She's going to ask how our visit went and you know she can see right through both of us. It would probably be better if you told her though," he advised.

When we were kids AJ always softened my mom up for me by telling her things I'd done from breaking a picture frame to sneaking out of the house. It was no secret that he was her favorite, so she'd usually calmed down by the time she dealt with me.

I shrugged. "If she asks and you feel compelled, you can tell her otherwise I'll tell her when I see her."

I picked a piece of lint from my velour sweatpants. "So, Rodney's in London? Did he leave Ernst & Young?" I inquired.

"Nah- he's actually there overseeing an audit or something like that but he said he's practically living there for a few months,"

"Did he um- did he ask about me?"

My brother sighed. "No. He wouldn't. I think if I would have started the conversation it would have given him an opportunity but I really thought it was over this time."

"It is," I said sadly.

"Sounds like there is still some unresolved stuff you need to handle,"

We talked for a few minutes before AJ stood. "I'm going to get some water. Go run a comb through your hair and put something shiny on your lips. Let's get out of this stuffy apartment and go get something to eat."

I smiled at him and got up from the couch to make myself presentable. Instead of doing anything fancy we just walked a few blocks over to get a couple of slices. I hadn't had pizza in ages. It felt good to get out of the house, sit outside and people watch with my brother.

"Hey, I think I might take your advice about seeing someone- a therapist." I said take a long pull from my soda. I looked at him judging his reaction.

"Good for you. I think it will help; I know it's helped me. And now you have all this extra stuff you've gone through," he shook his head. "Still can't believe you didn't call us,"

"I'm sorry," I said again.

He balled up a napkin and threw it at me. "Don't let it happen again!"

"Trust me, it won't," I wasn't necessarily promising that I wouldn't keep something from him again but I definitely wouldn't be getting pregnant again, which meant no more miscarriages. I couldn't handle going through that more than once.

AJ ended up spending the night with me and taking the train back to Philadelphia the next day. A few hours later, my mama called.

"Hey Ma," I said and prepared myself for her scathing words.

"Hey, how you doing? AJ still there?" she asked, which meant she hadn't talked to him.

"I'm good. He left a few hours ago. Have you tried to call him?" I asked concerned.

"Oh no, I'm sure he's fine. I was just asking, calm down." She laughed lightly. "It's just when the two of you get together you tell each other more than you tell me. Just trying to get some information."

Mama never pretended, she didn't know how. She always said what was on her mind.

"About him or me?" I asked.

"Whoever. I've always had to rely on second-hand information. But what I really want to know is what your brother was doing in New York? Said he had a business meeting. Is he trying to move there? He's got two sons, he can't just take up in another city and leave them. They need him around especially with a mama like

Paula," she said and I could tell by her tone that she was more afraid of my brother leaving her.

After all, that's why she'd moved to Philly– to be closer to him. And my dad followed to be close to her. Although they both tried to say they'd moved there to be closer to their grandchildren, I knew the truth.

"He's not moving to New York. It was just a business thing, he's trying to cut ties with Paula." I reassured her.

We talked a little more and my mom kept asking if I was okay, giving me plenty of chances to talk to her but I didn't. I hadn't wanted to admit my failures to her or to myself.

July

*O*ver the next few weeks, I'd started to get back to normal at work and had found a therapist to talk to once a week. Dr. Melanie Walker was helping me work through my issues and according to her, I had a lot of them.

"Why do you think your career is so important to you?" she asked during one of our sessions.

I shrugged. "Because I'm good at it,"

"According to who?"

"What do you mean?" I asked for clarification.

"What makes you think you're good at it?"

"I've been told- I've gotten results, met deadlines, great appraisals," I said with a hint of pride.

"And why is being good at your job important?"

"I don't really understand where this is going," I said in an exasperated tone. She was trying my patience. I came there to talk about my relationship issues and losing my baby, not work.

"I think that perhaps you feel defined by your job and you use it as a crutch," she said nonchalantly and I was instantly offended.

I folded my arms across my chest. "A crutch for what?" I didn't appreciate how she kept referring to it as my *job*, I mean I knew technically that's what it was but I also thought of it as much more than just a job. It was a career, my livelihood.

"That's the question *you* have to answer. But I'll pose another question first– if you lost your job today, what would you do?"

She'd asked me that after our second meeting. I didn't have an answer for her, so she'd given it to me as homework to seriously think about if my job was more important to me than having a relationship. I thought about it for the entire week and had an answer for her when I returned:

"My *career* is important because I'm good at what I do and I can manage the expectations of my role. Even if I no longer have a place at the Estee Lauder companies, I am confident in my abilities and skillset that I can find something else."

She eyed me. "It's about control. You believe you have some measure of control in your professional life that you don't have in your personal life or in your relationships, do you think this is a fair assessment?"

I shrugged. "Maybe."

"Tell me about your childhood. Did you live with both parents?"

"Yes, my parents were married," I said strongly. Not sure why I felt defensive especially since their marriage had ended in divorce before I graduated high school.

She smiled faintly. "Would you say they were happily married?"

I hesitated but told her all about my parents and their marriage.

"I think you have this deep-rooted belief that all romantic relationships between a man and woman are one-sided. That you will have to sacrifice your desires for your man and that once you've done this, he will leave you with nothing," she said simply.

I didn't argue and she continued. "Angela, all relationships just like all people, are different. And I know it sounds cliché but for any relationship to work, communication is vital. If you meet someone that you feel could become important to you, then you must have an honest conversation about expectations. There will most certainly be men who are looking for a conventional relationship where he works and his significant other stays home. But if this is not something you want, there is absolutely nothing wrong with that." She said strongly.

"You shouldn't beat yourself up for wanting to do more because there are also men out there who will support your goals and dreams outside of the home."

Tears filled my eyes as I thought about Rodney.

"But what happens if I have children?" I sniffed.

"There is paid childcare, sometimes you can enlist family to help if that's an option, and if not– both mom *and* dad should work together to adjust their lives and schedules to help take care of the child. There are no written rules that say a child has to become one hundred percent your responsibility."

"I don't think I'd be a good mother. I don't have *any* maternal instincts and I don't want to end up resenting my child,"

She chuckled.

"Every woman that has become a mother, even the ones who look perfect to the outside world, will tell you they were scared and they still are because you're essentially making it up as you go along. No one can predict what a child will grow up to become no matter how much nurturing they receive. And trust me, if you were to become a mother that maternal instinct kicks in automatically. You start loving that child before they are even born."

I thought about the baby I'd lost and knew that was true.

"And if you don't want children, that's okay too. You don't have to feel guilty or feel like you need to have an excuse handy for why."

"I think I'm just scared,"

"Of what?" she asked.

"Failing,"

"Unfortunately, failure is an inherent part of the human experience. You won't always get it right but hopefully you'll learn from your experiences and do better the next time,"

I continued seeing Dr. Walker once a month because I was undergoing an awakening and for the first time had started to see myself clearly. Dr. Walker was right, I had been clinging to my *job* and letting it define me. I felt without it, I would be nothing and I would have nothing. And worse, I'd convinced myself that if I didn't have a job I would have no one and nowhere to turn– that I was all alone in the world, which was not true at all! I had a family who loved me very much and would do anything for me if I needed them. But I believed asking for help was a sign of weakness.

Therapy had helped me understand it was okay to make myself vulnerable and that depending on someone was not a sign of weakness. I was strong and capable but it was okay to allow someone to take care of me every now and then. I'd also realized that I had been using my parent's marriage to sabotage my own relationships and justify my fear of commitment. Yes, my parent's marriage had been flawed but it didn't have to become my reality. Dr. Walker also said I should let go of the guilt from the miscarriage and that it was my choice whether or not to tell Rodney.

Honestly, I was afraid to tell him because I knew he probably hated me and it broke my heart because deep down, I still loved him. I knew it would take some time to get over him but I hoped eventually I'd find someone who I could experience the best of life with, someone to care for me and someone I could care for when life wasn't so great. I wanted a supportive partner that I could count on. I also wanted a chance to be a mother.

After my miscarriage, it had been on my mind a lot. It was a privilege to be able to bring a life into the world and although the world could be a shitty place sometimes, I still wanted to have a family and raise a little human. I wanted the opportunity to create a new family history, develop traditions, leave a legacy and prove that not all families were filled with dysfunction. So, I wasn't completely giving up on the idea of finding love again or having a family. I had faith it would happen one day and when it did, I'd be ready. Until then I'd keep working on myself and loving the woman I was becoming.

August
2014

I hadn't seen Xavier or Rodney since May but one night while watching TV, I saw Xavier on the red carpet at the BET Awards. He was with a woman who looked very similar to crazy Brenda. I didn't know if she was someone he was dating or not and I didn't care. I quickly turned to another channel and started watching a movie.

I visited my mother the following weekend and my brother was hosting a poker game at her house- correction, her *and* my father's house. AJ had purchased a fixer-upper and was currently in the middle of renovations. Since he was already spending money on the house, he'd moved in with my parents to save money.

"Can you take those sandwiches down to the basement?" my mom asked.

I decided to mess with her. "You think if I undo a couple of buttons, I'll get some tips?" I started unbuttoning my shirt.

She laughed loudly. "Girl, with them little tater tots, you'd have to be topless!"

I threw a nearby dish towel at her before picking up the tray and heading to the basement. When I returned to the kitchen she wasn't there, so I started arranging the wings on a platter. I heard somebody come in behind me and assumed it was her.

"I started putting these wings on the platter but I wasn't sure if this is how you wanted them," I turned around and my heart stopped beating for a full second. Rodney stood in the doorway of the kitchen.

"Hello, Angela," he said softly.

My mouth fell open but no words came out. Before I could compose myself, AJ appeared. I narrowed my eyes at him.

"I didn't have anything to do with this! I didn't know Rodney was coming to the game," AJ exclaimed.

"It was all me!" my mom said behind Rodney. He turned and she hugged him tightly. "Hey baby, you're looking good. How have you been?" she asked.

"Good, I'm good," he smiled down at her.

"Glad to hear it. Hopefully before you leave, you and Angela can catch up." She smiled and glided past him into the kitchen. My brother and I were shooting daggers at her but she ignored us.

"Come on Rod, let me get you a beer," AJ said as Rodney turned to follow him from the kitchen.

"Mama! What were you thinking! You are so out of line for this!" I confronted her after they'd left.

"And you were out of line for not telling anybody about your miscarriage," she said angrily and I recoiled. I knew AJ had told her but she'd never said anything about it.

"I'm sorry, I didn't mean for it to come out like that," she said softly. "I know you think I'm a weak, old-fashioned woman. I catered to your daddy, left him only to end up marrying him again. And I know you think you're a modern, strong woman clinging to your career because you're afraid to depend on anybody."

I sighed harshly and turned away from her.

"But I'll tell you something I've learned after my many years of living– in the end, nothing matters but love. If you find someone who loves you and they treat you right and take care of you- that's all that matters. Your daddy isn't a perfect man and I'm not a perfect woman. But no man has loved me more than your daddy and no woman has loved him more than me. And at this point, that's all *we* care about. We're willing to forgive and forget the past, and just do better with this second chance we've been given. But you're not me and your brother is not your father. The two of you have to figure out a way to make your own relationships work without blaming us," she said chokingly.

I turned around and looked at her.

"I just want you to find some long-term happiness that doesn't involve work," she said gently as tears filled her eyes.

I thought about the conversations I'd had with Dr. Walker about releasing my parents from the responsibility of *my* mistakes.

"Mama, I don't blame you or daddy for anything. I take full responsibility for my life and my own mistakes. You and daddy took great care of me and AJ and I'm proud that you're my mom," I smiled at her. "Even when you poke your nose all up in my business, I know it's because you love me. And I'm happy, right now where I am with what I have." I said as my voice cracked.

She shook her head and started to cry. I hugged her tightly before my dad interrupted us.

"Hey, I was um- are the wings ready? I can take them in," he said.

Mama wiped her eyes and smiled at him. "I got it- I'm working for tips!" He shook his head and laughed at her as she picked up the tray and shimmied out the kitchen.

"You okay?" he lingered in the doorway.

I nodded. "Yeah. Hey, I just wanted to say I'm glad everything is working out between you and Mama the second time around," I smiled at him.

"So am I, kiddo," he smiled leaving me alone in the kitchen.

After the game started I grabbed Mama's latest issue of Essence magazine with Michelle Obama on the cover and headed to the front porch. I wanted to disappear so that she wouldn't ask me to take anything down to the basement. I wasn't ready to face Rodney again but about twenty minutes later, the door leading to the house opened and he appeared.

"Hey," I said softly.

"Hey, you mind if I sit?" Rodney pointed to the empty chair next to me.

"No, sure," I said as my pulse quickened. I closed the magazine and stared at him.

He sat down and looked out into the front yard. "So, how have you been?" he asked.

I wondered if my mom or AJ had told him about the miscarriage. I couldn't understand why he was trying to make small talk.

"Okay," I said softly. "What about you?"

"Good. Working in London for a while,"

"AJ mentioned something about that. Another promotion?" I asked.

"No, just a project."

He turned and looked at me. "Are you sure you're okay?"

I narrowed my eyes at him. "Did my mom or AJ say something to you?"

"About what?" he asked genuinely confused. "Your mom just asked me to talk to you and I get the feeling something's going on because she was pretty insistent."

It was now or never. I knew I could probably take this to my grave but it would always be something that would eat away at me if I didn't tell him.

I cleared my throat. "There's something you should know," I

started. "First off, I'm sorry I left your apartment that day. I should have been clear about-,"

He frowned and held up a hand to stop me.

"Rodney, please I have to say this,"

He exhaled harshly and returned his focus to the yard, which made it easier for me to talk without having to look at him in the eye.

"The only reason I wanted to talk to Xavier was to break up with him. I wanted to do it in person, so that there was no confusion. I never intended on staying with him. But then he started making all these confessions and told me he wanted a future with me, so I told him I'd slept with you,"

Rodney lowered his head.

"I told him there was no future for us, because I still loved you. I flew back to New York that same night, but it was too late to call you. So, I came to your apartment the next day to talk. . .but when I saw that woman, I assumed I was too late and that it was time to let you go for good. I was a mess for a few weeks unable to eat or sleep and then one day, I fainted at work,"

"What?" he turned to me eyes wide in shock.

"Yeah, the onsite nurse asked me a battery of questions and at the end of it she suggested I take a pregnancy test,"

Rodney sat back in the chair and ran a hand over his head. "Angela, I don't know that I want to hear this," he muttered.

But I continued talking, this time turning my attention to the yard.

"I figured she was crazy because there no way I was pregnant– oh, I should back up here, Xavier has not one but *two* children from two random relationships and he got a vasectomy after the second one." I exhaled harshly. "Anyway, I went to Duane Reade and bought a test and it confirmed that I was pregnant," I took a shaky breath.

He stood. "Angela, what are you saying?"

I stood to face him, determined to finish. "I went to my doctor a week later and she did additional tests but couldn't find the baby's heartbeat-," I paused and bit my trembling lip as I stared down at the discarded magazine in my chair. "I was in the process of losing the baby. I had a miscarriage," I said with my eyes trained on the image of the First Lady.

"Was the baby *mine*?" he whispered.

I nodded.

"Oh god," he groaned. "Why- why didn't you call me?" he asked angrily.

"I was going to but the baby died," I cried. "And I thought you'd blame me."

He was silent and when I looked up at him, tears were streaming his face.

"I- I don't know what to say. I'm so sorry you had to go through that alone," he said remorsefully. "Were you- you were going to have the baby? I thought-," he his face was twisted in confusion.

I shrugged. "I couldn't have destroyed a life that we created together. It was hard- still is when I think- I never thought I could be so shattered by the loss of something I always told myself I didn't want," I admitted through my own tears.

He stepped forward, pulled me to him and wrapped me in a tight embrace.

"I'm sorry," I said clinging to him.

We held on to each other for a few minutes mourning our loss.

Rodney was the first to let go. He wiped his faced and stared down at me.

"So, how are you- physically. You okay?" he asked carefully.

"I'm good– the doctor said it was pretty common especially with first pregnancies. She said I shouldn't have any problems in the future,"

He nodded his head. "That's good, wow, I still can't believe–," he sighed heavily before clearing his throat. "Is it really over between you and Xavier?" He asked. I could tell by his tone, he was skeptical.

I wiped my face and sniffed. "Yes. I haven't seen or talked to him in almost four months," I looked him in the eye. "But things were over long before then."

He scratched his head and turned his attention to the yard again before looking back at me. He exhaled and took a few shaky breaths.

"I'm about to go on a beer run. You want to come?" he asked.

I smiled at him and got a strange feeling of déjà vu. This was exactly how things had started between us all those years ago.

There's always another side of the story. . . .

Xavier

I stood under the shower and let the hot water run over my head, shoulders, and down my back. I closed my eyes and reached for the controls to increase the pressure. The force of the water combined with the temperature felt good against my aching muscles.

After washing up twice, I turned off the water and stepped into the steam filled bathroom. I dried my hair and upper body before wrapping the towel around my waist. When I wiped away the condensation on the bathroom mirror and my face came into view, I winced. I looked like shit. The eye mask treatment I'd gotten earlier hadn't worked. I guess sleep was what I really needed to get rid of the bags and dark circles.

I opened my medicine cabinet and grabbed the Visine. I put two drops in each eye and blinked as the liquid ran out.

Soul Skylight had been on tour for almost a year and we still had five dates left. After my meltdown in Berlin, we'd taken two-months off and two weeks ago we started up again. I thought I'd have a chance to get back on track, dry out and spend some much-needed time with Angie. I would have never *ever* thought that she would not only break up with me but also tell me she had fucked her ex behind my back.

I remembered when I first told the band that I wanted us to play at my high school reunion:

"Are you fucking serious? A high school reunion?" Eric had asked angrily. "What's next? Are we going to start doing weddings and birthday parties?"

"For real! What the fuck, man?" Chris chimed in.

"This is about that chick, right? Angie?" Johnny asked.

Johnny knew me too well. "What? No- why you trippin'? It's my fucking high school reunion. I just want to do something nice. We'll do three songs and be out. No big deal."

"Bullshit, how much we getting paid?" Eric asked.

"If you guys do this favor for me- I'll give up my L.A. split," I offered because I knew money motivated those greedy bastards!

After I'd convinced them to perform, we finished rehearsal and were headed our separate ways when Johnny stopped me.

"So, what's up, man? Why you still hung up on some chick you fucked in high school?" he asked.

I didn't bother telling him I'd never had sex with Angie. We came close but I ended up not going through with it because I was young, stupid and in love with her. I'd let something I overheard her say actually hurt my feelings. I couldn't believe what a dumbass I'd been.

"I told you, I'm just doing a favor for the school, this has nothing to do with her," I lied. It had everything to do with her. I only wanted to do it because I hoped she would be there.

"Okay, whatever. Does she know you have a drinking problem? Huh? Or what about your kids?" he'd asked smugly.

Of course, she didn't. I hadn't seen her in over fifteen years. And during that time, I had changed a lot and not necessarily for the better. When it came to anything that would make me feel invincible against the increasing pressures of being in this business or numb the pain of loneliness– I overindulged. That included women, alcohol and occasionally drugs. It was a weak man's move but it helped me cope.

Johnny wasn't throwing my failures in my face because he was a dick- well, he actually was a dick sometimes but he was also my friend and didn't want me to set myself up for disappointment.

"For the last time, this has nothing to do with her," I packed up my guitar and left the studio.

I had almost ten months to prepare before the reunion, so I went to rehab (for the second time), hired a nutritionist and a personal trainer to get in shape just in case she was there. And I really wanted her to be there. I'd always felt our time had been cut short. But at the same time, I wasn't sure that we would've made it back then. She was headed to college and I barely graduated high school. We probably would've ended up breaking up anyway but I hated I'd walked away from her.

I don't know why I'd wanted to see her so bad. I guess because I'd been holding on to the idea of her and writing songs about this perfect girl I used to know and I wanted to see how she turned out. Or if she'd thought about me as much as I'd thought about her.

The thing I'd always admired about Angie back in the day, was that she seemed so unfazed by the external things like appearance or being popular. She was her own person. Not to mention, I could talk to her about anything and never worried that she would judge me or tell anybody my business. I hadn't had a friend like her since high school.

Two weeks before the reunion, we performed at a Saudi prince's celebration in Abu Dhabi and while out sightseeing the day before, I ran into one of Angie's friends from high school. This skinny chick named Sharon, who talked entirely too fucking much. Sharon wasn't so skinny anymore; she had packed on some serious weight, I barely recognized her. She told me Angie was engaged and I was pissed but tried to act unbothered when she told me. It was crazy as hell for me to be mad about Angie being engaged, I mean she was my high school girlfriend for one year and I hadn't seen her in fifteen years, so of course, she had moved on with her life. But to hear that she had a fiancé and not a husband- it was like I could've still had a chance up until he put that fucking ring on her finger. I wanted to back out of performing at the reunion but after I'd made such a big deal about it to the fellas, I was stuck.

By the time the date of the reunion rolled around, I'd made a complete physical transformation and looked like my old self but I was still disappointed about Angie's fiancé. I knew he had to be legit because the girl I remembered didn't take any shit or play games. He was probably some corporate guy with all kinds of degrees.

After we'd performed at the reunion, I told the guys that I was going to catch up with some old friends and sent them back to the hotel. Then I spent twenty minutes peeking through a slit in the stage curtain to see if I could spot Angie. There were quite a few people in attendance, more than I thought would show up. But I suppose a free concert was the incentive.

I was about to give up when I spotted her talking to a group of people. She looked over her shoulder towards the stage and for a second, I thought she saw me but she turned away and a minute later headed out the side door of the auditorium instead of the main exit.

I walked down the narrow backstage hallway that led from the auditorium to the band room and then snuck through the kitchen and out the back door to make my way outside. Nothing could have prepared me for coming face to face with her after all the time that had passed. I'd still felt that same spark and unexplainable feeling of safety, like I was home.

It was obvious that she'd changed, at least on the outside. She was a beautiful, grown woman now. Her brown skin glowed, her deep-set eyes made her look like she had some dark, dirty secrets and those lips of hers formed the perfect, kissable pout. She'd always had a nice ass but not much up top in the breast department however her small waist and hips more than made up for it.

When she told me she was no longer engaged, I couldn't hide my excitement. *She wasn't taken.* I only had one thought: make her mine.

I couldn't believe she'd agreed to come to my hotel room that night, probably because I'd told her I didn't expect anything but truthfully, I wanted her naked the moment I found out she was available. And I'd gotten my wish.

Honestly, I thought the sex would be better our first time together but she was probably nervous and part of her was still a good girl at heart. But she had potential. All good girls wanted a man to bring that freak out of them and I was definitely up for the challenge.

Since I'd just gotten her back and didn't want to lose her, I did something incredibly stupid– I told her I wanted a relationship with her. I knew I would be on the road for at least six months and it would be challenging to be in a relationship but whenever I was with her my better judgment went out the window.

I didn't tell her about my kids up front because I knew if I told her, she wouldn't have given me a chance and I really wanted another chance to be with her. I just hoped that we'd be able to make a long-distance relationship work.

Once the tour started, it had been easy to dodge the women but dodging the alcohol and occasional drugs was a challenge. I'd did it for the most part with only one or two slip ups here and there at the beginning of the tour. And considering my previous record, that was pretty fucking spectacular.

But soon the distance started to become an issue and she wanted to know where the relationship was headed. I really enjoyed being with Angie and the sex did get better but I didn't know if I could see myself married to her. First of all, if I ever got married, it would probably be after I turned forty and I wanted a wife who would be available to me. A woman who would drop everything to come see me or be waiting for me at home. I wanted to be the provider. Angie was way too focused on her job. She talked about it all the time and I didn't even really understand what she did.

After a few months, the performing started to wear me down, I think mostly because I'd never performed so many shows in a row. My fingers had started to blister and swell from playing the guitar. I had to soak them in ice water after every show. As time went on, me and Eric started arguing during rehearsals and after shows, and for the first time I started to think about a future without Soul Skylight. My manager told me I should do a solo album while the group was still hot and I was still relevant.

After the solo album, I could move behind the scenes and produce. I knew Angie would be supportive of me not performing because she wanted us to settle down in the same city. But I sure as hell wasn't moving back to New York.

The day before the band was supposed to leave for Amsterdam, I'd found out I was about to be served with papers to appear in court to renegotiate the NDA and child support payments for my son, Gabriel. I called Angie that same afternoon to finally tell her about my kids. I'd never planned on keeping it from her so long but I didn't see her that often and when we were together we were busy catching up and planning the next time we'd get to talk or see each other, so it never seemed to be the right time.

When I called, she didn't answer but she'd texted me a little later and told me her dad was in the hospital. When I got the chance to talk her, she sounded really scared. She and her father weren't even that close, so I didn't understand why she was so upset. But that gave me the perfect opportunity to leave town before the process server caught up with me. I'd told the guys that I was concerned about Angie and would meet them in Amsterdam.

Her family had always reminded me of the Cosby's. Even when her parents divorced I got the feeling her dad was still around in some way. I'd never even met my father. Before my mama died, she told me he was a drug addict who had been and in and out of jail. I ended up going to live with my grandmother and I'd turned out okay. Not to mention, I had avoided all the bullshit family drama in the process. Except for one time this chick showed up at a radio station claiming to be my long, lost sibling. Truthfully, she probably could have been my sister but I'd lived over thirty years without a brother or sister at that point and wasn't interested in gaining one.

Angie's brother was an overprotective asshole. That's probably how she had managed to stay a virgin for so long when we were in high school; he seemed like a world class cock blocker. Her mama was really nice looking for an older lady, I saw where Angie got her looks.

I'd expected to meet the two of them at the hospital, and maybe even her dad but I hadn't counted on seeing her ex. *Rodney.* Corny ass name for a corny ass dude. He didn't really seem like her type. Too straight-laced and serious. But he had probably let her run all over him, which is why the relationship more than likely ended. I could tell he was just as shocked as she was to see me at the hospital. He tried to play it cool but I could see it all over his face, he was big mad and jealous. I totally wasn't worried or intimidated by the fact that he was there in Philly with her. He'd had his chance and lost it.

Me and Angie had a brief conversation about the future and she'd said she didn't think she wanted to have children, which was perfect since I couldn't have any. I'd almost told her about my kids during that conversation but it seemed inappropriate since her dad had just come out of surgery. She probably wouldn't have handled it well. Not that it was a big deal, a lot people our age had kids and it's not like I had custody of them. She'd never even have to see them if she didn't want to but sometimes women flipped out over the smallest shit.

I stayed a few hours with Angie at the hospital and after it looked like her father would be okay, I'd made arrangements for a flight and car.

We went back to her hotel room across the street when visiting hours were over and had sex against the bathroom counter with all our clothes on. I had tried not to come before her but I couldn't hold back knowing I was about to be abstinent for almost two months unless she flew to Europe to see me. I didn't understand why she couldn't take time off from her job. If it was me, I would've jumped at the chance to see another continent for free.

The international tour started off great but I couldn't outrun the family courts. I was subpoenaed to come back to L.A. for a hearing. The night before the hearing I'd met my attorney, India for dinner to talk about our strategy. Somebody must have posted a picture on social media because the next thing I knew, there were paparazzi outside the restaurant and one of them was from TMZ.

The thing about TMZ was that they didn't just post random pictures, they investigated and added a story, which was usually true. I decided to jump in front of it and called Angie to tell her but I'd lied and said it was a business meeting. It all came back to bite me in the ass a week later. Angie had done her own investigating and found out I had a kid. And she was pissed.

I knew the media was about to have a field day with my ass and it would no doubt cause bad PR for the band. I needed to have someone with a solid reputation in my corner. I needed Angie to help get me through this but when she hung up on me, I figured it was probably too late.

That same night I made a very bad decision and hung out with Eric. I started drinking again and for the next few dates, I smoked a shitload of weed before going on stage. But one night I felt like I was crawling out my skin and I needed something to take the edge off so, I did a couple of lines of cocaine before performing three shows back to back. The effect of that shit in my system plus the fatigue and growing anxiety about Angie breaking up with me was too much.

I remembered going on stage in Berlin and after about two songs, the entire stadium started titling, my vision blurred and then everything went dark. I woke up almost six hours later in a German hospital hallucinating and had to be restrained. I was losing my mind and in that moment, I had an overwhelming desire almost a primal need to see Angie. She was my safe place; she always had been. I didn't want to become a cliché, a dead singer OD'ing on drugs or getting burned out on alcohol.

I wanted more out of life. I needed to get my shit together. For her. For me. I told the fellas I wanted to take a break from the tour. I had to get back on track. I decided to come clean to Angie about everything– both kids, the alcohol and substance abuse because I believed I loved her and we could have a nice life together.

And then she came and shit all over my dreams.

It's been months but I still think about her and her betrayal. Out of all the women I'd ever been with she was the one I never expected to cheat on me. I guess the reason it fucked me up was because I'd been totally faithful to her.

I put on some body spray and lotion before pulling on my faded jeans and a t-shirt. I tried to get the thoughts of Angie out of my head. That relationship was over and I needed to move on. I think had we reconnected in another five years I would have been more stable, mature and ready for a relationship with a woman like her. But I guess I'll have to always wonder. How fucking ironic!

"Mr. Ross, the car is here," Julia knocked on my bedroom door just as I finished putting on my shoes. She'd been my personal assistant for the past year, running my household and taking care of me. She reminded me of my grandmother but she was only around fifty-five.

"I'm nervous," I admitted when I opened the door.

"It's going to be fine," she smiled. But I wasn't totally convinced.

I was headed to a supervised visit with both my kids.

Gabriel was five and I'd met his mom at an after party right as Soul Skylight was taking off. We'd won a best new artist Grammy that year. I was drunk and barely remembered being with her, so when she showed up six months later saying she was pregnant I totally denied it. I didn't even know her name. But after Gabriel was born I took a paternity test and it came back at 99.9% positive. I was so fucking mad at her; she was a gold-digging bitch trying to ruin my career. I'd offered her some money, which she eagerly took, and a monthly stipend to sign a non-disclosure agreement, so that she wouldn't tell anyone I was the father.

Two years later a similar situation happened but this time I knew the woman and had been hanging out with her off and on. I'd told her about what happened with Gabriel's mom and how it had devastated me, so I never thought she'd be telling me the same thing less than two years later. I wasn't even going to bother with a paternity test for Zachary but my attorney had insisted when it was time to set up monthly child support payments.

I couldn't believe I'd let *two* women get me back to back with babies. The last time I'd gotten somebody pregnant was in high school. My girlfriend, Kim got pregnant during our junior year. But she got an abortion and then her family ended up moving that summer to Atlanta. I'd tried to be careful after that but most of the time I had sex I was drunk or high, so wearing a condom wasn't always the first thing on my mind. I guess that should have been a sign when I met Gabriel's mom. I mean what self-respecting woman lets a man she just met- celebrity or not- fuck her raw? I felt like I had learned my lesson but just in case, I scheduled an appointment for a vasectomy. Johnny had been angry at me for that decision.

"Are you for real? Man, you're only thirty-one! Why the fuck would you do something so stupid?" he asked angrily.

"Because I don't want any more kids from random women,"

"Well stop having sex with random women, dumbass! Or have you never heard of condoms?"

"Why you so fucking worried about what I'm doing? It's my dick, my decision!" I'd yelled at him.

"First of all, it's not your dick, it's your scrotum and the fact that you don't know that means you shouldn't be doing it and second what if you meet a woman, ten years from now, that you want to marry and she wants kids? That shit is permanent, X,"

Despite Johnny's objections, I'd had the procedure done and so far, I hadn't regretted it. However, I didn't use my vasectomy as an excuse to have unprotected sex, there were some nasty ass women out there and not the good kind of nasty. I wasn't trying to get any STD's, so I still wrapped up even though I couldn't get anybody pregnant.

Hopefully whoever I ended up with had kids or didn't want any kids, like Angie. I still couldn't believe how I'd fucked that up.

"Here, this one is for Gabriel he loves Spiderman. And this is for Zachary he likes cars," Julia gave me two gift bags with stuff for the boys.

I was glad their mothers had allowed the visits to take place together. It would not only be a chance for them to meet each other but it would also save me time. I had to be in the studio the next day to start working on some solo material.

I was still under contract to do one more Soul Skylight album but I was done being at the mercy of what the guys wanted to do, which usually wasn't what I wanted to do. Plus, I needed to be in a different, more positive environment. Me and Eric were currently beefing because I was one hundred percent sure he had given me some funky drugs that had put me in that hospital in Berlin. He swears he didn't but I'll always believe otherwise.

I think he was mad at me because he'd found out that I'd actually had sex with Brenda. But in my defense, it was before he started keeping her around like she was his woman. When he asked me, I lied and she'd been lying too but after Brenda had one too many drinks one night, she'd confessed. I think she was intentionally trying to start shit because after I slept with her that one time, I pretty much iced her out. She wanted to keep hanging out and I'd turned her down, so I guess she thought being with Eric would make me jealous. It didn't. I believe seeing me with Angie in Denver is what pushed her over the edge.

"Gabriel, Spiderman. Zachary, cars. Got it. Anything else I should know?" I asked Julia.

"Yes, this is not a business meeting. These are *your* children. Boys need a strong male role model and it's your responsibility to be one. Time to stop being selfish." She said sternly.

I nodded my head after her chastisement because she was right, it was my responsibility and I had to own up to my mistakes. Besides I had a lot in common with them already. They didn't ask to be born and I didn't ask to be a father. Okay, maybe that was a bad example. But I was hopeful that we could find something to bond over. I'd never really been into superheroes, so I didn't know shit about Spiderman and I wasn't really into cars. I actually employed a driver even in L.A. I also didn't have a father growing up, so it's not like I'd had a good example to follow.

Once we arrived at the Zimmer Children's Museum my driver, Teddy opened the door and I got out and squinted at the sunlight before putting on my sunglasses. I walked away from the car and heard Teddy clear his throat behind me, "Mr. Ross," he called.

I looked back over my shoulder and he held the gift bags toward me.

"Thanks," I took the bags and sighed heavily. As I slowly walked to the front door, I seriously thought about turning around and telling Teddy to take me to the airport. I could get on a plane and disappear for a little while. But if I left, I'd never come back and I didn't want it on my conscience that there were two boys out in the world with me for a father and they didn't know me or worse they did and thought I was a piece of shit.

I decided Julia was right, I needed to stop being selfish. I was going to prove to everyone that I could be a good father, a good person. That I was more than Xavier Ross, lead singer of Soul Skylight. My boys wouldn't have to look up to Spiderman, they would have me. I would be their hero.

Rodney

"*N*ext in line," the customer service representative called out. She was a mousy looking girl with freckles, jet black hair and thick glasses.

I looked around to make sure I was next before I walked to the counter.

"Hi welcome to Hertz, how can I help you?"

"Yes, I have a car reserved for Rodney Anderson," I said as I handed her my printed reservation, credit card, and driver's license.

"Great, let me take a look," she smiled. She took the paper and the cards from me before entering information into the computer. "Here we go, Mr. Anderson I show we have you in a full-size car for two days, is this correct?"

"Yes,"

"Awesome, we have a Nissan Altima available and a Chevy Malibu would either of these cars work for you?" she smiled.

"The Altima sounds good."

"Got it. Mr. Anderson are you in San Diego for business or pleasure?" she asked as she typed more information into the computer.

I chuckled before answering, "A little of both,"

I was actually in town to see my mother. I hadn't seen her since Christmas when I came to visit her and her husband, Harold. They'd left Sacramento and moved to San Diego almost ten years ago.

When I came to visit at Christmas my mother was both surprised and somewhat relieved that I was alone. Even though Angela and I had been separated for almost a year at this point, I'd never mentioned our break up to my mother. I'd even told her that Angela had moved to Houston with me.

I hated lying to her but she had this irrational contempt for Angela. She felt I could do better.

"She's selfish. And she won't make a good wife," My mother had said this to me, in private, after the first time she'd met Angela. I figured she was just finding it hard to let her only child go, it never occurred to me that she might be right.

I merged on the I-5 and my thoughts started to wander as I focused on the road ahead. It had been a crazy year and a half. After my breakup with Angela, I had found it hard to truly move on. Mainly because I was still in love with her but I'd also invested too much time and energy into that relationship to just walk away.

I was thirty-seven at the time and the thought of starting over with someone new gave me anxiety. I'd always thought I'd be married with at least one child by the time I was forty but it just wasn't meant to be.

When Angela and I first got together, I immediately liked her because she was smart, ambitious, extremely supportive, kind and she had an unusual sense of humor. Finding out she was a foodie and liked going to Broadway shows and art exhibits convinced me that she was the perfect woman for me.

Not to mention, she was beautiful. A natural, classic beauty who didn't have to do much to accentuate her looks. She had flawless, golden brown skin and deep-set eyes filled with wonder and her body was like that of a goddess.

Even though I'd believed she was the perfect match for me, she had her flaws. She was horrible at communicating her feelings and she was also a little insecure. I understood that her parent's marriage had been an awful blueprint for her own relationships but I thought the more I loved and supported her, the more she would see it was okay to trust me.

And for a while, I thought I'd won her trust and that we were on the same page about our future. We'd both keep advancing in our careers after getting married and eventually having kids. I never had any expectation that she would become the sole caregiver. I'd asked her to marry me, she was my best friend and I truly wanted to spend the rest of my life with her. She'd said yes but would always stall or come up with excuses about setting a date. I'd wanted us to have a couple of years together alone before we had kids. Then she started with the incessant comments about how great it was *not* to have kids.

We'd traveled to Paris the month following our engagement and were standing at the top of the Eiffel Tower looking out at the city when she turned to me and said, "We definitely couldn't do this is if we had kids." I'd disagreed with her because the kids could stay with her mom, my mom or her brother, or if they were old enough they could travel with us.

When we were out at one o'clock in the morning looking for pizza she'd said, "Aren't you glad we don't have kids. Otherwise, you couldn't be out here at one o'clock in the morning looking for pizza."

And she'd made similar comments if we were drinking cocktails at home or watching R-rated shows on HBO. So, one night I confronted her about it when we were getting ready for bed. I stood in the doorway of the bedroom after brushing my teeth, "Angela do you want to have kids?" I asked. It was a simple question. And only required a simple answer of yes or no. But she'd replied with a shrug of her shoulders.

"Is that a no?" I'd asked for clarification.

"I don't know- I'm not sure whether or not I want to have kids," she said softly.

"But you told me you wanted to have kids. *Several times.* We even joked about what our kid would look like and whose personality traits the child would have," I reminded her.

"I'm not cut out for motherhood," she said firmly and that was the end of the conversation.

I didn't say anything else. I told her I was going to do some work in the office and for the first time since we'd moved in together, I slept on the couch and she slept alone in our bed.

Things became tense after that because I felt she'd misled me. It was her prerogative not to want children and I wasn't going to try and convince her otherwise or make her feel guilty, but it made me rethink our entire relationship. Could I sacrifice not having kids to be with Angela for the rest of my life?

I wasn't certain that I could. Or that I wanted to.

When I'd heard about the assignment in Houston, I'd volunteered because it wasn't long term and I'd needed some space to contemplate my next move. I never really thought it would be the end of the relationship but subconsciously maybe that's what I'd wanted.

I asked her to come with me and pretended to be upset when she said she didn't want a long-distance relationship. But neither did I. Maintaining a relationship when you lived in the same apartment or the same city with a person was challenging enough but another state it would be virtually impossible.

In my mind, I suppose I thought we were taking a break. I'd even told her to keep the engagement ring. When I first got to Houston I was so busy I didn't have much time to reflect on the relationship and pretty soon, months had passed and I hadn't really been in contact with Angela and I started to miss her. She'd called me a few times to ask questions about something at the apartment, which she'd kept, but the conversations were awkward as hell and lasted only a minute or two at the most.

Whenever something happened that I thought she would find interesting or funny, I realized I could no longer call and tell her about it. So, I'd decided to call and apologize for leaving the way I did. She cried and said she was sorry too. I assumed for lying about wanting to have a child.

A month later, I was in New York on business and after the meeting, I'd met Angela for dinner. We had a great night out reminiscing about the good times and I realized that I'd made a huge mistake by leaving her. We ended up at her apartment and it felt so good to have her wrapped in my arms, I thought we were on our way to reconciling but she pulled away and told me she didn't think we were each other's destiny. I had planned to prove her wrong. I never anticipated that she'd start seeing someone else before I got the chance.

I felt so betrayed and stupid for longing for her and trying to win her back despite the fact that she didn't want kids. I couldn't believe she'd started a long-distance relationship with a former high school boyfriend that was a musician.

After I'd moved back to New York, I kept my distance from Angela because I hadn't wanted to interfere with her new relationship and I needed to focus on finding someone who wanted the same things I wanted out of a relationship. I met a few nice women but none of them were really my type. At least that's what I told myself. But the truth was- none of them was Angela.

I hadn't been in contact with Angela for a couple of months when I got the text from her brother about the monthly poker game he was hosting at his apartment. It had been a while since I saw Allen and the rest of the guys, so I decided to drive to Philly for a guy's night.

Allen and I had a strict rule about not discussing Angela, so neither of us brought up her name. But their mother, Ms. Gloria had stopped by to pick up Allen's kids and Allen told me she was probably going to tell Angela she'd seen me. I'd shrugged it off because I was more than certain Angela didn't care about me playing poker with her brother.

It wasn't until she showed up at my office the following Monday, that I realized I was wrong. She came under the pretense of telling me to stay away from her family, which if she were serious about she could have called or texted. But I knew the real reason she had come– she missed me. Probably just as much as I'd missed her. I didn't fully understand her relationship with the musician but Angela was a very outgoing person and him being unavailable was definitely going cause problems in their relationship.

When my assistant interrupted my meeting to tell me there had been an accident and Angela was hurt, I thought she'd lied just to get me to talk to her again but when I saw her on the paramedic stretcher, my heart leapt to my throat. Although it was only a sprained ankle, I didn't like the idea of her being hurt in any way. I took her back to her apartment after we'd left the emergency room and she'd practically begged me to be her friend.

I knew without a doubt that wouldn't be enough for me but I felt as long as the door was open and she was inviting me into her life, that I still had a chance. We went to a play together, had a few phone conversations and even texted while watching our favorite show. It started to feel like old times and then her father had a heart attack.

Allen called and asked me to bring her to Philadelphia and I didn't hesitate. I never thought for a second her boyfriend would show up. I understood that he was the one in a relationship with Angela, but he just didn't seem all that reliable. *Xavier*. I wondered if that was even his real name. It sounded made up. Women probably found him attractive but he looked rough and worn out to me.

I knew by the look on Angela's face she was shocked to see him and had no idea he would show up. But it still hurt and was just another reminder that she wasn't mine anymore.

I had gone on a few dates with a lady I'd met at the gym named Janet but avoided moving too fast because I still had feelings for Angela. But after coming face to face with Xavier, I was determined to let go of the fantasy in my head about being with her.

Janet and I started spending more time together. She was an attractive and outgoing woman, actually two years older than me with a teenage son. I doubted that we had a real future together but she was a good distraction. One weekend while her son visited his father, she invited me over for a home cooked meal. It was delicious! Angela was a terrible cook. I dabbled in the kitchen but could only make a decent breakfast, so it was a good change of pace.

After a few glasses of wine, she mentioned it had been almost two years since she'd been intimate with anyone. She hadn't had sex since she got divorced. It had been almost a year for me. So instead of going home that night, I stayed with Janet and we had sex on practically every surface of her apartment.

The sex was wild, uninhibited and satisfying but I'd felt empty afterward lying next to a woman who I felt no real connection to, she'd just helped me satisfy a sexual itch. I lay awake listening to the soft sounds of her snoring wondering where Angela was in that moment.

Janet and I continued to go out but I'd started to get really busy at work, so we didn't see each other that often, which was for the best since I felt things had started moving too fast.

It was almost two months before I saw Angela again, she'd showed up at my apartment drunk and we had a long overdue conversation about what had really brought our relationship to an end. I was even more conflicted after we talked, and I think she was too. I decided not to push since we both were seeing other people.

I was surprised when she came back to my apartment later that morning. Janet and I had worked out together and she'd left my apartment about fifteen minutes before Angela showed up. I answered the door wearing a towel because I'd just gotten out of the shower. Angela asked to come in and find her phone. I knew her very well and seeing me in nothing but a towel had flustered her. My ego got a kick out of it and for reasons beyond my comprehension, I started flirting with her and she flirted back. One thing led to another and soon we were naked in my bed. It felt like no time had passed between us. It was mind-blowing and beautiful.

I was convinced that making love meant we were getting back together. I would break up with Janet and she would break up with Xavier. But instead, she told me she needed to talk to Xavier and let him explain why he had lied to her about having a kid even though she'd said the relationship with him was a mistake. I didn't understand why she couldn't do it over the phone. I figured if she went to see him, he'd find a way to make her stay with him.

My heart couldn't take it anymore. I told her I was going to take a shower and I wanted her gone when I got out. The entire time I was in the shower I prayed she would still be there but she wasn't. I stayed in bed for the rest of the day wrapped in sheets that still smelled like her. And I suddenly remembered we hadn't used a condom. But Angela was adamant about not wanting kids, so I'd assumed she was still on the pill but still mentally chastised myself for being so careless.

The following week Janet came over and we were watching a movie on Netflix when someone knocked on the door. I went to answer it while Janet was in the bathroom, I thought it was the pizza we'd ordered. I was stunned to see Angela. She stood on the other side of the door smiling at me. It really pissed me off that she'd had the nerve to not call me for over a week and then come to my apartment smiling like I should be happy to see her.

Before she could say why she was there, Janet appeared at the door looking for me. I'd never even told her about Angela. Well, not specifically, I'd mentioned I'd been engaged before and things hadn't worked out.

After Angela left, Janet had asked me who she was, I'd told her a crazy ex-girlfriend that I hadn't talked to in a long time. It was mostly true. I could tell Janet wasn't happy about another woman showing up at my apartment but we hadn't defined our relationship as being exclusive, so I left it alone and tried to salvage the rest of the evening.

When I'd returned to work that Monday our managing partner asked me to assist with the opening of another office in London the following month. I considered it divine intervention and the perfect way for me to get away from New York to clear my head again.

I broke up with Janet, mainly because I was going to be working overseas and also because I didn't feel the same way about her that she felt about me. She deserved someone that was going to make her a priority.

I stayed busy in London and time passed quickly. However, unlike when I had been in Houston, I didn't miss Angela with such an ache and intensity as before. There was a part of me that would probably always love her but I was finally learning to live without her. I didn't know if she'd broken up with Xavier, but I hoped so. Not so that we could be together but because she also deserved someone who would make her priority.

When I'd gotten the group text from Allen about the monthly poker game, I'd initially declined. I hadn't expected his mom to call me.

"Hey Rodney, how you doing?" she asked and I could tell by her voice she was smiling.

"Hi, I'm fine. How are you?" I asked confused by the call.

"I'm great but my daughter not so much," she sighed.

"O. . . k, well you know Angela and I aren't together anymore," I said a little more tersely than intended.

She chuckled. "Technicality. But you'll always be her only true love."

A lump formed in my throat. "I don't know about that,"

"When's the last time you talked to her? You really need to talk to her. She has something important to tell you."

"My number hasn't changed," I said. I wondered what was so important that her mother had called me. Maybe she wanted to tell me she and Xavier were getting married.

"She'll be at my house during Junior's poker game. Maybe you'll see her there," she said hopefully.

I'd had absolutely no intention of a being back in the States on the Saturday of the poker game but I guess the universe had other plans. There was a shareholder meeting in New York on Friday morning and I was expected to attend in person, which meant I'd be back in New York and able to attend the game. If I wanted to.

And I'd told myself I didn't want to for the entire two-hour drive to Philadelphia. I questioned what I was doing and wondered when I had become such a glutton for punishment. It's not like I didn't know Angela was going to be there, her mom had called and told me she would be there, so it was more than apparent that she was the reason I was going. I couldn't explain the hold this woman had on me. My love for her hadn't faded despite everything we'd been through.

When I arrived, her mother met me outside. Unlike my mother, Angela's mother had liked me from the beginning even before Angela and I started dating. But I thought her behavior was a bit excessive even for someone who lacked boundaries like Ms. Gloria.

"Thank you so much for coming Rodney. I know it wasn't an easy decision but the right decisions are usually the hardest," she smiled faintly.

I was about to ask her why she had been so insistent that I come to Philadelphia and if Angela had anything to do with it, but before I could speak, she gently squeezed my hand and walked back into the house. I hesitated a few minutes and followed her. When I entered the house, she was in the foyer pointing towards the kitchen. As I passed the dining room, I saw Allen from the corner of my eye.

"What the fuck!" he said as he hurried towards me. But he was too late to intercept me as I stood at the entryway to the kitchen. Angela's back was to me.

When she turned around surprise was apparent on her face. Allen came in claiming not to have known the two of us would end up there together. But I'd tuned him out, my eyes were fixed on her. She looked like she'd lost weight, I didn't like it. She was too thin, I missed her curves. I was about to ask her how she'd been but her mother interrupted us and Allen pulled me away to the basement.

"Man, I am so sorry. I cannot believe my mama- I mean she's always crossing the line but this shit, this wasn't cool." He said angrily.

I smiled. "It's fine, no worries man. How have you been?" I quickly changed the subject although my thoughts were still with Angela.

We made small talk about work and soon all of the players had arrived. I played a couple of hands and lost because I was so unfocused knowing she was upstairs.

"Rodney, I need you to make a beer run, please." Ms. Gloria announced from the top of the stairs. Allen sighed harshly.

"Oh yeah, sure," I stood and glanced at him before Mr. Barnes started dealing the next hand. Allen shrugged his shoulders but didn't make eye contact with me.

"Angie's on the porch, you really need to talk to her." She said once I'd made it upstairs.

I opened the front door and stepped out on to the porch. I sat next to Angela and asked her what was going on. Nothing in the world could have prepared me for what came next. She had been pregnant with my child and had a miscarriage. All during the time since I'd last seen her.

I was heartbroken but I could tell it had devastated her. I couldn't understand if she'd never wanted kids why it had affected her so much. But I held her in my arms as we both cried over our loss. I wanted to keep talking to her, so I asked her to take a ride with me. She smiled and agreed, obviously remembering when we first met.

"So how long are you going to be in London?" she asked as she stared out the car window.

I shrugged. "It could be anywhere from three to six weeks. Things are wrapping up."

"You coming back to New York?" she asked softly.

"More than likely," I focused my eyes on the road.

"Well, whenever you're back in town I want to treat you to lunch or dinner. There's a new place I've been wanting to try called Dirty French. I hear the food is amazing," she smiled.

I thought carefully before I responded. I wasn't going back down the same road with her. I believed we finally had a chance to get it right, but I didn't want there to be any lies or second guessing.

"I mean- you don't have to feel obligated. Just forget I said anything," she said quietly.

Once I had pulled into the parking lot of the grocery store, I parked the car. When I didn't make a move to do anything she looked at me.

"Are you okay?" she asked.

"Are you?" I challenged.

"I don't- what, why are you asking me that?" she laughed nervously.

"Angela, we've known each other for a while now, we've lived together, we were engaged and now we've lost-," a lump formed in my throat. "No more games. No more pretending, for once let's be one hundred percent honest with each other,"

She shrank away from me with her back pressed into the seat. She was silent and I was about to tell her how I felt but before I did, she spoke.

"I've been miserable without you but I didn't try to contact you because after I saw you with that woman– I wanted you to be happy even if it wasn't with me," she stared out the front window as her voice trailed off.

"We broke up," I announced.

A faint smile appeared on her face.

"What are you feeling right now, right here in this car?" I asked.

"Scared," she said softly.

"Scared?" I asked confused.

She shrugged. "Scared I'm not going to do or say the right thing this time,"

"There is no *right* thing. Say what's on your mind,"

"I miss you. I miss our life," she said looking at her lap.

I gently grabbed her chin and forced her to look into my eyes. "I want to get married and have children," That hadn't changed.

She exhaled. "I want that too. I'm so sorry it took losing you and losing our baby for me to realize it." She whispered.

I took a chance and once again put my heart on the line. "I still love you, Angela and I want us to be together. But I need to know you're in this all the way this time. I don't expect you to sacrifice or give up your career to be a wife or mother. I know how important it is to you and I've always supported you. All I expect is your love, respect, honesty and support in return; that's the only way this will work."

She threw her arms around my neck and hugged me tightly. "I love you too, I love you so much. I'm in, all the way!" She declared.

We'd sat in the car talking until her brother called to make sure we were okay.

Fast forward three months and I was in California visiting my mother to tell her that I'd not only decided to be with a woman who she wasn't really fond of, but to also hand deliver her invitation to our wedding next month. Angela had wanted to come and even insisted that my mother would respect her more and maybe she was right, but the conversation I planned on having with my mother was long overdue and wasn't going to be nice or polite.

My mother had found love twice, so why didn't I deserve a shot at it myself? But it didn't matter what she said, the only thing that mattered was that Angela and I were *finally* on the same page and that she was going to be my wife and one day the mother of my children. We'd both changed a lot in the past year and a half but our love and friendship was even stronger than before and I knew this time we'd get it right.

March
2016

I looked at my body in the full-length mirror and smiled. I actually had cleavage. I placed my hands on my breasts and pushed them up higher and laughed.

"Hey, you ready? What are you doing?" Rodney laughed coming into the room.

"I hope they stay this way," I stared into the mirror again.

He smiled and walked up behind me. "A, B, C or D cup, I don't care. You're still beautiful and I love every inch of you," he kissed my neck and my entire body erupted in goosebumps. "And how are you doing in there? Taking it easy?" He asked after grabbing my waist and turning me towards him. He leaned down and directed his question to my stomach.

I was six and half months pregnant and we were on a babymoon–our last vacation as a childless couple before our baby arrived. We'd decided that we didn't want to know the gender but Rodney had started calling the baby "he" and "him". I didn't actually have a preference, I only wanted him or her to be healthy. And I prayed that I'd be a good mother. I already knew Rodney would be a great father. But we were a team, so I was pretty confident the kid was going to be okay.

After our parking lot conversation in Philadelphia, Rodney and I had gotten back together and five months later on January 20, 2015, we were married. It was a very small ceremony in New York at Ink48. We'd reserved the penthouse suite and there was a spectacular view of the city. Rodney's mom and her husband flew in for the wedding; it was her first time visiting New York since Rodney had moved to the city almost ten years ago.

I was prepared for the usual cold shoulder from her but she'd surprised me when she approached me at dinner the night before the wedding.

"Angela, I know that you and I haven't had the opportunity to get to know each other very well but I love my son and I trust his judgment. He loves you very much and despite the trials that the two of you have faced, you're still together," she paused and actually smiled at me, something I'd thought she was incapable of doing.

"I pray that you have a long and happy marriage and that your love for him is just as strong as his love for you,"

I smiled in return. "I love your son very much and I'm so honored to become his wife tomorrow."

I thought she would hug me or something but instead, she just nodded her head, turned and walked back to the end of the table where her husband was waiting.

"What did she say to you? Because if she's starting shit-," my mother had appeared out of nowhere ready to pounce on Rodney's mom.

I rolled my eyes. "Mama, no! She was actually nice," I laughed.

"Well, she better be I'd hate to have to drag her ass all over this nice restaurant," Mama chuckled.

The next afternoon, I walked down the aisle in a lace, off the shoulder, long sleeve wedding dress with a train, on the arm of my father. I stared out at the incredible backdrop of the New York City skyline overlooking Central Park and smiled. Eight million people in the city and I'd found The One. All the sights and sounds around me begin to blur as I focused on the face of my teary-eyed best friend, Rodney James Anderson.

I met him at the end of the aisle and we eagerly vowed to spend the rest of our lives together for better or worse, richer or poorer and in sickness and health. After we'd exchanged vows, had our first dance, and cut the cake- Christina cornered me just I was about to toss the bouquet.

"Hey, I wanted to say again how extremely happy I am for you," she said tearfully. I wasn't sure if she was so happy for me that it had brought tears to her eyes or if her hormones were out of whack due to her being seven months pregnant.

"Aw, thank you so much! And thanks for always being there for me and being such a true friend," I got a little teary-eyed as well.

"You know, I always knew you'd end up with Rodney. He's the real deal. That other guy, who shall remain nameless," she paused after referring to Xavier. "He's a fantasy type guy and reality is a thousand times better than fantasy." She winked.

I laughed and pulled her into a big hug, well as much as I could with her protruding stomach in the way.

Rodney and I mingled with our guests for a while before my brother whisked me off to the dance floor. A slow song was playing and it was very weird to be dancing so close to my brother.

"This is weird!" I laughed. We'd never danced that close before.

"It really is, maybe I picked the wrong time." He laughed and then became serious. "I just wanted to talk to you for a minute. Just to tell you how proud I am of you, how much I love you and how so very happy I am for you and Rodney. You deserve all this happiness and more," he said and his voice cracked.

I looked at him and immediately started to cry. I knew it was the ugliest cry in the history of ugly cries.

"Come on don't do that- especially with that face," he laughed as he pulled me close and hugged me.

"Shut up! It's your fault," I laughed. "Thank you, I love you too," I kissed his cheek.

We moved around on the floor for a few more seconds before it got too weird again and we left the dance floor. Soon it was time for Rodney and I to leave the venue and head off on our week-long honeymoon in Barbados.

We had an incredible time soaking up the sun and beautiful beaches in Barbados and when we returned we moved into a large brownstone in Park Slope. Six months later, I'd found out I was pregnant. We hadn't actually been trying to get pregnant but we hadn't been doing anything to prevent pregnancy either. We both definitely wanted children, so it was a welcome surprise although I was a little nervous after my miscarriage last year.

We'd waited until I was out of my first trimester to tell our family. I'd waited even longer to tell my team at work. I was already showing when I made the announcement and several people had figured it out, and a few rude assholes said they thought all that eating out had caught up with me and I'd just gained weight.

Although my pregnancy was considered high-risk because of my age, it had been pretty typical– a little morning sickness early on, mild discomfort as my body tried to make room for the human growing inside of me and of course, I had to pee nonstop!

My therapist, Dr. Walker had suggested the babymoon since Rodney and I were no doubt going to be sleep deprived and a little crazy during the first year and probably the years that followed. She said it was important that we stay connected as a couple.

I decided I would continue working after the baby was born. We'd worked out a plan where I would work from home two days a week and Rodney would work from home two days a week. We'd also interviewed a few nanny's and had a wonderful woman in mind to help us out a couple of days a week. Plus, my Mama volunteered to come to New York and help out during the first few weeks after the baby's birth.

I totally understood that saying, "it takes a village, to raise a child," now more than ever.

I hadn't talked to Xavier in well over a year but I did hear on Entertainment Tonight that he'd left Soul Skylight and gone solo. I also saw a picture of him with a woman in a magazine that called her his "new love." I hoped it was true. I hoped that he had found love and also established a relationship with both his children. I had no animosity towards him, being with him is what had led me back to the love of my life.

"Now put some clothes on woman, so we can go and eat!" Rodney said playfully swatting me on the ass.

We were in Sedona, Arizona staying at the L'Auberge de Sedona. It was an incredible resort with the most picturesque views of the Arizona mountain ranges. I'd never felt so relaxed in my life. I wondered if we were making a mistake raising a child in the hustle and bustle of New York. Maybe somewhere more laid back like Sedona would be better.

I pulled on a multi-colored caftan and slid my feet into my leather Manolo mules before running my fingers through my short-layered haircut, "my pregnancy hair" is what I called it. Super low maintenance. Once I put on a coat of lip gloss, I was ready.

"Beautiful," Rodney said as I emerged from the bathroom. He still had the ability to make me blush after all these years.

"I don't even have on any makeup," I smiled.

He shook his head. "You don't need it. Are you ready?"

I narrowed my eyes at him, "Is that why you're saying I don't need makeup because you're ready to go?"

He laughed. "I am ready to go but that's not why I said it,"

"Whatever Mr. Anderson," I grabbed my purse from the bed and passed by him.

He placed a hand on my hip and pulled me towards him. "You know the sooner we eat, the sooner we can come back here and try a few new positions, Mrs. Anderson," he whispered in my ear and a shiver of anticipation went through my body.

Sex with Rodney had always been extremely gratifying, but sex after we got married, went to another level and pregnancy sex took it to even higher heights. However, getting the right position got trickier the more my stomach grew but I was definitely up for the challenge.

"You know we could always order room service," I suggested as I turned to face him.

He gently grabbed my chin and tilted my face to meet his before kissing me tenderly.

"I get the feeling not much food will be eaten if we stay in and I need to make sure my son eats," he said rubbing my stomach.

I rolled my eyes, a little upset the romantic moment had been interrupted. "Or daughter, right?"

"I'm just trying to put a boy out in the universe for your sake," he took his wallet from the nightstand and put it in his back pocket.

"My sake?" I asked confused.

"Yes, if we have a daughter I'm going to totally be at her mercy. A son I can try and mold into a strong man but my daughter will be a princess that can never do any wrong," he said somewhat seriously.

"Well, for everyone involved let's hope we have a son," I said sarcastically.

We finally left the room and walked hand and hand to the Cress on Oak Creek, a restaurant on the property. It was breathtaking. An open-air restaurant situated on the banks of a babbling creek. I barely ate my food because I was so taken with the view and hypnotic sounds of the water.

At one point, I looked across at Rodney and he was looking at me. I smiled. "Do you realize we are going to have a baby in three months," I pointed to my stomach.

He smiled faintly. "Yes, that sounds about right,"

"Aren't you the tiniest bit nervous?"

"Honestly? I'm terrified," he grabbed my hand across the table.

My eyes widened. "Really? I can't tell. You seem to be so calm and prepared,"

"I'm doing all of that for you," he shrugged.

"Huh?" I asked confused.

"You're doing me the extreme honor of carrying my child- *our child*- I don't want you to have to worry about anything but staying healthy and having a healthy delivery. So, I make sure you've got whatever you need including a husband who appears to be on top of things and confident,"

"So, it's all an act? You're totally freaked out?" I challenged. I didn't really believe him. Rodney was usually very laid back and rational but it would be a relief to know that I wasn't alone in feeling that I was completely unprepared to take care of this child.

"I'm more excited and grateful to God than I am freaked out but if you must know, I did Google to compare about forty-seven strollers and car seats complete with watching YouTube product testing videos before I suggested the Nuna. And I've pretty much memorized all of the baby products on the recall lists and did you know that sometimes babies can forget how to breathe if-," I reached over and covered his mouth with my hand to stop his rambling.

"Shut up, you lunatic!" I laughed.

I could feel him smiling beneath my hand. I moved my hand and smiled back at him.

"I love you," I said.

"I love you too and this kid is pretty damn lucky to be getting us for parents," he winked.

"Yeah, pretty damn lucky," I agreed.

I wasn't perfect and neither was Rodney but we'd found our way to each other and back again, and were creating a life where we both felt loved, respected and supported. There was no way to predict the future but I felt confident after all that had happened, we would finally get our happily ever after.

Acknowledgements

To the readers, THANK YOU for taking the time to lose yourself in my stories and for your continued support! To my family, THANK YOU for always listening to my ramblings and encouraging me to keep writing. To my fellow writers, (both published and unpublished) I love being a part of such a cool tribe of wordsmiths and storytellers. Writing is not an easy task– it's often solitary, time consuming and criticized but we continue to write because there is something deep in our souls that compels us and it makes us feel alive!

This book is dedicated to the black authors who emerged in the 90's and early 2000's. You made me become a voracious reader with your stories. You gave voice to the contemporary black experience and introduced us to characters that were well developed, articulate, flawed but redeemable (sometimes), diverse and often relatable: Terry McMillan, Lolita Files, Eric Jerome Dickey, E. Lynn Harris (RIP), Virginia DeBerry, Donna Grant, Bebe Moore Campbell (RIP), Kimberla Lawson Roby, Benilde Little, Trisha Thomas, Reshonda Tate Billingsley, Victoria Christopher Murray, Omar Tyree and countless others! Thank you for your words and inspiration!

Questions for Discussion:

1. Do you think exes can be platonic friends? Why or why not?
2. Why do you think Angela agreed to a long-distance relationship with Xavier?
3. Do you think the way you're raised can affect your relationships?
4. Should Rodney have given Angela another chance?
5. Is it possible to have a successful long-distance relationship? If so, what advice would you have given to Angela?
6. Have you ever attended a high school reunion? If so, was it a good or bad experience?

Be sure to check out the Pinterest board for *Here You Come Again*. There are inspirational images, a dream cast of characters, a listing of all the restaurants mentioned in the book, a book trailer and a song playlist! https://www.pinterest.com/TracieMomie/

Thank you again for reading! Be sure to leave a review on Amazon.com. Reader reviews help give authors exposure. You can leave a review even if you didn't buy the book on Amazon. The review can also be anonymous!

ABOUT THE AUTHOR

Tracie Momie is an author and freelance graphic designer who lives in Houston, Texas with her husband and two children. Her five-star rated books on Amazon include: *What Was Missing, Nothing I Can Say and An Emotional Appeal.*

You can visit her at www.traciemomie.com or connect on social media:
Instagram, Twitter & Pinterest- @traciemomie
Facebook- Tracie Momie Creative

www.ingramcontent.com/pod-product-compliance
Lightning Source LLC
Chambersburg PA
CBHW071250170626
46809CB00001B/153